VERITAS

Charles D'Amico

VERITAS

First edition May 2020

Cover & Interior Design: Blue Handle Publishing, LLC
Editing: Ben Goldstein

ISBN: 978-1-7347727-0-8

For all those that have stuck with me through this journey.

My loving supportive wife.
My mother, looking down on me.
And the literary inspiration, whom I wish to write a hundred books for, my sister.

1

Had I known that the call would come so early . . . I probably wouldn't have stayed so late trying to hydrate with vodka.

The secretary at the main desk has a familiar smile, one I remembered from years earlier. Good to see not much has changed on the twenty-sixth floor.

"Neil Baggio, I had a feeling we'd be seeing you back here."

"Are you kidding me?" I asked. "I was afraid I'd never see your face again. How are you, Jen?"

"I'm doing pretty well. They're paying me well now, plus the benefits are all right for a change. How are *you*? I've read quite a few stories in the paper that had your company's name in them. It sounds like running your own shop is keeping you busy these days."

"Yeah, but I mostly just sit back and enjoy the show now that I have a lot of talented people working for me. I have a few ex-military guys, and a couple of veteran investigators, including an ex-cop. Business is booming, as they say."

"All those cheating, rich husbands must be keeping your

lights on."

"And for that, Jen, I thank them. Because of those cheating, rich husbands, I can finally enjoy a decent life."

"Well, let me tell Agent Garcia that you're here. You know the way—it's your old office, after all. Though from the looks of it, she's done a far better job with it than you did."

"That's not saying much, considering I never did a thing to it while I was here."

"That's true. As I recall, you seemed to prefer unfinished drywall and folding chairs to a nice paint job and a leather sofa. Maybe you never planned to stick around in the first place."

"You got me there. It was good seeing you again, Jen."

"You too, Neil. Don't be a stranger."

After all these years, the offices of the FBI's Detroit branch still had the feel of death in them. The hallways were filled with mildew as much as ever, and the only noticeable change since I last worked out of the McNamara Federal Building was the new carpet. When I was here, it was just linoleum flooring and white walls. I think the building was designed that way on purpose, to ensure that the agents spent most of their time out in the field, instead of trapped in this soul-sucking, overly lit, fluorescent box.

Could it be any brighter in here? I mean fuck! I swear I'm seeing spots right now, and my head is killing me. Of course, that could also be due to the hangover I brought in with me this morning. One can be careless and stay out a little too late when you own your own business. Having a flex-time schedule is just one of the perks of running a private investigation and security firm. Unfortunately, none of these perks was helping my head get out of the hangover's vice grip.

The fact that I'm not bringing my A or B game was cemented by the incessant ringing of my home and cell phones this morning. No one likes to be rudely awoken from a deep sleep, let alone at 5:00 a.m. and by the FBI, no less. I already knew the bureau would want to bring me back in for this case, should it ever be reopened. Had I known that the call would come so early after the latest development on Trumbull Avenue I probably wouldn't have stayed out so late trying to hydrate with vodka. The biggest question that was running through my head was, how much of my help did they actually need? The first step toward solving that mystery was meandering down the hallway to Agent Garcia's office, trying not to look like a lopsided cartoon character.

My first impression of my old office was utter amazement. To say that Garcia made a few adjustments would be an understatement. It looked as if she had changed everything, including the favorite wall I used to punch, which doubled as a hiding spot for paperwork I had yet to turn in. I know, I know— look at the meathead G-man who can only express emotions with his fists. But at the end of a crazy workweek or -month, paperwork was the absolutely lowest priority for us agents. Fortunately, Jen saved my ass on more than one occasion.

Taking dictation as I ranted around the room, and making sure those papers were filed on time, one way or another.

"Come on in and take a seat, Mr. Baggio, I'll just be a moment," Agent Garcia directed me while standing off to one side of her desk, ear pressed to her phone.

At first glance, everything about Agent Maria Garcia's appearance was planned and executed to the last detail. From the crisp tailored suit she was wearing, to her catalog-worthy hair and makeup, to the way she straightened her posture as I entered. She had an air of someone who was hyperaware of the way they are perceived. It's a double standard, but government jobs such as these do tend to carry more scrutiny and hurdles for women than they do for men. After all, a male agent could drag into the office rumpled and unshaven. Nobody would say a word about it, especially if he had been up all night working a case. For female agents, their image and the bureau's image were intertwined.

I sat down in the leather chair in front of Garcia's desk and couldn't help but admire what she had done with the place. To me, having an office was an obligation I never asked for, and I treated it as nothing more than a place to store boxes of case files. For Garcia, the office was another carefully curated extension of her persona. For starters, she had a handcrafted oak desk made by the Amish. You may ask yourself how I know that, and I'll tell you: it's because there's a small tab on the desk that says so. But amid all of that amazing woodwork, Garcia had a simple metal folding chair behind her desk. As expected, all of her degrees hung on the wall, alongside photos of herself with several political figures and local celebrities. My favorite was her picture with Thomas "The Hitman" Hearns, the legendary boxer and local hero, who still shows up at the Kronk Gym on Mettetal Street from time to time to growl encouragement at young fighters.

The way Agent Garcia put such an emphasis on detail in her office got under my skin. It just seemed too nice a workspace for a field agent; it looked more like a politician's office. Then again, I knew she might have aspirations in that direction. The persona that she broadcast screamed political figure. Even her oak squirrel paperweight fit perfectly with everything else in the office. Judging by the wood grain and the color of the stain, it was likely handcrafted by the same Amish family who did the desk.

"Sorry about that, I had some loose ends to tie up," Garcia said. "It seems as though some of my superiors aren't too happy that you're here right now."

"Let me guess. Bob Hendrickson?"

"Very perceptive, Mr. Baggio. Is there anything else you picked up eavesdropping while I was on the phone?"

"Honestly speaking?"

"I'd have it no other way."

"You appear to have a problem with your image; you worry about it too much. That's probably why you're so good for the

FBI. I was never image conscious, myself. I just wanted to work the case, and I couldn't care less which politicians I pissed off in the process."

"Oh, is that a fact? It looks like you've deduced quite a bit from just one phone call."

"You also keep staring at your chair."

"My chair?"

"It doesn't exactly fit your aesthetic, does it? My guess is that you were supposed to have something much fancier delivered this week; however, it didn't come in, so now you're stuck sitting on an unstylish leftover from the supply closet. If you're going to throw around words such as 'deduced,' then I'll be happy to show off my Sherlock Holmes impression. It's always a crowd pleaser."

I knew I was pushing it, but I thought a little charm might break the tension. I have a tendency to try to disarm any situation I'm in, from simple conversations to criminals pulling a firearm on me.

"Nice job, I'll give you points for the chair. An old colleague and mentor of mine ordered me a new one as a gift; I got my first big collar last month."

"Congratulations. Gracin?"

"Gracin, what?"

"He's still giving out those Eames executive chairs. Let me guess: merlot-colored leather with extra lumbar support."

Agent Garcia narrowed her eyes at me suspiciously—a look

I've seen on the faces of more women than I care to admit. "How did you know?" she said.

"Because I can see the order form on your desk. Sorry, Agent Garcia, I was just having a little fun at your expense. I'll try to keep the *deducing* to a minimum."

"Old habits die hard, I suppose. Now let's move on to the business at hand. Have you been following the news?"

"Close enough to know why I'm here."

"Well, let's get straight to the point then, shall we?"

I'd been following this thing for months, but I wasn't going to tip my hand quite yet, because the less they thought I knew, the more freedom I'd have in gaining information. Plus, if Garcia found out how much I actually knew about the case, she'd be very curious how I came across the information. I wasn't willing to tell her, at least not at this point. It was much better to keep her and Hendrickson in the dark.

The first time I worked the Cappelano case, it took a long time to get a handle on him. Because of his obsessive nature and his highly personal approach to murder. For instance, he would burn an insignia into the skin of each victim using a branding instrument, and each branding stamp was individually made. Cappelano enjoyed the intimate process of customizing each victim's stamp. Along with knowing that there was someone out there blissfully going about their day. Completely unaware of the horror that was in store for them. He was and is a sick and twisted individual. What kind of man can kill innocent people and, in his head, think he's doing the world a favor? It wasn't as if he thought any of the people he killed deserved to die. Instead, he believed that his firsthand "research" on the psychology of a murderer would bring humanity to some greater understanding.

"Well, you called me here, so why don't you start?" I said, getting comfortable in my leather chair.

"First things first, we believe 'Veritas' has come out of hiding to continue what he started back in ninety-eight."

"That's a good guess. Do you have any evidence to indicate that this is, in fact, Cappelano, and not a copycat killer?"

"We are almost certain this is 'Veritas,' based on—"

"Please call him by his name," I interrupted. "I can't stand that tag. His name is Franklin Cappelano."

"Apologies. I didn't mean to strike a nerve. Anyway, we know he wants you on this case, and we think he'll keep killing until we bring you back in."

"Fuck, Cappelano always did have a hard-on for me."

You never know what will inspire a serial killer's lust, but sexual gratification is almost always a driver of the violent act. The physical appearance of the victims could trigger a killer's dark urges, or it could even be the personal attention they feel from being hunted by individual detectives. Their motivations can even evolve from one trigger to another over time. Which is why I often think of the serial killers I chase as pansexual; there are few defined boundaries to their lust.

"Mr. Baggio, watch your language. The reason you're here is that we want you back, and we're willing to pay you substantially in return."

"Substantially, please—the bureau doesn't pay substantially for anything. But I hear you. I guess I only have one question before I take some time to think this over."

"I know what you're thinking. And yes, Bob Hendrickson is still running things around here. No, he's not entirely happy about this move to bring you in, but then again, this decision goes over his head as well."

She had no clue what I was thinking; she wasn't there when the case fell apart, and she had no idea what it did to me. Hendrickson was one of the reasons I'd been gone for so long. I was doing my job with handcuffs on because Bob Hendrickson didn't want any bad publicity. When it comes to a murder case, all I care about is getting the offender off the streets. If I wanted to get into politics, I would have chosen a different path than working serial homicide cases for the FBI. I've always felt one of the reasons our justice system has become so crippled is because of its ties to the political system. It's hard to shoot straight when you're worried about the votes those in office will gain or lose because of it. Instead of making the right choice, we end up choosing the safest path so that no one important looks bad. I wanted no part of working within that system anymore.

"Really, why don't you enlighten me on what I'm thinking?"

I asked her.

"I know how you feel you were treated. It was just standard bureau practice, you know that."

Bureaucratic practice would be more accurate. Pulling me off of the Cappelano investigation was nothing but a political move on Hendrickson's part. He was more concerned with the political and public fallout of my plan—and sure, maybe the financial cost of it too—than he was about catching a crazed killer. But hey, that's why I don't have a position in leadership; I don't think of the cost, I get too tied up in the catch. It just seems to me that the citizens whom Hendrickson claimed to serve would be more interested in us catching the guy than in how we did it. As long as there was no collateral damage.

"The ball is in your court, Mr. Baggio."

"Well, I need a day to think about it. How about lunch tomorrow? I have to set some things in motion at work if I'm going to do this."

"That's fine. Say, noon tomorrow at Mama Rosa's? Do you remember the place?"

"Yeah, I know the place. Sounds good. I'll see you then."

Of course, I didn't *actually* need time to think about it, but I had to do some posturing because I didn't want them to understand how eager I was to get back on this case. If they knew how fixated I'd been on chasing Cappelano and how I fantasized about putting the cuffs on him they would use my eagerness as a form of control. Acting like I could take it or leave it gave me bargaining power. If I played my cards right, I could get the bureau to give me nearly complete control over the case. Instead of having to play a supporting role, taking orders like a rookie on a ride-along.

I got a sudden vision of Bob Hendrickson fuming in his office, and not just because the bureau wanted to bring me back in for this case. But because he's always known that he wouldn't have a shot at catching Cappelano without my help. It's bad enough to let a killer get away once in the public eye; it would be an unmitigated disaster if it happened twice. So, for once, Hendrickson's political reputation and the high profile around this case were going to help me instead of hindering me. It's sad that the two of us couldn't set aside our personal problems and work together on this, but then again, we are both stubborn-ass men. I know it's not a good excuse, but the simplest explanation is usually the best one.

"Well then, I guess we're done here. We can cover the Trumbull case tomorrow. I'm still waiting on some more details from the assigned case agents" Agent Garcia said, flashing me a professionally rehearsed smile. "I'll see you tomorrow, Mr. Baggio?"

"I'll be there with bells on. And it's Neil."

I know you're asking yourself about the murder on Trumbull that brought me here. When dealing with Cappelano, the bureau, like myself, thinks this case is merely another way of Cappelano working his way back into the fold. They are going to let the team already assigned to work on it. If they think they find anything new, they'll let me know, but I'm assuming at this point is more about the next case. With Cappelano, there's always a next case.

Walking out of Agent Garcia's office, I knew that I had accomplished what I had set out to. Garcia and I established some level of understanding, I got my foot back in, and they got a carrot to dangle in front of me. Before I could even exit the building, my cell started to ring. It was Ken calling from the warehouse.

"Neil, how'd the meeting go?"

"Ken, you called quick. I could still be in Garcia's office right now."

"Come on, I've known you for too long, bud. We both know you keep it short, especially when you're trying to get your way."

"I guess you do know me pretty well, since that's exactly what I did, but I was in there for twenty minutes, not fifteen."

"Why do you think I waited to call you? I figured they might have tried the old stall technique. You know the one where they have the secretary call them as you walk into the office, and they act like they are on an important phone call to make you wait."

"Nice job, Ken; that was exactly how she played it. How is everything out at the warehouse tonight? Anything major going on?"

"Nothing too special. Are you coming in so we can schedule

things up for this case?"

"I'm heading out there right now, and since I'm already downtown, it shouldn't take me too long to get there. I'll see you in about fifteen minutes."

"All right, sounds good, Neil. See you in a bit."

It was about May 2001 when I met Ken, and I was frequenting a small bar not too far from my house called Kelly's. I had been there a lot, not drinking, I just liked the atmosphere, and it gave me a chance to get some work done outside of the house. I used to bring in my laptop and some old unsolved case files and just work. That's when I met Ken; he used to own the bar as a retired army ranger of twenty-three years. We got to talking, and he told me he wanted out of the bar business and would love to help any way he could with some of the cases I was working on. Eventually we worked together a few times. The first time he helped me out was on a case where a company was concerned that one of their warehouse managers was stealing.

Ken and I rotated an eight-hour shift for six days to stake out the warehouse. We got to know each other and eventually worked together a lot more. Ultimately the business kept coming in, and we had to hire more help to keep up with demand. He called some of his old military buddies, who, in turn, brought in some ex-cops. Eventually CB, Inc., was born. The "C" stands for Chamberlain, Ken's full name is Kenneth Maurice Chamberlain, and never call him Mo or Maurice, he'll hurt you, he hates that name. The "B" stands for Baggio, as in Neil Baggio. Coincidentally, the company that hired me for that warehouse job ended up closing the warehouse and moving out of state, allowing Ken and me to purchase it.

It wasn't until a year or so had passed that we had enough money and clout to turn a two-man operation into half a dozen men. For a while there, we were operating out of Ken's bar because we had no other place to set up shop. It wasn't until the summer of 2002 that Ken and I decided to find a place to set up shop; the warehouse just happened to fall in our laps. We drove around looking for properties and saw that it was for sale, so I called the owner. Because of our relationship, he was nice enough to sell it to us for next to nothing. Ken sold his bar, and we used that money along with some money I had been saving up to remodel the inside from top to bottom. When we bought the building, it was completely gutted; it was just a shell of a building, but it was just what we needed.

Today the outside of the warehouse still looks the same. It's the inside that we've done all the work on. We fixed all the weak points in the structure and built new doorways just inside of the other ones. Technically the doors on the outside are always unlocked, but once you walk in, you are in a small hall with another door than can only be opened by key card access. Even the car bay has to be opened by card key. We did this so that we can keep track of who is opening what and when if there is ever a worry. Everyone's office is locked by the same keypads to allow people security for everything that is theirs. This way, if someone does use their card to break into the building, they can only open a few other doors in the building. Most of the surveillance equipment is locked in a separate room to which a small number of people are allowed access. If an investigator needs a piece of equipment, they must check it out. I know it is a little elementary, but it works, and it keeps our costs down; it forces people to take care of things. No one wants to have to pay for a new camera or high-powered night binoculars.

The meeting with Ken is going to be nothing of great importance tonight. It is just the two of us looking at where everyone is at on cases and see who we might want to use in this case. I know I'm working for the bureau on this case, but I don't trust them as far as I can throw them. For my sanity and that of the people around me I'm going to be using my guys where the bureau can't always go. In other words, where the bureau must follow legal procedures to gain the evidence, my guys don't have to. It allows me a little bit of movement within the investigation that I would otherwise not have.

The meeting didn't take but thirty or so minutes, and most of the time Ken and I were just bullshitting around and making fun of the FBI. It was mainly the two of us making sure that we were going to be on the same page entering this investigation so that we didn't step on each other's toes.

2

It's always nice to know I have two ladies ready to attack someone at any point in time.

There's nothing like coming home and realizing you forgot to put your bedsheets in the dryer. We all love that feeling you get when your home is as well managed as your business, but right now my mind and routine are as organized as a toddler's room. I guess it isn't out of the ordinary for me to forget things from time to time. It's just really annoying when all you want to do is walk in the door and crash in your bed. It's moments like this that remind me of the conversation I had with Sheila a couple of months ago when we went shopping. She asked me if I had bought a second set of sheets yet, and I told her that I didn't see the need for it. Well, tonight I see the need, and I really wish I would have bought that second set of sheets.

I live in a place called Clinton Township, which is about half an hour northeast of Detroit. Looking on a map, you'd find that it's made up of all the leftovers that no other town wanted to claim. I live in a ranch-style house that I just did some remodeling to last year. Since my ex-wife was kind during the divorce, I can still afford nice things; all she asked for was the bungalow we remodeled together when we were married and some child support. One of the biggest reasons that I can afford a house is because CB, Inc., has been doing well as of late. Success can breed freedom. I'm in a position to cherry-pick cases that need my full attention. Plus, the added income from the FBI will be nice for a while.

My ex-wife Sheila and I have a daughter together and still get along quite well; we just can't live together. Sheila always worried about me when I worked, and I've never gotten used to having someone worry about me. I understand how silly and unhealthy that is, but such is life. I would be lying if I said that Sheila's concern for my well-being was the basis of our divorce, when in truth it was a bunch of small incompatibilities that built up over time into something we couldn't overcome. Still, we've more than made it work for Carol Lynn, our daughter, who is about to turn seven, born only a year before my divorce with Sheila. The day she was born will always live on as the greatest day of my life. Your life changes when those innocent eyes look to you for protection and love; you can't help but think differently from that day forward. As for Sheila and me, we've become better friends over time, and we absolutely still love each other. It's just a different kind of love.

I finished throwing the sheets into the dryer and started to make my way up the stairs when my house phone went off. It's not like Sheila to call me at home this late during the week; she usually calls my cell. I'd bet any amount of money it's that brown-nosing jackass Hendrickson. After taking a look at my custom-built caller ID, I could see it was a call from the bureau's office in Detroit. It had to be Hendrickson. He's the only guy I know who would have the testicular fortitude to call me this late from the office's main phone line. He has this theory that if he calls you when you're in bed or heading that way, he'll have the upper hand because you won't want to take the time to argue with him. He must have forgotten that I'll argue with anyone for any reason.

"How's it going, Bob? What are you doing at the office this late?"

"How did you know it was me? And this line should be blocked."

"Come on, Bob, give me some credit. You know I have the tools to track any call that comes in—even the blocked ones. And you guys aren't bouncing calls off satellites from the office."

"That doesn't surprise me. You always did love your high-tech toys. And you were pretty good at your job, too."

"Wait a minute. Can you repeat that so I can record it with one of my toys?"

"Can you not be a dick to me for one second?" Hendrickson said in that flustered voice I loved so much. "I'm trying to get past the fact that you drive me up the fucking wall in every way, shape, and form."

"To quote the magic eight ball: it is highly unlikely. It's too much fun pissing you off and getting under your skin, Bobby Boy."

"So, what do you want from me, Neil? What is it I have to do to get you back in here? And let me first say that if it were my choice, we wouldn't be having this conversation. This goes above me."

"You know, I might come back to the bureau just to drive you nuts," I said, reveling in the opportunity to get under Hendrickson's skin. "It's not like I need the money, but I sure could use a good laugh."

"If the chance at driving me nuts will be your main reason for coming back to the bureau, I'll take it."

"Don't be so self-centered. It's not always about you. I'm coming back because I want Cappelano dead or behind bars, and I'm not going to let my general distaste for you get in the way."

"Self-centered? Who are you talking to? You're the egomaniac. I don't even know why I called. Trying to have a conversation with you is pointless."

Judging by the dial tone on the other end of the line, it was safe to say that Hendrickson hung up, although I saw our verbal sparring session as just a little light entertainment. It was going to suck for Agent Garcia in a few minutes when Bob decided he needed to take out his leftover aggression on someone lower on the food chain. I bet Garcia is lying down right now, trying to get some sleep, and Bob's going to start calling her until she answers the phone. He's not someone who enjoys leaving messages since he can just keep calling. The arrogant prick likes knowing that he can exert control over you at any moment. I think he can sleep better if he knows he's made someone else's day that much worse.

I finally put the phone back on its base to charge and made my way into the living room, which is my home away from the bedroom. There have been more nights than not when I've fallen asleep in my big brown leather chair and ottoman, which Sheila gifted me for our divorce. I know it sounds weird to get a gift for a divorce, but to be honest, the two of us have been happier divorced than we ever were married. The chair was a gift to say thank you for making things easy, both on her and our daughter. I just couldn't see throwing away all the years of love we shared simply because we couldn't live together. It was a problem of proximity; our marriage might have survived had we just separated. But it was probably best for Carol Lynn that Sheila and I decided to end our marriage entirely and just have a healthy friendship. It's less confusing for her that way. At least, I hope.

In the quiet of the house, my thoughts turned back to Cappelano. Franklin Cappelano used to be one of the FBI's most gifted and well-respected agents; his superiors looked to him as the second coming of J. Edgar. He was an avid study of the human mind, especially as it pertains to human behavior when taking a life. His interest started with the study of historical documents on famous killers. It soon moved on to psych evaluations of actual serial killers currently held in our federal prisons. A lot of people looked to Cappelano as a pioneer in criminology. Yet, in the end, it was his desire to know more that drove him over the edge. I remember watching the videotapes of the interviews he had done, and you could see over time that his original intrigue turned into an obsession. His line of questioning began to change; instead of figuring out the killers' motivations, his primary objective during interviews shifted to understanding how it felt to take a life without remorse. It was obvious that he reveled in their stories, that the grisly details excited him.

Watching Cappelano go from top-tier agent to bonafide serial killer was one of the hardest things I've ever witnessed. The best way to describe it is by watching someone you care for, love, and respect fall apart from drug addiction. Seeing them become a shell of themselves, completely fixated on their next high. The Cappelano case had its hooks in me on many levels, one of them being the guilt of watching it happen.

Going through the issues of this case, sitting in my front room, or as I like to call it, my makeshift study, has me becoming one with my big leather chair. Already starting to get the worn-in spot where I can simply fall back into a state of relaxation and beach-like comfort.

I'll probably end up falling asleep here tonight. As I said, I've been spending a lot of my nights in this chair. Ever since the divorce, it's just been too hard to sleep on an empty bed, maybe because it reminds me of what used to be. That's why I was looking forward to spreading out in bed with the girls tonight. Right now, they're curled up in front of the fire, a pair of sister Doberman pinschers named Jackie and Danielle, which came from a breeder who only deals in police and government dogs. I don't know what I'd do without those two. It's always nice to know I have two ladies ready to attack someone at any point in time. Hell, we all know women are more vicious than men; go ask any man who's been divorced.

Just as my eyes started to close, I heard my cell go off. I have a ring tone set for whenever she calls me, so I know it's her.

"Hey babe," I said. Pet names are a hard habit to break. "What's up? Why so late?"

"I couldn't sleep after I saw the news. They said the FBI is certain the killing wasn't a copycat. He's back. And I know he's doing it for you."

"You know he would never harm me or my family, Sheila. I think we're the only people he won't kill. When will you stop worrying about me?"

I say that like it's certain—that Cappelano would never come for us—but at this point, I'm not so sure. I don't know what to be sure of anymore. I'm full of anger at him, distrust of my own instincts, and guilt for letting it get this far. It's a fucking mess.

"How about never?" Sheila said. "I don't want our baby to grow up without her dad. I just worry about you. I always will."

"Speaking of Carol Lynn, how was the parent-teacher conference? Sorry I couldn't make it."

"It's okay; you make it to the important things. The teachers know you're involved. It was the usual, she's getting all As. And the teacher said she's always willing to help others in her class."

"That's good; Carol Lynn has always loved to help. Maybe she'll get into law enforcement like her daddy."

"Over my dead body. But enough about Carol Lynn; that's not why I called. I was thinking, would you want to come over for a little late-night session?"

"Do I want to come over? Why wouldn't I?"

"I don't know if you have a new lady. It's hard to keep track. I mean, you're a little player."

"Oh, shut up. We both know that's not true. Is Carol Lynn asleep?"

"Yup, she's out like a light. We're so lucky that she's a heavy sleeper."

"I know what you mean. It's made for some fun nights. Give me ten minutes."

"Sounds good. I'll see you in a few."

I got off the phone with Sheila and headed to my bedroom, making my way through the kitchen to drop off my glass. I can't stand dirty glasses lying around; I don't know why, but it's always driven me nuts. As I continued down the hall toward the bedroom, I caught a glimpse of the girls. They seemed to be taking the night off from guard duty, on account of the fire that was holding them hostage. Let's hope no one stops by tonight while I'm gone. I don't think they'd be able to put up much of a fight.

I grabbed my jacket and was about to head out the door when I realized I was forgetting something. That's right, condoms; can't forget those. I wasn't worried about anything, it's just a matter of being responsible. One daughter is enough for me to handle right now. Don't get me wrong, I love my daughter and Sheila to death, but I couldn't handle another child while I know Cappelano's out there. My mind would always be somewhere else. I threw another log on the fire for the girls before I left, just to keep them nice and toasty tonight. It's not as if they are going to be moving anytime soon, so I might as well make sure they're warm.

I grabbed the new pack of cigarettes I bought earlier today off my dashboard, rolled down the window, and lit up. It's been four years since my last cigarette; if you're doing the math, that means I haven't smoked since the last time I chased down Cappelano. He always finds a way to drive me back to some of my worst habits. Obviously I needed to catch him because he's crazy and dangerous, but I also needed to catch him because it would be the best thing for my long-term health.

In our neighborhood, Sheila and I still live close enough to each other to share a neighborhood; it has your typical midwestern vibe to it—green lawns, sidewalks, old oak trees, and potholes. It's great for us, for our daughter, and it makes us feel like a family, even if it is unconventional. As I approached Sheila's driveway, I threw the car in neutral and rolled in almost silently. I wanted to make sure Carol Lynn stayed asleep. Every time we got together like this, it reminded me of sneaking into a girl's house when I was in high school or coming home after curfew. As I walked to the door, I saw a note:

"Quiet. Just come upstairs, I have a surprise for you."

Who would have thought that a divorce would spice up my sex life with Sheila? We've spent more time in that bed divorced than we ever did married.

The house is a colonial with four bedrooms, three of them upstairs, with the master bedroom on the ground level; this has come in handy for our late-night trysts. The other smart thing I did was listen to my dad for once and double-insulated the house so that each room held heat and noise that much better.

The part of the house I miss the most is the kitchen, and not because I designed it myself. There are stone tile floors and granite countertops, and the rest is finished in oak and stainless steel. I had the cabinets custom-made by an Amish family in northern Indiana, and the workmanship is amazing. The basement is finished, which gave us enough room to put a bedroom on the first floor. There's a full bar built into the side of the wall, a big-screen TV, and a top-of-the-line entertainment system. It's absolutely perfect for having people over.

As you approach the house, you're not overwhelmed by its size but instead welcomed by its warmth. The house really is a home; it's not a matter of cost or size but instead one of love. Sheila and I decided it would be better to buy a home under our budget. That way we could personalize it with all the little touches we've always wanted. In my case, it was the dream kitchen that I could cook family meals in and show my children how to make Grandma's spaghetti sauce. For Sheila, it was having a beautiful garden and well-kept yard in which we could entertain. With the help of my father-in-law I built a beautiful wood deck that wraps the entire back of the house and leads into the yard. I can still smell the freshly cut oak we used to build it. We decided to just stain it and keep the beauty of the wood as the focal point of the deck. Wow, I miss this house more than I thought.

After a small trip down memory lane, I made my way across the main room to the master bedroom, where I found more than an eager ex-wife. Sheila is a five-four bombshell, brunette, with hazel eyes and the body of a teenager. She prides herself on her ability to fit in the same clothes she wore in high school. It's not as if it comes easily to her; she's always watching her diet and working out regularly. I opened the door to her lying there in some lingerie I bought her for Christmas last year. I'd describe the sight of her in more detail, but it's for my eyes only;

you'll have to use your imagination here. I sometimes wonder how on earth I could have ever messed up our marriage. I know it wasn't all my fault, but it still wasn't healthy that I buried myself in my work and didn't make time for anyone else.

"Damn, I must have done something right in this world. What's the occasion?"

"Do I need one? I can dress up whenever I feel like it. As I recall, you bought this for me last year."

"I know I did. And no, you don't need a reason. But you usually dress up when you want something. Am I right?"

"Shut up. I was just feeling sexy tonight. As if you care what my motives are. I'm wearing it, right?"

"Trust me, you are sexy as hell. And you're right, I could care less right now what your motives are. I'll worry about it later."

"Then what are you waiting for? Come on over here and give me a kiss."

It really is an amazing thing how you can be with someone for so long and still get excited like a kid on prom night. That's just what Shelia does to me; she always finds a way to grab my attention. It's not just about sex, either. She has become my best friend in life, and that is the greatest gift she could ever give me. I would take her friendship over sex any day. I know it's not the typical guy answer, but it's true. I can talk to her about relationship problems, and she can give me answers that make sense because we were together for so long. After an hour of kissing and playing around, we finally finished up and fell over on the bed, panting like two dogs in the summer heat.

"Wow," Sheila said. "What was that all about? You haven't done that to me, well, ever."

"You know I love a good striptease. And you got me all riled up."

"Hell, I should do it every night. Where did you learn some of those new moves? Have you been practicing with another girl?"

"Nope. I finally went through and started reading all the magazines I've been getting to the house for the past couple of months. There's a lot of good information in some of those magazines."

"You're telling me. You should do some more reading. I liked it a lot."

"Yeah, I could tell. For a minute there, I thought you were going to suffocate me."

"Sorry about that, I wasn't really in control of my body at that point."

"No problem. Maybe next time I should bring a snorkel?"

"You are an ass. You know you loved every minute of it."

"That's true. But then again, I always feel at home between your legs. If I could, I'd fall asleep between them every night."

"We might be able to work something out if you keep up the effort you put in tonight."

"Are you serious, or are you just playing with me?" I said.

"It's a good thing that Carol Lynn's a heavy sleeper. I think it would lead to some hefty psych bills if she heard any of that."

"Speaking of sleep, you should go home and get to bed. You have a big day ahead of you tomorrow."

"I have a tough couple of weeks ahead of me. Maybe months if Cappelano has gotten even better at hiding his tracks."

"Get some rest. I'll call you tomorrow if you're lucky."

"Sounds good, babe. Thanks again for tonight."

"Thank you, Casanova."

"I'll lock up on my way out."

"Thanks. I don't think I'll be going anywhere for a while."

During the short drive home, I couldn't help but replay the night's events through my head over and over with a big grin on my face. Although my smile quickly turned into a frown when it dawned on me that I would still have to pull my sheets out of the dryer when I got home and make the bed before I could actually go to sleep.

Tomorrow I'll find out if Agent Garcia and the bureau will actually put their words into action. I'm meeting Garcia for lunch downtown, I forget where, but I know I have it written down back at the house. I'm smoking again, drinking again, and stressed out beyond belief, but that's the Cappelano regimen when you get diagnosed with his crazy ass.

3

The dining room of Mama Rosa's had about as much charm as an old high-school cafeteria.

With the smell of coffee in the air and the annoying scream of the alarm ringing in my ears, I finally made my way out of bed. I actually don't mind waking up early in the morning; it's my body that has a hard time doing it. Just like the old adage says: the mind is willing, but the body isn't able. It takes a combination of alarms to get me out of bed in the morning, the most important one being the coffeemaker. I say that because if I can't drag my barely awake ass to the kitchen in the morning to a fresh cup, then I won't wake up at all. I have two alarms on my phone, one on my radio, and one old-fashioned alarm clock, but all would be futile without the coffeemaker. Together they create an auditory and olfactory symphony for me every morning that even Vivaldi would be proud of.

In the kitchen, I began to pour that ever-so-important first cup of the morning. It took such concentration it felt like I was shooting free throws in the waning seconds of a championship game. All I was missing was the sweat; and the crowd as well, I suppose. As I sat there leaning against the counter with my hands gripped around my cup, I heard the pitter-patter of eight little canine paws making their way down the hall. The girls very rarely leap out of bed in the morning. They don't wake up completely until they feel the morning sun on their face—their own version of a hot cup of coffee. I opened the screen door to a rush of cold air that reminded me I was wearing nothing more than boxers and a T-shirt.

As the girls began to wake up and wrestle with each other, I decided to make my way over to my laptop on the kitchen table and read the morning newspaper. One might ask why I don't just get the paper delivered like any other avid newspaper reader. I'll tell you it's because Jackie and Danielle tore up too many copies of the *Detroit News* before I could ever get to it. I tried to train them on how to retrieve the paper in the morning, and they did a good job until they started to fight over which one would bring it in. By the time it was in my hands, it would be covered in drool and torn to shreds. For a while I had *two* papers delivered to my house at the same time so that they would each have one to bring me, and they still fought over who would get theirs to me first.

The shower is my safe haven. It's where I do my best thinking and where I spend more time than most. It's been that way my whole life. When I was a teenager, my parents thought

I had a chronic masturbation problem because I showered so much. Lucky for them, I just like being clean and smelling good. I have more confidence in myself when I'm looking and feeling my best. Plus you never know when you're going to meet a woman you want to impress; you can't really do that with a foul odor leaking out of your armpits. As I leaned my head back into the hot stream of water pouring from the shower, I felt that sense of relaxation I had been looking forward to ever since I woke up this morning. There is just something so invigorating and energizing about a good shower. It's like a reset button on your life.

The girls were starting to tear up my screen door with a vengeance, which meant I had about two minutes until they started barking. My neighbors don't like the barking, so I guess I needed to cut this shower short. As I scrambled to throw on a towel and let the girls in so I could start cleaning off their paws, Danielle quickly bolted from me and took off after her sister to start another game of tug-of-war with my socks. As I turned to yell at her, I noticed the clock and saw I was running very short on time. I needed to get out to Mama Rosa's very soon for my meeting with Agent Maria Garcia.

The drive was uneventful, with nothing much in the way of scenery except the usual combination of orange construction cones and potholes. Luckily, it only took me twenty minutes to make the ten-minute drive downtown. I walked through the door at Mama Rosa's and saw Agent Garcia sitting at a corner booth, one of only six tables in the place. She waved me over while on her cell phone. I swear she was always on that thing; then again, it seems like everyone is these days.

Mama Rosa's is not your average mom-and-pop Italian eatery. For instance, under my table, you'll find a historic museum dedicated to used chewing gum. I think some of the gum may even predate the establishment because the tables look secondhand. I could be sitting at a table that has gum under it older than I am. Normally you would find murals of Italy all over the walls of a place like this, along with Italian flags everywhere. Not here. The dining room of Mama Rosa's had about as much charm as an old high-school cafeteria. Of course, people don't come to Mama Rosa's for the ambience, they come for the food.

"Nice of you to join me. Running late, are we?" Agent Garcia said, rolling her eyes.

"You'll soon find out that the only thing I'm on time for is my job. At least the important parts of it. Sorry for being late, Maria.

"It's okay. I've been stuck on the phone with your buddy Bob all morning."

"He actually waited to call you until this morning. That was nice of him."

"Not really. He did call me last night, but I told him if he called back, I'd send you to his house."

I couldn't help but laugh. It was nice to see that she had a little fight in her, and where it counted, too; she wouldn't let Bob push her around just because he outranked her.

"All of a sudden, I think I like you a little more," I said.

"What you didn't like about me before?"

"I'm just giving you a hard time. What did Bob have to say?"

"The usual. He told me that if this thing blows up in the bureau's face, it's all on me."

"And if it works out, he'll take all the credit. Good old Bob, that miserable turd hasn't changed a bit."

"Watch your mouth. He's *your* boss, too, although I doubt you'll listen to a thing he has to say."

"Enough about Bob. Let's talk about you and me. We need to get to know each other if this thing is going to work. The more I know about you as a person, the more comfortable I'll be around you, and vice versa."

"Does this mean you're willing to come back?"

"For another shot at catching Cappelano, of course I am. On a contract basis, at least. Let's start there, and we can discuss a more permanent return later. Who knows? We chased him for four years last time."

That only counted my time at the bureau; it didn't include every waking moment I had after I left. Those dark, aimless years that killed my marriage almost ended my life and put me into the wrong side of a Jack Daniels bottle in Mexico. Which makes me wonder if that's where this story is going to end up again. I've always felt Cappelano went down to Guatemala or some other Central American country to work with the cartels, to fund his lifestyle and find protection. I mean, it makes sense for a man with his cravings and talents.

"Good point," Garcia said. "Where would you like to start?"

"Start with where and when you were born and catch me up to right now."

We sat there talking for hours about our parents, our lives before the FBI. Maria Garcia was born on July 27, 1976, to a Cuban mother and a Spanish father in Orchard Lake, Michigan. Her father was always a prominent figure in politics. He started out with local community involvement but worked his way up to city council. Then district attorney, and finally he retired after being a circuit court judge for twenty-five years. Both of her parents were well-educated high achievers, and both carried JDs from Harvard Law School, which is where they met, incidentally. Maria was educated at the University of Michigan as a prelaw student, then went to Harvard just as her parents did and graduated with a law degree. But unlike her parents, Agent Garcia was more drawn toward holding people accountable to the laws than helping to write them. Starting in 1998, her career with the bureau started and has taken off ever since.

While I didn't grow up rich and affluent in Orchard Lake, Maria and I had something in common. I went to high school out there at Orchard Lake St. Mary's, an all-boys Catholic school. I grew up in East Detroit in a small brick home. The house had felt so much larger than it really is; I'm still amazed when I go home to visit my parents. Looking back, we had a very humble lifestyle with few luxuries, but we never thought we were "underprivileged." The community looked out for each other so much that you never realized what you didn't have. It's depressing to see how places like this changed over the years, as people stopped caring about their neighbors. Today, everyone just looks out for themselves.

My father was an Italian butcher shop owner, which you'd think would make us well-to-do, but not in those days. My mother was an Italian stay-at-home mom, which in many ethnic families is more than a full-time job. I put myself through college working at the butcher shop for my dad during the week, and then on the weekends working at local bars as a bouncer or bartender, depending on the night. I finished my undergraduate degree in psychology and criminology from the University of Detroit Mercy in three short years to save money on tuition, then received a master's degree in clinical psychology from Wayne State University. I started working for the FBI shortly after that in 1996, two years before Maria started working there. If you're wondering, that makes Maria twenty-nine years old and me thirty-three, a good match of a veteran and an up-and-coming bureau prospect. I guarantee that someone higher up took time to think through this partnership and as many variables as they could connect.

Our getting-to-know-you session was interrupted by the buzzing of Maria's cell phone, which she answered in the clipped tones of her professional persona. Back to "Agent Garcia" like the flip of a switch.

"Neil, that was Hendrickson," she said after ending the call. "There was another body found this morning, a female victim down by the river, and they're pretty sure it's Cappelano's work. Looks like the Trumbull murder will have to wait. We'd better get going. I'll drive."

There was no way I'd be getting into a car with Agent Garcia, and it's not because she's a female driver or anything like that. It's just because I can't stand being in a car unless I'm driving. Some may say it's because I have a problem with being in control, but I just say I like having an out for any situation. When you're a passenger in a car, you are at the will of the driver. If you ride with someone to a party, you have to stay as long as they want to because they're your ride home. I just prefer to be in control of my own situation.

"Why don't you let *me* drive down there, since that's where I grew up," I suggested. "I know the area pretty well. I don't know if you've been downtown too much, seeing as you're from the Upper East Side."

"Are you trying to imply that I'm spoiled rotten? I don't know if I like that tone."

"I wasn't trying to imply anything; I think I was pretty straightforward. Why don't we both drive? We'll worry about who's going to be driving the rest of the time when we get back to the office."

"That's fine; we can discuss logistics later. Try and keep up—I hate slow drivers."

If this were any sign of what's to come, this could be more fun than I had originally anticipated. I had a feeling Agent Garcia had a bit of an attitude, but this is a nice surprise; she hates waiting around for people, just like I do. Especially when driving.

We headed outside, and as I watched her get into a 1957 Corvette, I immediately made two observations. One, she has incredible taste in cars. And two, can you say Daddy's girl? I'm serious: her license plate says MI477AV; it's not as if I was just guessing. She has it written across the back of her car, for crying out loud.

"Hey Maria, nice license plate."

"Just get in your car. Less sarcasm, please."

"Calm down with the bossy act. It doesn't suit you well."

Maria briefly shot me a *what the hell did you just say to me?* look, and I could tell she was mentally calculating whether to scold me again. Luckily, she eased up. "Sorry about that, Neil. I've just got a lot riding on this case; it has me on edge."

We both do. Don't get me wrong, probably me more than she. Maria can always use me as the scapegoat; it just depends on how she plays it.

"Trust me, I've been there, and I know what you're going through. I let Cappelano get away once, and there's no way I'm going to let that happen again."

"It's not you I'm worried about. I'm afraid Bob is going to try and pull rank again at the last second and fuck everything up. Pardon my language."

"No need to censor yourself around me. And I take it you did read between the lines on the case. Let me worry about pushing his buttons, and you can be the buffer between us so that he doesn't do something stupid. In the end, we'll both take credit for catching this crazy fucker."

For the first time since I met her, Maria gave me a smile that felt genuine. "Sounds like a plan. The *only* plan, to be honest. Now stay close; I hate having to wait for someone who's following me."

This could get interesting. My Jeep runs fine, and I usually drive it with a heavy foot, but it's not every day that I have to keep up with a classic sports car designed for one purpose, speed. I know I'm making plenty of money to buy a new car, but I just don't see the need right now, not to mention the seats are just starting to get worn in. I'd been following Garcia for a few miles. I was already terrified at the prospect of riding shotgun with her, and this is coming from a guy whose driving record is as full as Nicolas Cage's IMDb listing. If I were a teenager in today's world, I wouldn't even *have* a license anymore. As we got closer to the crime scene, I felt my phone vibrate with Agent Garcia's number on the caller ID.

"So why are you calling me when I can see we're almost there?" I said. "Is there something I should know before we pull in?"

"I was just letting you know that we're here, and to find a spot with the TV crews since you don't have your credentials on you yet."

"All right, I guess I can handle that, but I still don't think a phone call was necessary."

"I don't care what you think is necessary. It's my job to tell you what's important when it comes to the bureau. You just worry about Cappelano, and in this case, let me worry about everything else."

I could hear the tension in her voice, and all of a sudden I wasn't sure what we were going to walk into.

"I'm going to hold you to that," I said. "I'm not going to worry about anything other than the case. That means no paperwork, no interviews, and definitely no bureaucratic bullshit, *especially* if it comes from Hendrickson."

"Trust me, I already know. I want you to do what you do best, and I'll do what I do best. Anyway, find a place to park, and I'll see you soon. Everyone should know who you are over here, so you shouldn't have trouble getting around."

I got off my cell and watched Agent Garcia pull into the staging area for the FBI's team and forensic van, which were set up close to the crime scene near the edge of the river. I, on the other hand, pulled off the street into a dirt lot, parked among a few news vans, and stepped out into a nice muddy puddle. Luckily for me, only the law enforcement people should recognize me; the last thing I need is a nice long walk in the cold, brisk air with microphones shoved in my face. On second thought, there is one person in the media circus who *does* know who I am and my connection to the case, and that's Christina Moore of Channel 4 News. Still, I don't have the time or the patience to talk about that now. I'm sure I'll have to deal with her shortly.

"Did you stop to get another cup of coffee? If you're going to be late, make sure you bring me one too."

"I took the scenic route on my way over. By the way, remind me never to ride with you, Maria. You drive worse than I do."

"Thanks. That means a lot coming from a guy who wrecked four government vehicles in one night."

"Hey, that doesn't count, I was driving only two of them. And I wasn't driving recklessly, either. I don't care what the report said."

That was a crazy night. Cappelano was there before he went rogue and all crazy. Come to think of it, I'm not sure he wasn't already killing, but I do know that he was still working for the FBI. We were on a stakeout, and it was like day four or six, probably six when some guys came upon us and started shooting. We got out of there, barely, and while we were being chased, our back-up vehicle also got wrecked. Technically I ended up in both cars before they got wrecked, so I see her point. Long story, different day. Back to the case.

"You're lucky that your ability to investigate cancels out the majority of your faults because sometimes I wonder why I'm putting my neck out for you."

"You can look at it that way, or you can look at it like I do—those faults *help* me investigate. By the way, where's the coroner? Have you talked to them yet?"

"He's the guy in the tweed jacket over there. Bright guy, horrible fashion sense. I haven't had a chance to be briefed by him yet."

"Why don't you go talk to Mr. Tweed?" I said. "I'm going to check out the body and track down the first person to the scene. We'll meet up later and compare notes. Sound good?"

"Fine by me, I'll catch up with you in a bit, Neil. Let's try and keep the excitement to a minimum for your first day back on the job, okay?"

"I'm almost insulted that you think I can't even make it through one day without causing trouble. I'll see you soon. Let's get to work."

Maria headed off to talk to the coroner as I made my way toward the body. More than likely, the coroner will tell Garcia that the body was dumped here. That the victim was probably killed twelve to eighteen hours ago, and that they can't say much more until the body gets back to the morgue. That's just my guess, but it's an educated one because Cappelano is consistent when it comes to his time frame with body dumps. He likes a clean scene; it's never pretty if you dump a body when it's fresh and there's blood everywhere. It's kind of pointless for Garcia to talk to the coroner this early, but I want to get a look at the body without her breathing over my neck. Plus I want to see if she'll trust me to wander on my own.

As I made my way to the body, I noticed something odd about the way it was positioned. Considering the temperature of the water and the rigidity of the soil along the banks this time of year, the body should have settled into the dirt at the river's edge a little more than it had. It looked as if she had only been there for a little while. I needed to find the first officer on the scene and learn how the victim was found. This wasn't some crazy super-detective detail; any good investigator should have seen something didn't look right. Imagine seeing a half-melted ice cube on a towel, but the towel is dry. It wouldn't add up.

Though her face was hard to get any detail from all the cuts, my heart kept telling me I knew her. The young woman bore an uncomfortably close resemblance to Ashley Gracin, Lawrence's daughter. There's no way that Cappelano needed attention badly enough to go after an old colleague's daughter; at least that's what I hoped. Lawrence Gracin still worked for the bureau; he's the guy who became my mentor after Cappelano disappeared. Then again, it had been four years, and Cappelano's habits could have changed a lot in that time. I couldn't let what I *thought* I knew about him blur my judgment. Still, one thing about Cappelano's methods clearly hadn't changed: burned into the victim's right ankle was an inch-tall "V" enclosed in a circle. I called Garcia's cell to ask her who the first officer on the scene was. Deciding it was okay to work as a team and follow the chain of command sometimes, even if it went against my better nature.

"Hey Maria, did you happen to find out the name of the officer who got here first?"

"Officer Stanley Johnson, from the Detroit Police Department. He's over by the reporters. The chief of police is about to give a statement right now. You should be able to sneak in there and talk to him without any issue. Any word on the body or an ID?"

"I'm not sure yet. I need to get a few questions answered before I can say anything definitive. I did see a brand marking on her body consistent with Cappelano. I'll track you down in a bit when I find something more concrete. Did the coroner have anything interesting to say?

"Nope, just the usual story. It was a basic Cappelano dump. They're looking for a way to ID the victim other than fingerprinting. It looks as if he hasn't changed completely since we last dealt with him. I'll see you around in a few."

The last person I want to talk to right now is a Detroit Police officer. Don't get me wrong, they do a good job, they just aren't the friendliest people to deal with. Then again, you wouldn't be too chipper either if you worked in one of the highest crime cities in the world, in a job that pays next to nothing. A lot of these officers will make less in a year that many of the criminals they're chasing will make in a month.

"Officer Johnson, I presume? My name's Neil Baggio with the FBI. I know officers and agents haven't always gotten along, but I'm not your typical agent. I'm not sure I *am* an agent, technically," I said with a friendly chuckle.

"I know who you are, and I know about your reputation," Johnson said with a respectful nod, but giving back nothing in the way of warmth. "It's a pleasure to meet you, Mr. Baggio. What can I do for you?"

"I just really need to know what happened from the time you received the call to the time that the next person showed up. Can you help me out?"

"I've told you guys already. I swear, no one knows how to communicate anymore. Luckily for you, I admire your work and your attitude when you do it. Would you like the long version or only the parts that matter?"

"I just need to know two things, actually. Were you the one who actually found the body, or did someone else beat you there? Also, where was the body when you arrived?"

"This scene is right along my route, so I was the first one called. The person who called it in was a passerby named Michelle Samson. If you're looking for her, she's the blonde over there by that ambulance. The one with a blanket over her."

"Thank you, officer. One last thing, do you happen to have the name of the victim?"

"I believe her name is Ashley or Amber Gracin. I have it written down if you need the exact name. One of the first responders recognized her. We don't have a definitive ID, but we're all pretty confident. Nothing will be released to the press, but it's how we're operating until otherwise directed."

"No, it's okay. Her last name is what I was most interested in. Thanks again for everything, Officer Johnson." So that settled it. Cappelano was now targeting the families of FBI agents. This was no longer a manhunt—it was a war.

"Before you leave, Mr. Baggio, do you happen to know Ken Chamberlain?"

"Yeah, we're partners. We own and run CB, Inc."

"I thought I heard your name outside of the FBI. I've read about you in the paper a few times over the past year. Your company seems to do some great work. How long are you back with the bureau? Is it just for this case, or is it permanent?"

"Just this case, for now. But who knows? It might be longer, depending on how long this case takes and how many toes I step on along the way."

"Hey, can I ask you something off-topic?"

"No problem, just make it quick."

"Are you guys hiring over there? I need to get out of this job. I can't survive on the pay."

"I'll tell you what. Here's my card, give me a call tomorrow, and I'll set something up with Ken and myself. We'll see about getting you in part-time to start."

"Thanks for your consideration, Mr. Baggio. I've been doing this for a long time, and I love the field, just not the pay."

"My pleasure; we are always looking for great people. The pay is usually how law enforcement loses most of the good investigators to private companies like mine. I look forward to hearing from you tomorrow."

As I parted ways with Officer Johnson, my mind returned to the body of poor Ashley Gracin. I wasn't buying that she simply washed up to the edge. With the current moving away from the shore, the way Ashely's body was resting on the dirt, and how carefully Cappelano had presented his previous murders, it just didn't make sense. The body was tied down here, I was sure of it. It had to have been moved by someone or something. Cappelano doesn't just dump a body to be found randomly. He sets up a crime scene like a photograph of sorts. Planning every last detail of his kills from picking the victim to dumping the body and how he expects it to be discovered. Every variable must be accounted for from beginning to end.

The other thing that threw me for a loop is that he did this to Ashley Gracin. To be honest, it scared me. I had assumed my family would be safe from harm's way, but this was a dramatic departure from Cappelano's old pattern. For God's sake, he was at Ashley's first communion when he was still with the bureau, and now she turns up dead with his signature on her. I can only hope there was some deeper motivation for it. Simply killing her for joy would mean he has crossed into a new level of killing, even for his psychotic ass. I can only hope that Ashley didn't recognize him while he tortured and killed her, since he has yet to kill someone without putting them through excruciating pain first. Who knows? Maybe being recognized by his victim was part of the fun this time. Before I got too upset thinking about the whole thing, I needed to go over and talk to Michelle Samson. According to the officers' notes, she was the one who called in the body.

"Good afternoon, miss," I said as I approached the shell-shocked-looking blond woman whom Johnson had pointed out. "Are you Michelle Samson?"

"I am. Is there something I can help you with?"

"Sorry. Where are my manners? My name is Neil Baggio. I work with the FBI. Can I just take a few moments of your time and ask you some questions?"

"I've already talked to the FBI, and I didn't lie about anything. What's this about? I'm not a suspect, am I?"

"That's not it at all. You have no need to worry. We know who did it. It's catching him. That's the hard part."

"What do you need to know, then? I answered everything they asked me," she said, her voice trembling.

"Where was the body when you found it?"

"It was on the shore, just like I told the other officers. I saw the body, leaned over, and checked to see if she was alive, and then I called nine-one-one."

"If she was on the shore, how did your pants get soaking wet? Did you fall in afterward?"

"When I approached her, I checked for a pulse and tried

CPR, and when I did that, I slid on the mud and fell in the water."

"You performed CPR on her? I thought you said you called nine-one-one after you checked to see if she was alive. According to the coroner, she was dead for more than twelve hours by the time you got to her. Rigor mortis had already set in. Are you sure you performed CPR?"

"Well, I used to work as an EMT, but I just started working at a senior community. Old habits die hard. I saw her and did the first thing I could think of, and then I dialed nine-one-one. I was pretty sure I did. I'm all confused right now. I'm sorry if I'm not any help."

"Thanks for your time, Ms. Samson. If you think of anything else, or if you just need someone to talk to about everything, here's my card."

"Thanks. What did you say your name was?"

"Baggio. Neil Baggio. And thank you, you were a big help. I'll make sure one of the officers gets you home safely.

"Thanks again, good luck with the investigation."

I tracked down Maria, and we finally got a chance to exchange notes. The coroner confirmed to her that the deceased was Ashley Gracin, Lawrence Gracin's daughter. I wasn't certain at first because her face was cut up beyond recognition, but Officer Johnson removed all doubt when he gave me her last name. Judging by the condition of the body, she had been killed more than twelve hours earlier, but she had been in the water only four to six hours. That meant Cappelano probably picked her up yesterday morning when she was on her usual morning run. Then took his time killing her, and then brought her body here at night to arrange the final display that we found today. This case was already personal, but now that mistake years ago has caused the death of a mentor's daughter. I just found another reason to put this fucker behind bars or just two in his chest. Maybe another in his skull for good measure. I've never contemplated murder, but I suddenly felt a rage I had never experienced before in, one that might only be satisfied with blood. Maybe it's better I'm on the outside working as an FBI consultant this time around.

As I continued to walk around the scene, I noticed a news crew making their way toward me with the utmost urgency. By the time I recognized Christina Moore from Channel 4 News, I didn't have enough time to make an evasive action. Christina is a vulture who helped ruin my shot at Cappelano the first time around. She constantly followed the other agents and me on the team while we were on stakeouts or when we'd get a lead on something or someone. Out of nowhere, she'd fly in behind us with a camera crew, trying to get the exclusive. Eventually we had to get a court injunction to keep her from inhibiting the investigation.

"Agent Baggio, Christina Moore with Channel 4 News. Can we get a moment of your time? Is it true that the body found was that of Ashley Gracin, the daughter of your old mentor in the FBI?"

"As if you're going to give me a choice of saying anything or not," I said, trying very, very hard to stay cool and not catch a felony assault charge with cameras on me.

"We are not commenting on anything at this time. When we have more information, we will make sure to keep you up to date."

"Agent Baggio, it's just a simple question. Has Veritas come back? Is he coming after the FBI? Why did he target Ashley Gracin?"

"I told you no comment. Now get out of my face before I make you. A girl has just been found brutally murdered, and you're acting like you've never covered a homicide before. Get these cameras out of here."

"We just—"

"Someone, please get her out of here right now."

I probably could have handled that better, but I figured if I made the story about me and not Ashley, it would better for Lawrence and his family. Keeping Ashley's name out of the paper for at least one day and giving them time to grieve privately is the least I could do for a man who has taught me so much. So I decided I would lean even harder into the old misdirection play on the media coverage. Time for Crazy Neil to make an appearance.

"Hey guys, why don't you get a nice close-up of the fucking body?" I yelled at the Channel 4 News crew as they were retreating. "I bet that would help pump up your story. You're fucking weak, Christina, you know that?" Lawrence will understand what I'm doing, Cappelano will see me on TV and won't be able to resist reaching out to me, and I always like yelling at Christina. She's actually great at her job, and a good person off-camera, I just hate what she does for a living.

"Baggio, calm down," Maria said, rushing over to pull me away. "What the fuck are you doing?"

"Don't worry, Maria, I'm just having a little fun at the expense of the news."

"I thought we were going to try and stay away from all the excitement today."

"Hey, I tried my best, but Christina ticked me off. The last thing Lawrence and his family need is Ashley's death being exploited for entertainment. This way, I become the story, instead of the body. I'd much rather see 'FBI Agent Goes Nuts at Crime Scene' on the news instead of Lawrence's picture."

"You old softie, I didn't know you cared. But did you have to go postal?"

"Probably not, but I got caught up in the moment."

After my fun little squabble with the Channel 4 News crew, it was time to calm down and get refocused on Cappelano. I made the rounds and talked to some agents I hadn't seen in a few years. I even called Lawrence Gracin and left a message of condolences on his voice mail. I'm sure he'll know why I went delirious on Christina tonight; he was the one who taught me how to manipulate and misdirect the media, after all. I just prayed that his family could get through this in one piece.

It was dark by the time Maria caught up to me again. "I think it's time to head out of here. What do you say, Neil?"

"Yeah, I guess you're right. It's almost nine, and we have a long day tomorrow."

"We have a lot of long days coming up. You know that. Go home and rest up."

"You too. I'll see you bright and early tomorrow. Say, ten or so?"

"Nice try. Let's make it eight tomorrow morning. I'll let you sleep in a bit."

"You're a peach, Maria. I'll see you tomorrow."

As fast as my thoughts are flying right now, I just hope I can get some rest, even if it's a simple two-hour nap in my chair.

4

He told me to stop chasing him or he'd kill them.

Being awake at four in the morning seems to be a regular event in my life lately, more so now that Cappelano is out of hiding. It's not like I'm trying to stay awake; there's just too much on my mind right now. Regardless of the reason for my insomnia, the problem is that it's late, and I need to be up shortly, whether I like it or not. I really need to talk to Father Roberts tonight. He always seems to find a way to help me refocus my thoughts. Father Roberts and I were born on the same block and in the same year. Our fathers were best of friends, and eventually the two of us would be as well. I found his number in my cell phone and dialed. He picked up after one ring, as I knew he would.

"Neil, it's been a while since you called me this early," Father Roberts said. "I'm assuming you know, after all these years, I haven't changed my routine?" He's always been a morning person, even when we were kids, but as a man of the cloth, he has raised it to new heights.

"Exactly, some things are a constant in life, and your morning routine is right up there with my need for coffee," I said. "I just really needed someone to talk to, and you're the only person I'm able to open up to, ever since the fight with my dad."

"You know your father is too stubborn to make the first move. You have to be the one to reach out. But I'm going to guess, as usual, you're calling me about one thing, but something else is bothering you, so why don't we skip the dance this morning and get right to the real issue."

It's hard to get away with anything when you share so much history with a person. He has a point, too. He knows my brain is great at multitasking and processing a ton of information at once. I also use that as a defense mechanism when I don't want to deal with something I should.

"This is exactly why I called you, Father Roberts. You know how to smell the shit in my voice even across the phone."

"Are you all right, Neil? I have a feeling you've got more than just your family on your mind. Let's talk about Carol Lynn; that always calms you down. We'll clear your mind a bit, then come back to what's really bothering you."

Now he's managing me, like a veteran hostage negotiator. I swear he missed his calling in law enforcement. The way he manipulates me gets me to slow my mind, focus on something simple that brings me joy. It calms my mind and allows me to find my center, which will allow me to focus on the root of the problem I called him about in the first place. I'm truly blessed to have a friend like him.

"She's growing up so fast," I said. "I'm already practicing my speech to give to the guys she brings by the house. With every passing day, she reminds me of her mother more and more."

We spoke about Carol Lynn, how she always has a way of making it all just wash away. Anyone who has kids can understand, and some who don't, can too. But when you hold the hand of your child, get a hug from them, or hear them tell you they love you, it just changes it all. When you work in the world that I do, especially when someone like Cappelano is out in the world with you, it can put stress and pressure on you like no other. My kid keeps me sane.

I know some of you are thinking, how does he not freak out and move Sheila and Carol Lynn to Canada to get away from Cappelano? The truth is, right after I left the bureau I went off the deep end and sunk everything I had into tracking him down. My money, my friendships, maybe even my soul. Cappelano *did* get to them, to show me that he could, to scare me. I think in a way to tell me to stop chasing him; more than in a way, he told me to stop chasing him or he'd kill them. I moved Sheila and Carol Lynn three times. He found them every time, I finally had to step away, accept to myself that it was no longer my job to track him down. It wasn't my responsibility, but I never let it go. It was like dealing with an injury you have to work around but never letting it heal.

"Now that you're relaxed, how about we talk about what's really bothering you?" Father Roberts spoke in the calming tone of an airline pilot reassuring you that it's just a little turbulence and you're already through the worst of it.

"All right, if there's anyone who will be able to understand, it's you," I said. "Your old man had a way of straightening my dad's head out, and you seemed to inherit his gifts. The way he could listen without judgment and find the source of a person's pain."

"I still have those two photos in my apartment, by the way."

"Oh, you mean one of you and me when we were in second grade and one of our fathers around the same age? They're kind of creepy if you ask me. It's like the same kids wearing different clothes. Wait, you did it again."

"Did what? Got you to relax and take your mind off of what's bothering you for a moment, so we can talk about it calmly?"

"Yeah, that's exactly what I'm talking about. I'm scared, man. I mean *really* scared. I don't know if I have it in me to make another run at Cappelano. The farther away I get from this case, the more I realize what it's all about."

What Father Roberts is already aware of is the details pertaining to me and Cappelano's relationship, how it started, and how I feel he groomed me specifically to be his rival. And now I harbor an unhealthy resentment for it if you haven't figured that out already.

"What are you afraid of? Failure? Afraid of how things ended the last time, what you had to accept, how you feel you gave up? Not every wrong in the world is yours to fix, you know that, Neil, not even Cappelano's. Especially his."

I mean, who isn't afraid to fail in general, now add to it the fact that your failure means that more people will be needlessly murdered, your peers will judge you. The guilt you'll carry will undoubtedly harm your ability to ever have a healthy relationship again. I guess you could say I have a little bit more fear in me than your average middle school kid on the bowling team. As for Cappelano, that's where the problem lies. I used to feel that it was my duty to stop him because I let his crimes happen on my watch. Then I realized he put me in this game without my knowledge, against my will, and I got resentful, wanted out, convinced myself I was done. Now I have conflicting feelings that push me in and pull me out constantly.

"It's more than just the fear of failure. I'm almost afraid to go to sleep at all. Every time I close my eyes, I have the same nightmare over and over. I just can't take it anymore."

"Is there a particular event in the dream that's disturbing you, or is it just fear itself?" He was trying to get me to examine my anxiety, not merely the summary points of the nightmare.

"In a way, it's the same thing over and over. I keep dreaming that Cappelano decides to come after my family because I won't go back to the FBI and play his sick game. I keep seeing my daughter getting kidnapped by Cappelano, and then I see her death."

"Ah, that old standby. It's been a couple of years since you've had this nightmare, is it not? Part of the problem is that half of it isn't a dream. He really *did* get to your family, but as he told you, he wouldn't harm them. He was only doing it for your attention."

Once I stopped coming after Cappelano, he started getting angry with me. He would apologize, then he would tell me it's not my fault, because the bureau set me up to fail. He told me I needed time to rest and be with my family. Then he would get angry again. I could hear him struggling with his own grasp of reality, with this thing he was becoming, or always was, and I just didn't see it until it was too late. It was during this time after I had left the bureau that I was able to see the whole picture for what it was. Cappelano had manipulated me from the very beginning. He hadn't killed me, but he had taken my life just the same.

"When I read in the paper about his first suspected killing in four years, I knew Cappelano was back and gunning for me. I just don't think I'll be able to handle the pressure, not this time. Not to mention, how am I supposed to trust his crazy ass? Knowing what I know now, how he played me and groomed me for this. He went after another colleague's daughter. What's to say he won't go after mine?"

"Still haven't gotten over the way things went down back in 2001, have you? Neil, how many times have we gone over this? This isn't something you'll ever get over, it's something you need to accept, something you need to use as fuel to catch him. Stop letting this resentment hold you back. When you're a man on fire, you're unstoppable. EMBRACE IT, NEIL!"

"You don't have to yell at me, Father Roberts. Then again, I deserve it. I need someone in my face right now, and I think that's what's holding me back. Everyone is waiting for me to act."

"I'll be praying for you, Neil. I'll tell you what, come to the church sometimes, I'll put you in your place really good, get those juices flowing. Anytime you need it, I'm here for you. That's what brothers are for."

"Brother from another mother, I'm lucky to have you in my life. When this is all over, I'm going to need a place to disappear somewhere. Maybe we can do a mission together somewhere."

"Don't tease me, Neil. You know I've been asking you to help me with one for years, I think it'll be great for your soul. Have a great day, Neil, and do me a favor: catch this asshole."

"For you, I guess I can do that. Thanks for listening to me. If I have a crisis of confidence again, I'll have you come kick my ass like when we were kids. Have a blessed day, Father."

Just like that, I was back on track. Father Roberts has a way of pushing me, getting me back to the center so I can focus. I know you're asking, how can you call your best friend "Father Roberts"? It took some time, but eventually you just get used to it. Sure, the formality of it is a little weird, but I can't call him anything else.

5

I knew there was a missing piece to this story.

It was 6:00 a.m., I'd already made it through my first three alarms, and now the aroma of coffee from the kitchen was arousing my nostrils. I rolled over in my queen-size bed and searched for the remote on the floor to turn on Channel 4 News. Not that there's any difference among the channels—I just wanted to see if they had captured my good side. Sure enough, there I was. A cameraman caught the tail end of my screaming but missed most of the good stuff. At least they weren't running with Lawrence's name all over the place. That was my intention, and I considered it a victory.

I was sitting there watching the news, dozing into and out of consciousness, when the final alarm in the series of four went off. It's the loudest alarm I have, and it launched my ass in the air. I sat up at attention and shot across the room to shut it off. I thought about climbing back into bed, but the smell of grounds and water brewing pulled me into the kitchen to start the morning.

I tried those energy drinks for a while, but they just didn't do it for me. I even tried caffeine pills, which only made me shake incessantly. I like my coffee, and I like it with plenty of cream and sugar; when I'm done, it doesn't even look like coffee anymore. With a warm cup in hand, I found my way to the bathroom for the first shower of the day. The bathroom is my second favorite room in this house, second only to the living room because of its fireplace, leather chair, and the Baker Street feeling to it. Now, I'm not Sherlock by any means and don't claim to be, but I do have a great memory and a keen eye for observation. I can't rattle off any insect species, but that's the literary detective. I'm the real thing.

As a kid, I had an affinity for my uncle, who was a cop. He was rarely around, but he made a permanent impression on me. He was also the one who introduced me to Holmes and Watson. The idea that a criminal's most diabolical plans could be completely blown apart by a detective who knew what to look for. It was Sherlock's problem-solving at a Hall of Fame level that drove me toward chasing bad guys. He had an amazing memory for the most minute details and an ability to draw information like he had a hardwired search engine at his mental disposal. I have a great operational memory that allows me to understand information at a glance, but not on that magical, almost fantasy level. I'm more like the know-it-all at a party who drives you nuts and can't cite any of his facts, but when you look it up, it's right.

Twenty minutes into my shower, and I could hear the girls

getting restless in the other room. I know I should have put them out before I got in. I made my way to the Jeep to start the vehicular obstacle course the city of Detroit has set up for us commuters. I started to feel guilty for not being the first one to make the call to my mentor about his daughter. I'm also a little surprised he hasn't reached out to me yet. Narcissistic, I know, but the thought is still running through my mind.

Several potholes and numerous orange pylons later, I pulled into a parking garage near the bureau. For once, I was on time. On my way up to Garcia's office, I began the usual good mornings: head nods to the guys and smiles to the ladies. Most of the people here are friendly. It's the assholes who ruin it for everyone else. I made my way down the hall to the canteen room to get another cup of coffee. For those of you counting, this will be my fifth cup of coffee of the day, and it's not even 8:00 a.m. I know I'm addicted to it, but it's better than the cigarettes I smoke and the whiskey I drink. Besides, I'll probably die at the hands of some guy I caught cheating on his wife. I don't have a death wish, I'm just realistic about the choices I've made in my life, that's all.

For example, Ken's grandfather smoked a pack of no-filter cigarettes every single day for his whole life. He drank a fifth of vodka a week for the better part of fifty years, and he lost his life on a fishing trip. He went out early in the morning to catch some walleye and didn't check the weather before he left. Then he got caught in a storm and flipped his boat. They found his body two days later washed up on the shore. The man smoked, drank, and kept a horrible diet, and none of it killed him. Instead, his death came from doing something he loved, something completely harmless. It just goes to show you that life can catch up to you regardless of how you live your life, so why not enjoy your life to the fullest extent? Of course, I'd be lying if I didn't mention that his drinking probably led to him missing the weather report in the first place, but come on, don't be that reader.

"How are you doing this morning, Neil?" said Agent Garcia when I entered the doorway to her office. She had her phone to her ear, as usual.

"Chipper as can be," I said, flashing the fakest smile I could muster. "I'm not much of a morning person, especially when I forget to go to bed the night before."

"Give me a second; I'm on hold with the coroner's office."

"Not a problem at all. Have they finished the autopsy report yet?"

"Almost. The coroner said he'll have his report for us in about an hour."

"Are you telling me I could have gotten in another hour of sleep? I guess I can't do anything about it now. Any ideas on how I can keep myself entertained for the next hour?"

"How about I show you to your new office. I think you'll really enjoy it."

"It's not like you guys to be giving out offices to outside

contractors. Not to mention, I thought this floor was at capacity already. Did you toss a chair into the mop closet or something?"

That got a small laugh from Maria, which I appreciated. "Dang it, how did you know? No, the truth is, if you're coming back to help, they want you back in full capacity. Hell, your new office is bigger than mine."

"Who are 'they,' and what are we talking about? Wait a minute—there are only two offices bigger than yours, and one of them is Bob's. Bob's gone, isn't he?"

"It seems that some people above the head of your buddy Hendrickson think you're worth something," Maria said, smiling in a way that suggested maybe she agreed.

I could really care less, but the point is they wanted me back full-time—not just for one case—and they knew this one case could take months, even years. Bob's office was still one of the nicest spaces on this floor, if not the entire building. I guess it's *my* office now, which is a waste of space because I'll almost never use it. Then again, if losing his office sends Bob Hendrickson into a spiral of rage and depression, I'll gladly accept it.

"Well, it's nice to know I've got some support, at least for now," I said. "What's the catch?"

"Catch? There isn't any catch. The bureau wants to keep one of their best homicide investigators happy, that's all. Can't you just accept the fact that we want you back because you're good?"

Like most political or governmental agencies, the bureau makes decisions based on a balancing act of three things: budget, politics, and talent. I mentioned talent last on purpose. Talent can only get you so far if the right people don't want to see you succeed. That was part of my problem when I started back in '96. I was an outsider who was outperforming people at the academy, a talented rising star who also pushed the boundaries. Cappelano noticed me and took me under his wing. At the time, he was the golden child of the bureau, coming off of some huge wins. The fact that he chose me as his protégé made top brass keep an eye on me, and middle management fucking *hate* me.

"No, I can't accept it, Maria, because for the past five years the bureau hasn't wanted anything to do with me. Why are they giving me Hendrickson's old office, anyway? You guys know I seldom use an office."

"He got promoted to a new field office in DC. You know how they like to play political favorites out there. I guess all that work got him where he wanted to go. Though, if you ask me, it's not much of a promotion."

"When did this happen? We were just talking to him yesterday."

"Last night. They said they needed him ASAP in DC, and they wanted him out of the office by this morning. You know how fast the bosses can move, especially when they want something." On the flip side, they can move slower than molasses in the dead of winter when they don't want to.

"So, who's going to be running things around here? Is someone getting promoted, or are they bringing someone in from outside?"

"They have a new guy coming in, on an interim basis. It seems the powers that be know that you are the key if we're ever going to catch Cappelano, and they want to make sure you're as comfortable as possible."

Damn! This is bigger than I thought. Apparently someone in Washington wanted Cappelano caught so badly that they were even willing to cater to me. If it weren't for Hendrickson, I probably would have caught that son of a bitch the first time. But he kept giving me this shit about doing it by the book and not leveraging the kinds of resources I needed. He was just pissed that I had an inside track, and he didn't. It got really annoying, and it slowed me down. And now Ashley Gracin is dead. I hope Hendrickson's replacement understands that I'm going to catch Cappelano this time, no matter what.

"So when do we meet this new guy?" I asked.

"Funny you should ask. He's right behind you. Neil Baggio, meet Michael Angelo Ponecelli."

"Hey Neil, you can just call me Mike. That's what everyone else calls me. And yes, I know, 'Michael Angelo' is a little nut, but my parents really love Italy."

Son of a bitch, this guy is big. Mike Ponecelli filled the door frame as if he were wearing it for a coat. He stood at about six-two and weighed at least 280 pounds, his huge chest twice the width of my own. A genetic freak, in other words. He had a high and tight and was dressed casually, not at all your typical FBI field-office supervisor. Usually, you're stuck with uptight Harvard grads who have barely been in the field. Not this guy. My new boss looked like he'd been through plenty of battles. I had a feeling that the two of us would get along just right. And with a last name like Ponecelli, I think it was safe to say he's Italian. How can you not like someone with Italian roots? I like me, and I'm Italian.

"It's a pleasure to meet you, Mike," I said, extending my hand, which immediately disappeared into his hand like my daughter's in mine. "We should sit down soon and go over the case so far."

"The pleasure is mine, Neil, but I need to get settled in first. How about we meet in the briefing room in an hour. See you there?"

"Sure. But I don't promise anything." Mike nodded warmly and retreated to his office. I think he already knew that if he was going to supervise me, he'd need to have the patience of a saint.

"Come on, Neil, let's get back to my office," Maria said. "I should have the faxed autopsy report on my desk at any moment. Plus the techs need to get in here to install your computer."

"That was great, our new boss is wearing jeans. By the way,

can you make sure I don't get a desktop computer? I like having a laptop so I can work anywhere at any time."

The information around the office is that Mike is the kind of guy who would rather bust a few heads and deal with the paperwork later, which might be what I need right now. I used to be crazy aggressive, but after all these years of chasing after Cappelano, I almost feel burned out on him. Don't get me wrong, I want that sick bastard. I just can't tell if I'm trying to outsmart myself and my approach to this case, or if I'm losing my edge.

"Bossing people around already, and you haven't even moved in. As for Mike being casual, I don't see the problem. He's the boss, he can do what he wants."

It seems Mike started out in the military in the Army Reserve. Then he received his bachelor's in criminology and picked up a master's degree in management and finished up with a four-year tour of Europe, Asia, and the Middle East. He'd been through some tough confrontations, both politically and literally, definitely someone I could respect. Word is he'd been with the FBI only a couple of years. After he successfully ran a field office out in the middle of nowhere. He was moved to Las Vegas as an assistant special agent in charge and is now back in control of an office here in Detroit. Maria continued to fill me in that his family is legendary in the FBI. His grandfather, father, and uncle were all agents, and his uncle still is. That explains why he's so young and in a position of leadership—he's been groomed since birth.

"Have a seat," Maria said when we got back to her office. "My assistant is bringing in copies of the autopsy report that was just sent over."

"Hey, did you see the news this morning? They buried the story just like I told you they would. Instead of seeing Gracin's face all over the news, you saw me screaming at the top of my lungs, making a scene."

"I seriously wonder about you sometimes, Neil, but I have to admit you were right. You looked good on camera, too. As for your acting skills, I wouldn't quit your day job."

While Agent Garcia was giving me a hard time for my little public freak-out yesterday, her secretary poked in and dropped off two copies of the autopsy report. I grabbed a copy before the papers even hit Garcia's desk. I was in a hurry to see if my hypothesis was true, that the victim was originally tied up in the river and not left on the shore.

"Thanks for your vote of confidence, Garcia. Now give me a second: I'm looking for something here. There it is. That's what I was looking for."

"There what is? What did you find?"

"There were no abrasions found on Ashley's back or neck, but they found bruising around her hips and torso as if something had been tied around her waist."

"Why is that surprising? I don't think I'm following you on this."

"There wasn't anything at the crime scene, no rope or other bindings that could have been used to tie someone up. I had a feeling that Michelle Swanson had removed it, and in all the excitement, forgot that she had done so. We need to get back to the crime scene, and right now."

"What about your briefing with Ponecelli? It's in twenty minutes. Don't tell me you're going to blow it off."

"I'll tell Mike. Just call the dive team and have them meet us out there."

"You're really going to ditch your first briefing? Picking right back up where you left off, I see."

"We don't have time to kill, Maria. The current is destroying evidence every second we waste. But you're right, we should sit down and talk about it in a group setting first," I said, sarcastically as shit.

I made my way over to Mike's office to fill him in on my hunch and where Maria and I were headed. He grabbed his jacket and told me he was coming along. He didn't just want to tag along, he also wanted me to catch him up on this case as much as possible. He told me he read the case files, but he wanted me to fill in the holes; he wanted the truth from me and where I saw this case going. I knew I liked this guy when I met him.

"Let's take my car. Would you mind driving, Maria? I need to talk to Neil without distractions."

"Sounds good, Mike. Safety first."

"There's my car right there. The bureau really took care of me in Vegas, and they let me bring this baby up for my new assignment. That reminds me: I need to have the registration decals changed from Nevada to Michigan."

He wasn't kidding about the FBI taking care of him. Mike drove a Ford Explorer that was tricked out with every gadget I could ever imagine in a car. Plus a mini forensics lab in the back so you could test for basics such as gunpowder residue and blood. That would help a lot if you had a suspect in custody, or if you needed to obtain evidence on site. It just didn't make sense that any department would spend the money on a vehicle like this, let alone allow Mike to take it with him to his new gig. He must really be part of a legacy. If the bureau let him keep a vehicle that was probably worth upward of three hundred thousand dollars after you added all the aftermarket upgrades it picked up in Vegas.

"Why don't you fill me in on everything, Neil? Tell me what was cut out of the files. I know something's missing."

"I don't know what you mean. I didn't leave anything out of that report. I can guarantee you that there wasn't one fact from the case that didn't make it into that file."

"I'm not saying that *you* left anything out. I'm saying someone went in later and 'disappeared' a few things. I can tell you wrote the majority of it, but then someone else made some cuts and rewrote it. This isn't my first time around the block. I'm ex-military, I've read plenty of chopped up files."

"After I left the bureau, a lot of the case files that I wrote were edited by FBI brass to keep privileged information out," I explained.

"Things like—"

"Franklin Cappelano is 'Veritas.' I figured that out after his third murder—things just started to piece together. But tracking him has gotten extremely hard over the years because he's gotten better and better. If it weren't for the brand that he put on each victim, we probably wouldn't know which murders were his."

"I figured that one out on my own. I didn't know his name, because those files are pretty much 'lost' to people like you and me."

"The other part that's missing is how I found a pattern after the Anna Walton murder."

"Anna Walton? She was number seven, right?"

"Close. She was number eight, his second-to-last murder, before I started to catch on to his movements and almost caught him. But there was a problem with the bureau."

"Problem? You mean you told them you figured out the killer's identity and you wanted to act on it? Then they said they needed time to analyze the situation before they could get clearance to give you that kind of manpower? Something like that?"

"Pretty much. It sounds like you know what you're talking about. Ever run into a similar problem?"

"Like I said, I was in the military. I came across those problems all the time. In fact, that's how I ended up in the FBI. I was told I had to transfer to another government branch or be discharged. So I followed my family name to the FBI. I figured that would help me get clear of the people I was constantly butting heads with."

"So how'd you get the job out here in Detroit? If you don't mind me asking. You're not the most qualified guy we've had come through this office, even if you do know your way around a case file."

"Trust me, I know. I was up for the job in Vegas, and the people out West were tired of my antics, so they shipped me out East. It just happened to be fortunate timing with Cappelano's reappearance and the FBI needing you back in to capture him."

"It's good to know I'm not the only one in the office now who pisses off my superiors. This relationship might end up being the best thing for both of us."

"I hear you."

As Maria guided our lab on wheels down I-94, Mike and I began to talk about the case and my history with the killer known as Veritas. I filled Mike in on my close, personal relationship with Cappelano, and the late-night phone calls from him taunting me and egging me on. After twenty or so minutes of us bantering back and forth, I saw everything click in Mike's head. He started to understand why I've been grinding this case out for so long and why I take small defeats so personally.

"I knew there was a missing piece to this story," Mike said. "The files made sense to some extent, but the way you and the bureau reacted at the end of the case just didn't match up, and that's how I knew something was up."

"It was really hard to have complete confidence from my superiors throughout the case. Then when I was actually close to catching him, they pulled the rug out from under me. It just drove me crazy."

"I want you to know that I have your back all the way, Neil. This case is going to make or break my career. Not to mention your future with the bureau rests on the outcome as well. I guess what I'm trying to say is, if you go down, then I'll be going down with you."

"Thanks, Mike. It really means a lot to hear that. I've had so many trust issues with the bureau and the people I work with. No offense to you, Maria, it's just hard to trust anyone from this office ever again."

"None taken," Maria said. "It looks like we're almost here, guys. I'll park next to the USERT van, and we'll go from there." Maria was referring to the Underwater Search and Evidence Response Team—the FBI dive team. I don't usually toss jargon around when layman's terms work just as well. Maybe Maria was just trying to impress Mike with her encyclopedic knowledge of bureauisms.

At the site where the divers were getting ready, I saw an extra suit and tank sitting there, as if they were waiting for a friend to join them. It wasn't like the divers to use more than two or three guys, so I didn't know what the extra gear was for until we stepped out of the car and Mike began stripping his clothes off. The man was full of surprises today. First it was coming along on our evidence-gathering mission, and now he was actually going into the river with the dive team.

"Neil, don't give me that look. While I was doing my four-year tour, I did more than a handful of aquatic missions. You could say I'd like to be as hands-on as possible because the more invested I am in this case, the more trust you can have that I'll go to the wall for you."

"You don't need to do this for me, but thanks anyway. Just be careful down there. You never know what to expect if you find anything that Cappelano has left behind."

"While I'm down there, you and Maria can keep an eye on things from the dive team's van. There are monitors in there that are linked to the tiny cameras on top of our masks. That way, if you spot something we miss, you can let us know through the radio."

"All these high-tech toys are going to take a little getting used to. Good luck down there, Mike. Try not to do anything too dangerous," I said with a sarcastic chuckle.

Mike and the rest of the dive crew entered the chilling waters while Maria and I monitored their progress in a warm van. After thirty minutes, give or take, one of the dive team members made his first significant discovery. A large metal box, possibly a safe; it was too hard to make out for sure on the video relay. Mike swam over to the box to take a closer look before allowing the dive team to retrieve it. We had to be extra careful when dealing with Cappelano because he was known for rigging key evidence with explosives. Years ago, we lost a lead because an overzealous lab tech didn't fully inspect a stack of receipts left at a scene, and by the time he got them back to the lab, they were a pile of dust. We still don't know how Cappelano pulled that one off. If we didn't handle this safe with the utmost care, we could ruin any chance of finding evidence from Ashley Gracin's murder, and maybe even get Mike killed on his first day on the job.

"Hey Mike, what's that writing on the front of the safe?" I asked. "It looks like there's something etched into the door."

"B-A-G-G-I-O," Mike said, his voice crackling through the radio. "Neil, are you missing a safe at home by any chance?"

"Yes, I had an old safe in my garage stolen a couple of months ago, but there was nothing in it, and it didn't have my name carved into it. This must be Cappelano's way of saying, 'guess who was in your house recently.' I'd still be careful, Mike. If I know Cappelano, that thing could blow if you make a wrong move."

"I have a bad feeling about this already, Neil. Wait a minute . . . everyone out of the water now!"

All but one of the camera feeds cut away from the safe and suddenly angled upward s the other members of the dive team scrambled toward the surface of the water. "What's going on down there, Mike?"

"It looks like there's a digital lock under a case. This is some high-tech stuff. I'm guessing the old safe combination isn't going to work. Since it's digital, he probably changed it."

"I wouldn't try the old combination, anyway," I said. "Knowing Cappelano, he'd set the safe to detonate internally if we used it. Hold on. Try 08-06-98; that's the date of his first kill. That's all I can think of."

There was silence on the radio for ten very long seconds. "That's a no-go. Hey, Neil?"

"What's up, Mike?"

"You have less than three minutes to figure out a combination that will work, or this thing will blow inside or out, can't be certain. He set it to blow either way. If we don't figure this out soon, we're going to lose any evidence that might be here. That clock just started counting down."

"Fucking Cappelano, I can't stand this asshole. All right, give me a second to figure this out. I'll get it."

What the hell could the combination be? I didn't have the slightest idea. It could be the date Cappelano left the FBI, or maybe the date he killed his nephew. FUCK! I wouldn't let him beat me, not now, and not this way. He's sick, twisted, and deranged. If I were those things, what combination would I set?

"Hey Mike, try 01-02-03," Maria suggested. "I know it sounds stupid, but just try it. Cappelano is just messed up enough to pull something like that. His idea of a joke at our expense."

"I'll give it a try. What's the worst that can happen?" Another nerve-wracking pause. "It didn't work. By the way, you're down to a minute and a half."

Goddamn it. Come on, I can do this. Think, Neil. Are there any other dates that would be meaningful to him? Cappelano wants me to come up with the answer. So what is it?

"Hey Neil, what's your birthday?" Maria asked. "You always said he claims he's doing all of this for you."

"That's right. Cappelano liked to tell me that I'm the focus of his life, as bizarre as that sounds. It's worth a shot. Try 06-19-72, Mike."

"Okay, trying it now. In case you were wondering, we have only forty seconds left."

"As if I don't have enough pressure on me, you go and say something like that."

"That wasn't it either. Now we've got only twenty-seven seconds. Any other ideas in that head of yours?"

"Son of a bitch, why didn't I think of it sooner? Put in 12-12-15. That's got to be it."

I could barely watch as Mike typed in the combination. Most guys I knew—even most FBI agents—would have been swimming their asses off at that point, trying to get to shore and hide under a canoe before the timer hit zero. Not Mike. His hands went about their business like he was making a sandwich or something. The dude had heart.

"Thank God. Good work, Neil, you got it! I'll have the dive team pull this thing to shore. By the way, what were those numbers?"

"Believe it or not, that's Frank Sinatra's birthday. Cappelano and I both love to listen to Frank. I got him started on his Frank collection."

"Thank God you figured it out because we were fifteen seconds away from losing anything that's in here. I'll have the safe opened at the lab, so we can pull any evidence that might be inside."

"Great job, Mike, just get up here and let's get you dry and warmed up. We'll talk more about it then."

The dive team used the wench on the van to pull the safe to shore. Mike wasn't kidding—that thing was high tech. There was a pressure switch encased in Plexiglas under the safe that allowed for certain shifts in weight from the current. Cappelano had always been on the cutting edge of tactical technology, becoming an expert on everything from surveillance devices to weapons. He gave me my first education in FBI field tech gear—before he went crazy, that is. To be honest with you, I was scared shitless of what was to come.

"The dive team will get the safe back to the lab, and we'll have a couple of hours to kill before they get it processed, if not longer," Mike said to Maria and me when he was out of the water. "Anyone have an idea of where to go?"

"I say we go grab a cup of coffee. We can go to my favorite place. It's out of the way, but we have the time. Is that cool with you?"

"Sure, I'm game for a cup of coffee. Maria, how does that sound to you?"

"Since you know where we're headed, Neil, why don't you do the driving this time?"

One thing I noticed during this crazy day was how adept Maria was at reading a room. I could see how she was able to move up the ranks so quickly. Not only was she smart, but also she took time and picked her moments to contribute. Although things are progressing, there is still a boys' club culture in today's bureau, but she hadn't allowed it to slow her down. I wish I had her conviction and self-awareness at that age and stage of my career.

"No problem," I said. "I could use a break from being a passenger of an Indy car driver. You scare the shit out of me when you drive."

"I'll have to second that notion, Maria, you drive pretty crazy," Mike said. "Hey Neil, maybe we should get her one of those bumper stickers that say 'Drive It Like You Stole It.'"

"Haha, I get it, but that's not going to get you guys moving any quicker. I'll just assume at this point neither of you can handle a fast woman."

6

They spend a lot of time alone and around dead people, so asking us to come in for some live conversation is okay by me.

Mike was on the phone most of the time during our drive, talking to people at the lab. We noticed when we got to the safe on shore that it only contained a CD, held in a sealed plastic case, which could have been faked; it's not hard to seal a CD case. There were no identifying markings or labels on the CD, so we'd have to wait and see what the lab techs at the bureau could pull off of it. With Cappelano even something simple like this can be a form of misdirection.

Walking into Bella Café, the first thing most people notice is the two plasma TVs hanging on the wall. One on the back wall by the pool tables and the other hanging over a fireplace surrounded by three large fabric chairs, which you just sink into. There's also a big-screen TV just chilling to the left of the main counter. I've never seen it on, and the cable cord sitting on top of it suggests that it's not currently operational.

Bella Café isn't your everyday coffeehouse. As a matter of fact, it's a lot closer to a small sports bar. Imagine the setting and atmosphere of a coffeehouse armed with an arsenal of entertainment. In addition to the plasma TVs and pair of pool tables, there are touch-screen game machines and a game room in the back. As amenities are concerned, they serve an assortment of coffee, tea, and smoothies as well as desserts and a few sandwiches. There are only four employees, and it's frequented mainly by eastern Europeans. If you come early enough on a Saturday or Sunday, you'll find them watching soccer matches from overseas via satellite. Most of the regulars are men, and almost none of the conversation is in English.

The girl working the counter is of Iranian descent, recently out of high school, and studying at the local community college, as I recalled from the few brief conversations we've had. She was a friendly face that I had seen here before. I probably didn't have to tell her my order, but I didn't want Mike or Maria to realize how much I came here for coffee. It's bad enough that they see me with a cup in my hand all day long. I don't need them to know that I frequent the same coffee- house nearly every day, even though it's nearly ten miles from my house.

"Hey Neil, how are you doing today?" the barista said with a smile. "I was worried when I didn't see you earlier. It's not like you to miss your morning white chocolate mocha."

"I had to get to work early this morning. But it's okay now

because I came back this afternoon, and I even brought you some new customers."

"Well, I know what you want, Neil, but what can I get for the two of you?"

"I'll take the same thing that Neil got, that sounds good, but I'll take a small instead of a large," Garcia said, taking the easy way out. "You're next, Mike. What do you want?"

"I'll take a double shot of espresso with medium white chocolate mocha."

"Holy shit, man, do you have enough caffeine in that mix?" I said, simultaneously shocked and impressed. "All that at once would spike and crash me. I'm a marathon caffeine drinker; I can't binge it."

"I'm with Neil on this one, and I might give you some 'new guy' shit if you fall asleep in your office later. Just saying."

"Okay, enough of the joking around. Neil, you weren't kidding, this place is really nice. Why don't we go take seats over there by the window?"

As I led us over to the seats like a proper host, I noticed Maria heading toward the love seat. Mike noticed the same thing and started to make a play for the spot next to her. Luckily for me, I already had the inside track and was able to hold him off without making it obvious to Maria. At this point, I can't tell if I'd be as interested in Garcia if I didn't think others were chasing her too. She's attractive, has a brilliant mind, and she's ambitious. To be honest, those aren't the traits I usually look for in a date.

The server brought over our coffee with some napkins and those little cardboard sleeves you put around your cup so that you don't burn your hands. I wonder who came up with that; those things are amazing.

"Could you have waited any longer before you figured out the code to the safe? I was freaking out down there, Neil." Mike was a little dramatic, but that was understandable.

"I was going to wait until the very last second, but that's so cliché. The hero always stops the bomb at one. I thought fifteen would be a nice change of pace."

Right as we were talking, I could feel my mind start to simulcast back to Cappelano. He found a way to give a steroid shot to my personality and my ability as an investigator. The issue is with anything that can push traits to the surface; it can be good and bad. The problem now is that he left me with some form of performance anxiety that Father Roberts hit on when we spoke.

I have to keep it light with Mike and Maria. They want this case to go right, they want me to excel, but I really need someone in my face. That ass-kicking from Father Roberts may have to come sooner than later. As I begin to snap back to the conversation about the safe and my impeccable timing, I heard Mike chime in.

"Very funny, smart-ass. Is he always this witty, Maria? As for you, Neil, do you have any idea what Cappelano may have left for you in that safe?"

"Knowing him, it will be something that looks mundane and stupid but is actually of great importance. He likes to hide things in plain sight. There's also the chance it's some simple, sleight-of-hand bullshit, where he's trying to send us on a wild goose chase only to waste our time."

"How about you, Maria. Any ideas?"

"I really don't have any ideas on the CD. If anyone's going to have the best guess, it's going to be Neil. He's the one who has a history with Cappelano." Maria was right, simple and to the point.

"I see where this relationship is headed with the bureau and me," I said. "I'll have to make all the big decisions on Cappelano, won't I?" I wanted the responsibility on my shoulders, but I was also a little afraid of the pressure that would come with it. On the other hand, fear can be a good motivator; it makes you aware and heightens your attention.

"You've been on this case for years, and you have a relationship with him," Maria said. "Why wouldn't we put our faith in you? The reason the case fell on its face the first time around is that the bureau didn't trust you enough. We aren't willing to make that mistake again."

"I agree with Maria. Neil, you're going to have to be holding the ball, there's going to be a lot riding on you and your ability to anticipate Cappelano's moves."

My real fear was this: what happens if they give me the

reigns and I can't bring him in? After I left the bureau, I went after Cappelano outside the law and still couldn't reach him. I know I didn't have the resources I have now with the bureau, but that's not a good enough excuse. Who's left to blame if he gets away again? Who's left holding the bag? Just me. At this point I might as well own it, wear it like a badge of honor.

"I'll take the lead and all the pressure under one circumstance, and I'm not willing to budge on it," I said.

"What is it? I'm sure Maria and I can accommodate you."

"I get to come and go as I please, and I get the final call on *all* decisions regarding the case, even personnel decisions. Do we have an understanding?"

"I don't see anything wrong with that, Neil," Mike said. "The only way it would be an issue is if some line of legality is ever crossed. Your history has never given the bureau a reason to think that would be a problem. Where do you stand on this, Maria?

"I don't think we have much to bargain with, Mike. Looks like we're at the mercy of our friend Neil Baggio."

With that covered, we all shook on it and spent the next couple of hours drinking coffee and talking about Cappelano. I told some stories about what he was like when we worked together, before all the killing. Until we knew what the lab came up with on the safe, there wasn't much to discuss on that front. Other than all the memories that haunted me in my sleep of the people Cappelano had killed and will continue to kill unless I can stop him. Just then Mike's cell phone rang, and from my end it sounded like the lab techs had called him with good news.

"We should head back," Mike said. "That was the lab with news on the safe; they said they have something to show us." A TV cop-drama stare had settled on his face; he was ready to go.

"I hate when the techs won't tell you what they found," I said. "They try to make it so dramatic, and it usually ends up being nothing."

"I sense some cynicism in your voice," Maria said. She could see I was a crank-ass. "You don't like those lab guys too much, do you?"

"They aren't my favorite people, but I wouldn't say I hate them. How about you, Mike? What's your take on them?"

"They are usually a little weird, but I've learned that the more eccentric they are, the better they are at their job. They spend a lot of time alone and around dead people, so asking us to come in for some live conversation is okay by me."

We were just about to head back to the office downtown when I realized we would be stuck in traffic the whole time. It was almost 5:30 p.m., which meant our fifteen-minute drive would take us about thirty or forty minutes. I love this city, but I hate the traffic, and I *really* hate the construction, a permanent feature of the Metro Detroit area that never seems to fix anything. The drive was the usual combination of assholes on their cell phones weaving into and out of traffic, and that's just Maria.

On the serious side, the drive was eerily quiet among the three of us. I was trying to get a read on Mike and Maria while they sat in the front seat. This time Mike decided to drive back, and Maria sat up front with him while I sat in the back playing on my cell phone. I could only guess what they were thinking up there while we drove, but I'd imagine that Maria was wondering if she had made the right move by bringing me back to the bureau. As for Mike, I would guess that he was doing a combination of taking in the scenery around him and wondering if he made the right move by taking the job here in Detroit. Who knows? Maybe I was just projecting my own anxiety onto them.

By the time I had finished a little psychological introspection of my own thoughts and those of my counterparts, we were already pulling into the parking garage at the lab. As we entered the building, I was met with an immediate rush of stale air mixed with ammonia; the smell just ran straight up my nose and to the back of my head. A cleanup crew was mopping the floor profusely as we walked in, as if something major had come in earlier that made a big mess. My guess is they had a body that was dug up from a crime scene or some other old and decomposed evidence.

I used to hate working old cases because the smell was like someone leaving eggshells in a garbage disposal overnight—just brutal. I don't care what anyone says on TV, you never get used to it. The lab techs will tell you that after enough time, the smell becomes second nature. You don't even notice it, but I've spent my share of time in buildings like this throughout my career, and I was noticing it quite well at the moment. It's an amazing thing that I don't get sickened by the sight of blood and guts at a murder scene, but the smell of formaldehyde ruins everything.

"Hey Baggio, you're looking a little green in the face over there," Maria said. "Should I get you an air sickness bag?"

"Very funny. I just never liked the smell of formaldehyde. I'll be fine, trust me."

"Maria, did you know your partner had such a weak stomach? He may be denying it, but judging by that look, he's about to lose his last four coffees."

"I'm glad my aversion to formaldehyde brings you both such enjoyment. Enough about my stomach, let's get to the lab so we can find out what else was in that safe."

"Speaking of stomachs, how about we all go out tonight for drinks after this," Mike said. "I'm buying."

"First you make fun of me, and now you want to make up and get me drunk? You're all right in my book, Mike. I don't care what anyone says behind your back."

"Do you need to be such an ass all the time, or can you let your guard down every once in a while?" Maria said. Maybe she thought Mike needed someone to defend him. Or maybe she was just going to be loyal to her superiors no matter what.

Good to know.

"Hey, I said I'm up for going out and drinking. I just said it a little sarcastically, that's all."

"So, what are you trying to tell me?" Mike said. "Are you coming tonight because I'm your boss or because you want to?"

"I'm telling you that I can drink like a fish, so bring your platinum card. I'm going to take full advantage of your generosity."

"Why don't we make it a little bit more interesting? Let's say the first one to puke has to pay the bill."

"All of a sudden you're not up for paying the tab?"

"I understand if you're worried, considering you have such a weak stomach."

"All right, guys, this isn't a dick-measuring contest, put it away," Maria said. "If one of you knuckleheads ends up dead from alcohol poisoning tomorrow, it'll ruin my entire week."

I laughed, secretly relieved that Maria had stepped in to defuse my and Mike's chest-thumping displays. "How about you buy tonight, and I'll buy next time?" I suggested. "Sound good?"

"I can live with that," Mike said. "Where do you want to go tonight?"

"I've got a better idea. Why don't we still use your money, but let's do pizza and drinks at my place. I'll prep it for a crash course on the Cappelano-Baggio case files—plenty of details the bureau doesn't even have yet. And before you go nuts, my guys are already preparing copies to deliver to the field office by tomorrow."

"Make it Buddy's Pizza and super casual, and I'm down," Maria said. "How about you, Mike?"

"Absolutely. Just text me the address so I can find the place. Now let's find these lab techs so we can figure out what I almost lost my life for."

It took us a few minutes, but we tracked down a couple of the technicians who were working on the safe and finally got some answers. I did most of the talking when we got to the lab, mainly to keep myself from puking.

"All right, guys, I'm hoping for some good news here. Did you find anything we can use from that safe?"

"To be honest with you, Neil, we didn't get much," said one of the techs. "Obviously it was going to be nearly impossible to pull anything from the outside of the safe. Being submerged as long as it was, especially with the current this time of year."

"How about the CD that was found inside the safe? Anything there?"

"Depends on what you mean by 'anything.' It was just a music CD, nothing of major importance, at least not to us." As the lab tech spoke, short and choppy, I was already thinking of different tests we could run back at CB, Inc., with our tech and team.

"You're telling me that Cappelano left me a fucking CD to listen to? Is it at least anything good?" I already assumed it had more significance than that, but I wasn't ready to throw that out there just yet.

"The CD is a Frank Sinatra's greatest hits album. It's a two-disc set, so we checked both discs, the inside and outside of the case, the booklet, and we couldn't find anything. No latent prints, no hairs or fibers, no secret messages. It's as if he had just bought the CD and threw it in there. We were hoping you could shed some light on the subject."

"I'm not sure offhand, but I'm pretty confident if I take it home and listen to it, I'll be able to figure out what he's trying to tell me. I have a feeling it might have come from my house; since he stole my safe, it's not out of the realm of possibility that he would have stolen the CD as well. I'll look around my house and see if anything's out of place."

"I don't think there's anything else we can get out of this CD, so I don't see any problem with you taking it. It's not like it's going to be a crucial piece of evidence tying our killer to the victim. Is that okay with you, Mr. Ponecelli?"

"I don't see why not," Mike said. "Without any physical evidence on it, it'll just be taking up space in an evidence locker. Just don't lose it. All right, Neil?"

"Since that's settled, I guess I'll take it from here and see where it ends up."

"Is there anything else from you guys, or just the CD that Neil is going to take with him?" Mike asked. "Even if it's something that seems pointless, it could turn out to be helpful."

"No, that's it. We dusted for prints on the inside of the safe, we did a full workup, and we even tried to think outside the box. Nothing."

"What about the timer?" Mike asked. "It was counting down as we were trying to open the thing. Was there a bomb?" He was hammering this point again, understandably.

"Yeah, it wasn't anything major, just a small amount of C four hooked up to the inside of the safe. You would have just lost a limb or two, nothing serious," the lab tech deadpanned. Not sure if Mike noticed his sarcasm.

"Thanks. I'll be able to sleep better tonight knowing that I would have only lost my appendages if the bomb would have gone off. It's a good thing I didn't know how badly I could have been hurt."

"I guess we're done scaring Mike and screwing up my stomach for the day," I said. "That doesn't look like enough C four to do any damage outside of the safe anyway. Am I wrong?"

"No, you're not mistaken, Mr. Baggio. And my apologies, Mr. Ponecelli, your safety isn't an appropriate thing to joke about." The tech realized his joke didn't land quite as well as he had hoped, which is why I aided him in walking it back.

"I guess we'll just meet up at my place, say six o'clock," I said. "That will give us all time to go home and clean up first. Is that okay with both of you?"

"I'll be there," Maria said.

"I don't see any problems with that, either. I should have plenty of time to take care of some odds and ends before tonight. I'll see you guys out there."

As we made our way to the parking lot from the stench that is the lab, I felt my phone vibrate. *Private call*. I hate when it says that; I'll just let my voice mail get it. As I was saying, we're making our way out to the car, and I noticed . . . fuck, *private call,* again.

"I'm happy with my long-distance provider; leave me alone. Seriously, you guys are vultures."

"Hi old friend. How are you? It's good to see the FBI knows what's best for them, bringing you back in. Congratulations."

Just his voice alone brings me to an instant boil. I will never forget it. No matter how much his face changes, that voice will stick with me forever, haunting me wherever I go.

"Frank, is that you? How'd you get this number? Never mind that, what the fuck do you want?"

"That's right, it's your old friend Cappelano. Aren't you going to thank me for getting you back in the bureau?"

"Thank you . . . thank you for killing God knows how many people? Your ego is getting out of control, Frank. You think you got me my job back because you're killing again?"

"I'm doing this for you, Neil. You belong in the bureau, with the best. When I'm through with you, you'll be the greatest homicide investigator the world has ever known. Did you get my gift?"

"I sure did. And I'm truly fucking honored that you're breaking into my home *and* taking the lives of innocent people to make me a better investigator. Anything special I should look for on the CD?"

"You'll know what to look for. I've taught you well."

"Wow. You haven't taught me a damn thing, Frank. But soon enough, I'll teach you what it feels like to take two to the chest."

"Obviously you can't hold a civilized conversation right now. Maybe you should talk to your priest again and calm down. I'll be in touch. Good night, Neil."

I heard the call go dead and saw Maria look at me with confusion. She doesn't understand my relationship with this crazy asshole Cappelano. He likes to jerk me around and call from satellite phones that bounce off every tower imaginable. I don't even bother worrying about tracing the calls anymore; I've learned my lesson on that one. The last time I was on his trail, I had this bright idea to trace his call and follow the signal. I tracked it all the way to a pay phone in the dressing room of a male strip club. He had a good laugh at my expense with that one.

"Neil, who the hell were you talking to?"

"Don't worry about it, Maria. It's not worth it."

"That was Cappelano, wasn't it? Why didn't you try to have us trace it? We have the equipment in Mike's car."

"There's no need to try. I've tried to trace his calls hundreds of times; it always leads nowhere."

"Our technology has improved in the past couple of years. We might be able to do it now."

"No, we can't. Cappelano is always a step ahead of the game. Leave it be. I'll see you guys tonight at my place. Just leave it be."

7

They were files from unsolved murders across the Midwest that he had actually committed himself. He wanted me to learn from him; it was a sick game to him.

I made my way home from the bureau's office listening to some local sports radio for a change. Instead of the usual ESPN station, I have tuned to my satellite radio. I stayed on the expressway as long as possible so that I could make good time. It was just after rush hour, so the roads weren't too congested, and it only took me about fifteen minutes to get home. I think some of Maria's driving skills were rubbing off on me. Walking up to my front door, I noticed a note on it. Please tell me it isn't Cappelano messing with me again; I can't take any more crap from him today.

Stopped by to see you, but you weren't here, so I put the girls out for you and fed them dinner. Sorry if you already fed them. I tried you on your cell, but you didn't answer. Have a good night.

Love,

Sheila

Ps. Thanks for the other night.

I love opening the door to my ladies in waiting, Jackie and Danielle. I know it's not healthy to name your dogs after your favorite drink, Jack Daniels, but I figure it's better than naming them Buffy and Muffy. I even had custom-made dog tags and collars for the girls that read "Old No. 7." I think they're cool; most people just tell me I have a problem.

Before I could get anything done in the house, I had to get in a little playtime with the girls; they love wrestling when I get home, especially after a long day. Shortly after wearing the girls out, I made my way to the kitchen to pour myself a Jack on the rocks that I would take with me into the shower. I'd say I'm a situational drinker. I'll go weeks and even months without drinking, but sometimes I just need a nightcap. While pouring myself the drink, I let the girls outside for a run and to get some fresh air before Mike and Maria come over.

I slowly made my way into the bedroom to get ready for that much-needed shower and turned my phone off so I wouldn't have any distractions. I just needed a few moments alone to clear my head. The warm water rushed down my neck and back, and I fell into deep thought, trying to figure out where Cappelano is hunting, where he's conducting his "research," as he would put it. Nothing seemed to make sense this time around. Why is he coming after me now, and what does he feel is unfinished? The only thing I could come up with is that he felt cheated, as I do, with the way the bureau kept me from capturing him. I guess it's time to revisit what happened right before Cappelano slipped away from us the last time and my exit from the bureau in 2001.

It was about two months before I left the bureau, and I had gotten into a shouting match with Hendrickson about strategy. It had come to my attention—let me rephrase, I finally *realized*—where Cappelano was probably going to strike next. I had gathered some reliable intel that I felt comfortable acting on, but it was a risk that the bureau didn't want to take. My information had come from a girl who had managed to escape Cappelano after being abducted and survived long enough for me to talk to her. I'll never forget her name: Anna Walton.

At the time, Anna was twenty-one years old and a college athlete attending Ball State University in Muncie, Indiana. She held several MAC records in distance running and was training to challenge the national records. Anna was a very tough kid who not only ran cross country but also had competed in several triathlons. It was her endurance training that drew Cappelano's interest in the first place. She took care of her body and mind, training in both yoga and deep meditation for several years. Because of Anna's rigorous schedule, which she followed every day, she was an easy target to plan for. She also lived alone, which gave Cappelano plenty of opportunities to strike. Since he made his move during Ball State's Christmas break, her apartment complex was almost empty.

On December 22, 2000, Anna woke up at 5:30 a.m. As she had done so many times before, she went about her morning routine, consisting of yoga stretches and core exercises to get her heart rate up before starting her run in the cold Muncie air. It was a snowy Indiana morning, primed and ready to be conquered by an elite athlete. Anna made her way out the door of her building and started running toward the campus. As she took her usual route through the darkened Worthen Arena parking lot, Cappelano made his move, jumping out of his car and grabbing her, then covering her mouth with a cloth that had been doused with chloroform. Anna was in a deep sleep before she fully realized what was happening. Cappelano threw her in his car and proceeded to drive back to her apartment. This run would be her last, and she would soon come to wish she had never woken up.

It was unlike Cappelano to take a victim back to their own home before they were dead. He usually had another location set up in advance that was sterilized and covered in plastic, or ready to torch when he left. He did this to cover his tracks and leave forensics in the dust. As a matter of fact, it was because of Anna's case that we figured out that all of Cappelano's victims were killed in separate locations than where they were found. His calling card was to abduct his victims, then take them to a location where he would conduct his research. Eventually he would dump the body in another location, to be found later.

We only found out they were connected to him from his notes.

As he pulled up to Anna's apartment with her unconscious on the floor of the backseat, he looked around. He noticed there was only one other car in the apartment complex's lot: Anna's. This gave him a false sense of comfort, as he thought he'd have all the time he would need to carry out his plan. He carried Anna into her apartment and noticed her cell phone showed three missed calls. All from her ex-boyfriend, who wasn't ready to end the relationship the way Anna wanted to. Cappelano knew it was her ex because he had been monitoring her phone calls for almost a week now. As well as tracking her every move.

Cappelano then proceeded to tie Anna up, which was easy because she was an avid rock climber and kept all her ropes and harnesses in her apartment. Cappelano tied her to her bed, then turned on the stove and placed the branding tool he had made onto the burner to heat it up for later. Cappelano liked to brand his victims before he began to torture them. When the brand was sufficiently hot, he took it off the stove and pressed it into the bottom of Anna's feet. Cappelano told me later that he was making a statement about her drive to perfection. I think his motivation was simpler: he was taking away her power so that he would have more of it.

Anna shot awake immediately and began thrashing around. As she lay there bound and gagged, in extreme pain from the branding, Cappelano started to make markings on her body with a permanent marker, indicating where he was going to cut her, not only because he was so meticulous but also to keep his victim in a constant state of anticipation of fear and pain. According to Anna, he kept looking back at what appeared to be a file or notes, as if he had planned everything out, down to the last cut. For someone about to be brutally tortured and already in excruciating pain, she was very observant. That could have also been a side effect of the adrenaline injections he was giving her. To make her regain consciousness every time she would pass out.

Cappelano proceeded to cut into her Achilles tendon, severing it with a swiftness that can only come from knowledge and practice. Screaming past the limits of her voice and bleeding all over her bed, Anna started to fade into and out of consciousness. Cappelano moved on to his next cut, into her abdominal muscles, carefully dissecting her body as if he were a butcher and she was a piece of meat. Anna's adrenaline kept her aware of Cappelano's habit of stopping for a moment between cuts, to make comments into a recording device as if he were studying how her body reacted to the trauma.

It was at that very moment that Anna was saved. Her ex-boyfriend had planned to surprise Anna when she came home from running; he still had a key to her apartment and was going to let himself in so he could be there when she came home, in hopes of patching things up. As he pulled into the apartment complex, Cappelano noticed the headlights flash in the window, as it was still predawn outside, and took a look outside through the blinds. He recognized the car as belonging to Anna's ex from the time he spent watching and planning for this attack. Not willing to settle for a rushed, compromised version of the murder he had so carefully planned, Cappelano decided to call it quits. He packed up his tools and ran to the kitchen to turn on the gas oven; he always covered his tracks, and today was going to be no different. Then he lit a cigarette and put it inside a book of matches, which would leave him enough time to get out of the apartment before it caught fire.

The ex-boyfriend (I can't remember his name at this moment) entered the apartment. He immediately noticed the blood on the floor, and ran to the bedroom, where he found Anna unconscious and still bound. He pulled his cell phone from his pocket and dialed 911. At that very moment, Cappelano slipped out of the apartment through the front door, which the ex had left wide open out of shock. Once outside, Cappelano knew he had to ditch his car quickly. There was no time for a clean job—he would have to destroy it, and fast. Luckily for Anna and her ex, the gas line in her oven had been giving her trouble lately, causing it to delay in igniting; she had meant to bring it up with her super that day. This problem would save both Anna and her ex as well as give me a chance to talk to the only victim of Cappelano to survive.

The ambulance arrived, and paramedics immediately attended to Anna while she was rushed to the hospital. Outside of the apartment building, police officers were quick to put her ex in handcuffs and proceeded to read him his rights. But before they could finish, Anna's ex told them he saw a white Ford Taurus with a Ball State plate and logo in the parking lot. It was the same make and model of the cars that Ball State officials and athletic coaches drove. (Cappelano had stolen one early that morning.) Just then, Anna's apartment went up in flames, her front windows exploding out into the parking lot. A fire engulfed the building as well as two members of the Muncie Police Department. Why they were in there, I'll never know. They weren't CSI, so why take the chance of compromising evidence?

It wasn't long before the Muncie PD started to piece things together. They could tell that Anna's abduction and the brutal assault was planned by a professional, and that's when I was called. I'll never forget the look on Sheila's face when I told her I wasn't going to be around for Christmas because I had to drive down to Muncie. By the time I had arrived at Ball Memorial Hospital, Anna had been out of surgery for only about an hour. This meant it was going to be quite some time before I'd be able to talk to her, but that gave me a chance to talk to the local police, the doctors, and look at the crime scene, or at least what was left of it. As it happened, I also got a surprise visit from an old friend.

It was about 11:30 p.m., and I was making my way to the local police department, when I saw a car on the side of the road with its hazards on that looked like it was starting to catch fire. I immediately called it in to the local authorities and pulled off to help the driver; who was standing about ten feet past the front bumper, waving me down. As I stopped behind the car, I realized the driver wasn't just a local in need of help, it was Cappelano. He knew I was in town, and he wanted to hand me the case files from all his crimes, but with his own personal touches and notes. To this day I have no idea how he got his hands on all those files. They were files from unsolved murders across the Midwest that he had actually committed himself. He wanted me to learn from him; it was a sick game to him.

Just as I was about to draw my gun, Cappelano turned and ran. The car blew up, and I was thrown backward. All I remember is the sound of a motorcycle peeling off from the scene. Some of the files were damaged, but all wasn't lost. Almost all of the information was put on a backup disk that Cappelano had left with me as well; he was very thorough. I rolled over and started to do a mental check of my body to make sure I was okay. No major injuries, just a few minor cuts and bruises. Oh yeah, and a damaged ego. He was right there, and I let him get away. It probably didn't help that I had been up all day and only survived the drive down to Muncie thanks to a lot of coffee. I finally made it to Anna's apartment, where I met up with Officer Harper of the Muncie PD. It turns out that Harper was a lot like me, meaning he pissed off all the wrong people and was demoted from head of SWAT in the tricounty area to a beat cop working the midnight shift.

"Sorry about my appearance; I had a little run-in with an angry motorist earlier. Officer Harper, I presume?"

"That's me in flesh and blood. By the way, what the fuck happened to you?"

"Long story. I'll fill you in after we get done here, maybe over a coffee or two?" Between the exploding car and the fact that I had intel on a dozen unsolved homicides stuffed into my inside coat pocket, I was feeling a little mentally scattered. I needed the caffeine to level me out.

"I don't see why not," Harper said. "Are you sure you're going to be okay?"

"No need to worry about me, let's just get this taken care of so we can grab that cup of joe."

"You got it. As you can see, the perp did one hell of a job covering up his tracks. I'm guessing you guys have an idea of who did this? I mean, they usually don't send a fed to Muncie, especially one from Detroit, unless there's a connection. Does this have anything to do with that killer the news is calling 'the Veritas Killer'?"

"It's nice working with someone who can put one and two together," I said. "You'd be surprised by some of the people I have to put up with in my own office. But yes, we're quite positive the attack was perpetrated by a known serial killer, but the name was one coming from the way the killer branded his victims; it's more descriptive than a name.'"

"The fire inspector said the explosion came from the gas

oven. He said it looked as though it started the old-fashioned movie hit man way—a lit cigarette in a book of matches."

"That sounds like something he might do. Did your guys come across anything else we can use?"

"They did find the cigarette butt that started it, which is a rarity, as you know."

"Thanks, Harper. The victim wasn't a smoker, I assume."

"Not at all; she was a real health nut. Give me a second to radio over and see what they've got on the cigarette."

"All right, I'm just going to look around. Don't worry, I won't disturb the crime scene."

"No problem, Agent Baggio." After a moment on the radio, Harper had an update for me. "The lab said it was a Camel menthol cigarette. Does that mean anything to you?"

"It does. That's the same brand of cigarettes our suspect smokes. Thanks, Harper, now we can almost be positive it was him."

"Thank the forensics team; those guys have made my job a lot easier over the years. I remember when we'd have to work off of hunches most of the time instead of hard evidence."

"Hey Harper, how did the victim get out of the apartment in time?"

"Apparently her stove was a piece of shit, and it didn't turn on right away. Also, her ex-boyfriend dropped by unexpectedly to try and salvage the relationship. It's not often a girl is *lucky* that her ex didn't know how to let go. Believe me, I've seen those situations play out a lot differently."

"So because her landlord's a cheap ass and her ex-boyfriend is a stalker, she's still alive?"

"Yeah, I know, crazy to think a girl was saved from one mentally unstable person by her mentally unstable ex."

I sensed some hostility in Harper's voice. He wasn't happy being stuck babysitting a feed, which is a job usually reserved for rookies and inept veterans; he was neither. Harper also grew up in Muncie and had a lot of pride in the area. Things like this rarely happen. They get their share of basic college campus crime—date rapes, assaults, theft—but nothing this brutish, nothing this planned.

"Do you have a flashlight I could borrow for a minute?" I asked.

"Sure; I have a lantern in the trunk. Give me one second to grab it."

I didn't need a flashlight per se, but I could use the light and wanted a little alone time to look at the scene without a chaperone. It took him a few minutes, but I was able to get a survey of what I wanted in a short time before he got back from his car.

"Thanks, Harper."

"No problem, Agent Baggio. Can I grab you anything else?"

"You can call me Neil, and not unless you have a beer back there."

"So Neil, do you mind if I ask why the feds are crawling up

our asses? It's not like the victim is someone special. I mean .
. . well, you know what I mean."

"I'm not supposed to say, but all right, I'll tell you. The victim
might not be 'special,' but the killer is. We've been trying to
catch this fucker for almost three years now."

Harper whistled, shook his head. "You ain't kidding, this is
one hell of a fucker."

"He is indeed. I probably would have caught him already,
but too much bureaucratic crap keeps getting in the way of a
good investigation."

"Trust me, I understand. Just six months ago, I was the head
of SWAT, and now I'm babysitting a fed on a case. No offense."

"None taken. I know the last thing you want to be doing is
keeping an eye on me all night long." I already felt like Harper
was a kindred spirit; we should get along quite well.

"The reports won't be done until morning, and you won't be
able to see Anna until tomorrow afternoon. Do you want to go
grab that coffee?"

"Yes, thought you'd never ask. Got any ideas?" I was in the
mood for a Peach Pit–type atmosphere. Something friendly and
wholesome to turn the night around.

"I'm sure we can find a place to relax, maybe even one with
a lively college crowd to keep us distracted."

"What do you have in mind?"

"I know just the place, Sunrise Café. It's right across the
street from a great bar in case we change our mind."

Harper called into the station, telling them he was going to show the fed (me) around town and fill me in on what had happened in the past twelve hours. He caught me up on the basics that they had gotten from Anna's ex. God, I wish I could remember his name; oh well, I always sucked at remembering names of assholes, and he was a big one.

Harper and I pulled into a parking lot and made our way across the street to the diner. It was in the basement of an older '80s-style shopping complex with pillars and popcorn-painted walls. It was as classic a midwestern diner as one could imagine, from the knife marks in the tabletops to the half-lit signs out front. But as long as we had room for some files and plenty of coffee, I'd be a happy man.

"Good choice, Harper. This will work perfectly."

"What it lacks in ambience it makes up for in great coffee and even better service. Hey Betty, two cups of your worst jet fuel, please." Right then, a lady in her late fifties, giving off that witty grandma who talks like a truck driver vibe, walked over with two cups of coffee for us and a smile. She dropped them off and didn't even say a word, just a smile.

"So Neil, you said you have some files you wanted to go over. Is there anything I can help with? Anyone who comes into our city and does this kind of damage gets my attention. I'm here to help in any way I can."

"I appreciate that, Harper. Tell ya what, let me go grab the box from my car, and we'll start organizing all the files by date and location and see what we can come up with. Do you have a notepad and pen in your car?"

Before I could even finish the statement, the two of us were out the door, grabbing what we needed to make the night more efficient. I had the box that Cappelano had left me, and Harper went to grab his notepad so we could start to map out all the information as best we could.

It was already past 1:00 a.m., and I could hear Sheila in the back of my head telling me that I'm no good to anyone when I'm burned to a crisp mentally. Still, I was just handed a gift, and I had to run with it. Harper was someone I wasn't sure I could trust, but at this point I needed help, I needed hands, and I needed them quickly.

"Harper, I'm going to start by simply listing off all the basic file info for each case on the top sheet. Then I want you to write them out in different file orders. Start by organizing them by location, then by the age of the victim, and so on, and let's see if we can find a pattern."

"Got it. I haven't been this amped up in a long time. Since I don't have the same knowledge you do, is there anything you want me to look for in particular?" I was about to give Harper a rundown of the Cappelano FBI profile when it struck me.

"No; better you look at it fresh. We've had so many eyes on this case, and maybe we're all too close to it. Having a fresh pair looking at the raw facts of this new information will help a ton."

Harper and I started digging vigorously into the case files, slamming cup after cup of coffee as the night wore on. After the fourth round, Betty just started leaving a pot at our table, knowing we were going to drink through it before it got cold. It was a good thing that we were taking extensive notes along the way because the night became a blur.

"Neil, I know there are seven files in here, and we have the case that we caught today and the others we know about, but doesn't this make you feel like there are way more than the ones you're aware of?" He had a great point, and once again I felt like Harper was sharper than many of the FBI investigators who had worked on this case.

"Harper, that's always been the fear with Cappelano. He's so methodical that I've felt he has only allowed us to know what he *wants* us to know. No more, no less."

It took us about two hours to go through the files and get them organized to see if we could learn anything. It was rough, but we could pick out a little bit of a travel pattern leading up to Anna's case. I was going to have to get these back to Detroit ASAP. Maybe I could double dip, head to Harper's station, use their scanner, and spend some time in their gym so I can work out all this caffeine and all the new information stuck in my head.

"Harper, you think I could go back to your station to use your gym and scan the files back to my station in Detroit? Heck, I'll take a fax machine if you've got one."

"Our station has a better gym then the local campus PD station, but we don't have a scanner. I'll run you by there first to scan your files over, then you can hit the gym at our station, and I can go home. Sound good?"

"Perfect."

Harper took me over to the campus station to use their computer system; it wasn't surprising that a university had better computers than a city-funded police department. The next stop was his station, where I could get in a workout, clear my head, and figure out where to take this case next. The police station was everything I expected from a small college town. It wasn't anything special, but it had everything needed to get the job done. The one surprising thing about the station was their gym, which was surprisingly nice and well equipped. They even had a heavy bag, which made my night because I had packed my wraps just in case; I found a bag I could whale on for a while. The officers on duty were really polite in showing me around the station and getting me into the weight room. As for me, I changed in the locker room, grabbed my wraps and music player, and just went to work on that bag for a good hour. By the time I was done, it was nearly sunup, and I was dripping sweat, but at least I had a firm grasp on the situation at hand.

After getting some rest at my hotel, I went to Ball Memorial Hospital and spent the first of several days by Anna's side, talking to her, trying to get as much information as possible. I'll never forget those days with Anna. She died shortly after her parents came to see her, from an infection probably caused by Cappelano's rusty knife. The doctors did everything they could to save her, but she just couldn't hold on any longer. They had to amputate her right leg from the hip down, and she lost a major part of her abdominal muscle, which created a noticeable abnormality in her figure. She remembered a lot of information from the cold winter morning, and it's because of her that I got as close as I did to catching Cappelano.

I can't allow myself to talk about Anna too much. Whenever I do, I just get mad because my failure in catching Cappelano led to her death. With other victims, you can move on a little easier, because you never meet them, at least not while they're alive. But Anna was very much alive when I met her, and it put even more strain on me and this case.

The cold water came rushing out of the shower as the hot water ran out, waking me from my memory. I must have dozed off in the shower. It felt like yesterday that I was in Muncie, studying the unsolved case files with Harper and trying to find some justice for Anna. I guess that's why I drink; it slows me down and allows me to reflect. There are plenty of times I don't drink, but I go through phases when it helps.

Anyway, now I need to get ready for Mike and Maria. I made my way into the bedroom, where the girls were passed out on the bed. I doubt that they'll stay that way for long, though. As soon as my guests make their way over, they'll get hyper for a bit. Mike said he'll bring the beer, Maria is bringing the pizza, I just need to clean up the house and start organizing all my notes and old case files on Cappelano. Tonight is the official, unofficial Cappelano class for Maria and Mike.

8

Sauce on the top is one of the few things the people in this town can actually agree on.

It was easy to tell when they pulled up, because all of a sudden the girls woke from their slumber and turned into the crazed guard dogs I pay them for. Then again, they didn't stop Cappelano a few weeks ago from stealing a safe from my garage, though they were probably inside. You may be asking why I am not mad or upset about Cappelano showing up at my house to borrow something without permission. You have to understand my relationship with Cappelano goes back a long time, so long that I used to call him Frank "The Collar" Cap. He was the Kobe Bryant of the FBI when I started out, and I was proud to call him my mentor. But then he turned into this crazed killer. That changed when I realized he was a psychopath, but we'll talk about that soon enough.

It looks like Mike is the first one to make it, not surprising since Maria went to get pizza from Buddy's, and they're probably slammed. I can't wait to dig into that thick crust, heavy cheese, and some ranch, it sounds so good right now. I heard Mike knocking at the door and the dogs going nuts, so I rushed over.

"Hey Mike, I hope you didn't have any trouble finding the place," I said with a grin.

"Nah, other than the construction from downtown, it's a pretty simple drive. I like the older neighborhood; the vibe is great. Here's the beer. I got one more in the car, give me a second." Mike handed me two twelve-packs of beer and walked back to grab a few bottles of wine. Granted, it was only 6:00 p.m., and there's a chance we could be here all night going over stuff. Don't worry, I have lots of coffee.

"Neil, I wasn't sure of anyone's mood, so I grabbed both wine and beer, figured it would be a decent gift either way for hosting us tonight. I know you're not big on sharing some of your private views with the bureau, especially after the way Hendrickson handled you and the case last time."

"Mike, I appreciate you understanding that. It's because of that and the way Maria has handled bringing me in that I'm willing to review my files with you. Let me give you some insight into him and our relationship, along with some of the issues Hendrickson's had with me on the case."

Bob always had a theory I was holding back on the case, allowing Cappelano to roam free. Not only was it insulting, but it also was one of many reasons Hendrickson put roadblocks in front of me continually. Claiming procedural issues, making me wait for basic things such as wiretapping or search warrants. He was convinced that I was trying to throw the bureau off scent out of some residual loyalty to my mentor, allowing Cappelano to keep doing his work. Bullshit.

"I think I just heard Maria's car pull up. Neil, do you have somewhere I can put the wine to chill for a bit? Can I just put it in the fridge?"

"Go for it, Mike. I'll let Maria in, then we can get settled and start going over some of the basics and grab some pizza. Then, after we eat, I can break out my old files and notes. I really don't want to get grease or sauce on them."

It was a casual night, which was very much needed. Mike showed up in jeans and a T-shirt with his sport coat, but he did come from the office, so his choices were limited. Not to mention, I doubt he had even unpacked yet. Maria, on the other hand, looked so cute, but then again, when doesn't she? I saw her walking up in jeans, heels, and a form-fitting zip-up hoodie. She's not rocking crazy heels, but she knows she's small, so she goes the extra mile to stand tall and stand out. She's fully aware of the image she portrays, but you have to when it comes to the bureau.

"Hey Maria, thanks again for grabbing the pizza. I hope it wasn't too much trouble."

"Neil, Buddy's is never too much trouble. I'd fight a bear for Buddy's Pizza. This is Detroit, where we put the sauce on top, and it's damn good," she said with a huge smile and a chuckle.

"Mike just got here a few minutes ago. I was telling him I'll go over some of the history of Cappelano and me, how we met, when I noticed he turned, and go from there. Sound good? I don't want to go over case files until after we get done eating."

"This is your show tonight," Maria said. "We're here as spectators, here to learn, get the view behind the curtain no one else gets to see. Mike and I are very grateful for it. If there is anything we need to keep private, just let us know."

"Yeah, Neil, the last thing we want to do is burn any more bridges between you and the bureau. Now let's eat. I'm starving, and this sauce on top has me intrigued."

We spent the next ten minutes simply explaining to Mike the sauce on top phenomenon that has taken over Detroit for as long as we could remember. Sauce on the top is one of the few things the people in this town can actually agree on. Eventually we got around to talking about Cappelano, and how he and I met in the summer of 1996, when I was fresh on the scene in the FBI. Cappelano had already had fourteen years with the bureau at that point, having started back in 1982 under Ronald Reagan, and quickly rose to prominence after doing a lot of the footwork on the "Pizza Connection" case back in 1984. I never fully understood why he sought me out. People told me it was because I was breaking his records, which had stood for more than a decade at the academy. What can I say? I'm competitive. I know, you're asking yourself, what happened to that edge, Neil? The answer to that is simple: Cappelano happened.

Back to the Super Mario Bros.–type relationship between two Italian plunger-toting *paesanos* such as Cappelano and me.

"Neil, slow down. Real cute, with the Mario and Luigi reference, by the way, but I never knew that Cappelano was part of the Pizza Connection case. That was a huge international heroin ring between the US and Italy, if memory serves me correctly." She *was* correct, as usual.

Back to the story, Cappelano saw himself in me for a multitude of factors, from our Italian backgrounds, my drive to beat his records, and my sometimes careless regard for the rules. I was just as often being praised for exemplary work as I was reprimanded for operating outside of the manual. My mother called it at birth, I have a problem with authority, which seems odd for someone in the bureau. But I wanted to catch bad guys, and that's where I felt I could do my best work.

One of my favorite stories shortly after I left the academy and was assigned to the Detroit field office involved one of the assistant special agents in charge. Essentially an assistant manager of the office. I was given an office, but never really unpacked, got set up, or used it the first week. This raging rule enforcer kept on my ass, telling me I'm never going to get anywhere with a desk like that. It was actually a month or so into my assignment that Cappelano took me under his wing. Looking back, with more spite than a scorned ex-wife. I can only assume he saw me as an easy target with little to no internal connections to the bureau, easily influenced.

"Neil, if you don't mind me asking, what was the first case you and Cappelano worked on together as lead and secondary where he really started to groom you?" Mike was really dialed in on the details of this part of our relationship. Maria seemed generally observant of Cappelano's progression from standout agent to deviant killer.

"That would have been a case shortly after we met; he gravitated to me, and vice versa. People oftentimes think we had a very long relationship. The truth is, it was more like a hot and heavy fling than a long, steady marriage, for lack of a better description." I know that sounds funny, but I really don't have a better way of describing it.

We hit it off immediately. Cappelano was fourteen years older than I, but we had a connection, almost like brothers only a few years apart. Sometimes you just meet someone and know that they are going to affect your life moving forward. There was a lot of animosity in the bureau over the fact that one of the top stars took a shine to a small-time kid like me. Who was just as likely to get charged with cherry bombing the bathrooms or making the dean's list. Our first case was to track down a group smuggling in high-end vodka and skipping the proper taxes. We worked in conjunction with the ATF, but it was a big case, and our first as a team. We ended up finding out that the group was dyeing the vodka blue, putting it in glass cleaner barrels, and bringing it through customs that way to dodge the alcohol taxes. Then once it was in the US, they would spin the blue out of the vodka and bottle it again.

"Neil, if the two of you started working on cases in 1996 and he left in 1998, that's a pretty quick turn of events, don't you think?"

"Maria, you're starting to understand my relationship with and hatred for the man. Someone who I thought was bringing me in under his wing was actually using me from day one. I have a theory that he was already killing or preparing to kill when he started grooming me back in '96."

"I guess I can see why you get so short when talking about him, where that animosity comes from. It's not simply the fact of him being out there, not catching him. It's the embarrassment of being fooled publicly. He tricked you."

Not just embarrassment—complete humiliation. In any big organization, there's going to be a rumor mill, a gossip chain. The bureau was no different. Add to the mix the political nature of the job, and a whisper could make or break a career. Jealousy from my peers when Cappelano was in the bureau quickly became pity or an assumption of guilt by association when he left. I was young, green, and didn't know any better, and now I had his name anchored to me forever, like a shit-covered "Kick Me" sign taped to my back.

I don't know why, but just hearing someone else speak the words put me a bit over the edge, and I walked out of the room, out the back door, and into my backyard. I let the dogs out and sat down, enjoying some refreshing cold Detroit air while I tried to regain my composure. I could hear Mike and Maria talking in the kitchen in the other room. I wasn't trying to be rude; I just needed a quick second; talking about this asshole all night really drained me.

"I should go apologize," Maria said, her voice drifting through the doorway. "I didn't mean to push him like that."

"Maria, give him a minute, I'm sure he's just tired. Talking about this is like talking about your ex cheating on you repeatedly. It's not fun for anyone. Just give him a minute."

I never thought of it that way, but Mike put it perfectly. Talking about Cappelano just makes me feel dirty sometimes, feel used, and then I get pissed. The funny thing about the night is, Mike brought over drinks for all of us to enjoy, and we barely even drank them. We've been sitting here nursing a beer or two and just talking most of the night.

After a few minutes of decompressing and clearing my head, I walked back inside the house. "Well, we already polished off a pizza and a half, but we still have another one and a half over here," I said, returning to the role of a gracious host. "Either of you have room for more? Or can I start cleaning up a bit?"

"Neil, if I'm full, I know Maria *has* to be full. I think she ate twice as much as I did. Impressive."

"Michael Ponecelli, you'd better not be calling me fat. I'll have you know that I can still fit into my high school cheerleading uniform."

"If he *is* calling you fat, I would hate to see what he thinks is skinny. If you were any thinner, you'd fly away in a strong wind. Now let's revisit this cheerleading uniform you mentioned; you said you still fit in it?"

"I wasn't calling you fat, I swear, Maria. I was just saying, it's not every day you see a petite girl who can put that much food away."

"Well, thanks. I was just giving you a hard time. And I love to eat, which is why I run every morning before work. As for you, Neil, you need to get your mind out of the gutter. Let me help you clean up, and then we can start going over those case files." Maria got up and started grabbing plates and heading to the sink.

"I need to step out and make a call to the office," Mike said. "I have a few messages to check."

After about fifteen minutes of Maria and I having some playful banter and cleaning up, Mike finally came back into the room. By that point I had a box on the dining room table with a stack of old case files in it.

"Hey guys, I hate to cut out, but it looks like I have some early morning meetings tomorrow starting at seven, and I have a briefing at six. I need to head home and get some rest. Maria, any way you can put together a memo of what you and Neil cover after I leave?"

"As long as it's okay with Neil, I'd be happy to put something together for you," Maria said, smiling. "I'll take notes and run things by Neil before I leave. Sound good, boss?"

"Perfect. Have a great night, Neil, and thanks again for everything. Sorry I couldn't stay." All I could think was, *Oh no, please don't leave me here alone with this beautiful lady in my house.*

"Have a great night, Mike; we'll manage. I'll cover as much as I can and set Maria up to brief you tomorrow."

The two of us jumped right in, Maria taking notes for the next three hours. Before we knew it, the clock was telling us it was midnight, and we should get some rest ourselves. By now we'd had a few more beers—not enough to be drunk, but enough to be relaxed. Was I actually bold enough to make a move on Maria? I guess only time will tell, but I think I'll need a little more liquid courage first. I still act like a junior high boy around the high school hottie with her. Before my mind could wander too far off, Maria started asking me about the current case of Ashley Gracin.

"Hey Neil, wasn't there another case years ago that involved another young woman, similar to this one but much more gruesome, I believe in Indiana somewhere?" Maria asked me.

"Yeah, Anna Walton, out in Muncie. Cappelano never got to finish his work. He was interrupted by her crazy ex-boyfriend. She died a few days after the attack, unfortunately. That's also when we were gifted case files on some of his work that helped us start to find a pattern, which led to more cases being tagged to him. Seven to be exact."

We talked for a few hours, going over old case files, most of the details still feeling firsthand and fresh. I explained how Cappelano never repeated a "type" of victim. What I mean is that to Cappelano, this is research. He needs measurable data points and variables to make each kill worthy of his time and risks. He chose his victims wisely, wanted to learn from their differences. That's what made the Gracin case stand out. It was out of character, it fit the mold of kills he had done before, and it had nothing to do with his research. It was simply and purely personal.

For example, we learned in the case files we obtained in Muncie those years ago that he started by killing easier targets. They were unhealthy, overweight, some even disabled to ensure he wouldn't have any trouble. People with no next of kin, cut off from family, one of them even a homeless man from Detroit whom we later found out to be Cappelano's first kill. As he grew more confident and honed his skills, he escalated his targets to ones who would present greater challenges.

As he put it in his notes, he wanted to learn the "truth" about the human spirit, what drove people, what weakened them. Cappelano was always driven by the idea of "Veritas," or truth. That's what inspired his research into the mind of a killer. He felt he was gaining knowledge that he could pass on to the bureau that would help us catch other killers and on to me. But at some point, he lost his soul. Though his tactics have always been inexcusable, I feel he has crossed over to an even darker side of killing for the pure enjoyment of it.

"Neil, one thing keeps driving me a little crazy about this case, and you a little bit. We don't have to talk case files anymore; we can just talk as colleagues having a few beers, if that's okay with you?" This is not a side of Maria I was expecting.

"I've never been one to turn down a request from a drinking buddy, especially not one as pretty or as powerful as you. Double trouble if you ask me." We both smiled and chuckled a bit. We were finally relaxing, breaking down our defense mechanisms, and just being ourselves.

"Seriously, Neil, if you're so pissed at this guy, why aren't you out there right now, turning over every stone, chasing every lead like a rabid dog? I feel like if I were in your shoes, I'd be going nuts, like a drug addict trying to score my next high. I'd find a way."

"You're assuming I haven't gone down that road already. What do you think I was doing all the time after I left the bureau? You think I just stopped looking for him? I ruined my marriage, almost lost my daughter, who barely knew who I was, what few friendships I had were almost all broken. I think many of them would have taken it easier if I was a heroin addict. That they would have understood, but the way I took on this case was brutal on me. It took its toll, and now I'm trying to come at this with a level head and a clear mind."

"I'm sorry. I guess I rushed to judgment. I didn't—" I cut her off.

"It's okay, stop there. Can we just sit here, enjoy the peace and quiet, and relax, maybe even pass out?" That's when she came over to my side of the room, sat on the couch next to me, and curled up into my arm. We grabbed a blanket and just sat there, sometimes talking and sometimes . . .

9

Each second that passes brings you closer and closer to that moment where you're looking at another dead body.

Searching for answers with the smell of coffee filling the air, I realized it was too early for my coffee pot to be brewing. My first alarm wasn't set to go off for another hour. What the hell was going on? As I tried to get my bearings and figure out what had happened the night before, I noticed clothing on the floor and realized the shower was running. Is there any chance I woke up in the middle of the night and turned on the shower? Back to the clothes, whose . . . wait a minute, Maria was wearing that last night. Holy shit, Maria was wearing that last night, and now it's on my floor. I guess that means I didn't follow through on not complicating this case any more than it already is. Just as the look of panic left my face, Maria came out of the bathroom with a big smile on hers.

"I'm sorry. I didn't mean to wake you. I was going to shower first and wake you up when I got out."

"What happened last night? And why are you up so early?" I

was playing a little coy; she's the kind of person you could never forget.

"I have to be at work, and I have to stop home first so I can change. It might look bad if I show up to the office wearing the same thing I wore last night."

"Holy shit, my head is killing me. I knew I shouldn't have mixed alcohol and coffee last night."

"You don't remember *anything* from last night? I find that hard to believe," she said with a smirk that told me she knew I was just playing.

"What should I be remembering? It'll get there eventually. Sometimes it just takes a second for the old brain to warm up. Some of that coffee might help."

"Are you asking me if we had sex? That's hard to say."

"What do you mean 'hard to say'? Did we or didn't we?"

"I had sex last night, and you were there, but apparently you don't remember it, so I guess I was the only one who had sex last night."

"Are you serious? We had sex, and I barely get to remember it?"

"Well, maybe I can catch you up on the highlights. You surprised me, you're quite a caring partner in bed, and for being drunk enough to forget your own name, you're a good kisser as well."

"Flattery will get you everywhere. I take it this isn't your first time with a colleague?" Not sure why my brain let that slip out. I really act like a teenager around her; I can't function.

"What are you trying to say? No, I'm not normally like this, but I was drunk last night, not to mention my personal life has been on hold for a while, with the job being as insane as it is. You know what it's like. Don't ruin a good night by overthinking it, Baggio."

At this point in the conversation, things started coming back to me in waves. It was like that feeling of déjà vu when your brain is reloading on you.

"I didn't mean it that way. It's just, it's not like me to hop in bed with someone I barely know, especially someone I work with."

You could tell Maria is a career girl at the bureau looking to do more than just "the job." I mean that as a compliment. There are plenty of men who can't handle this job, and women deal with way more scrutiny. To her, we are simply two people enjoying a moment in time. I can respect that. I remembered from the past couple of days her mentioning that she went through a pretty rough breakup last year. In this job, it's hard to sustain a relationship with someone who truly doesn't understand that the case will often come first over everything, even them. Heck, even those who understand it can still get hurt and affected by the life.

I'm still trying to wrap my head around this. I know I'm attracted to her, but I've never been one to get involved with a colleague. I have a wild night of alcohol-induced sex, and I barely remember a thing; this sucks royally. I mean, Sheila and I have had a lot of good times when my memories weren't exactly crystal clear the next morning, but she's my ex-wife; that doesn't count. I needed a cup of coffee and some Tylenol. I worked my way to the kitchen and let out the girls, who were looking at me as if I just stole their favorite dog bones. They are disappointed in me, to say the least. I cheated on them, after all. I brought a girl home, and they couldn't sleep with me.

I poured myself a cup of coffee as Maria walked into the bathroom with nothing but my robe on. She still hadn't gotten into the shower. Maybe I could salvage the night after all and go for a morning refresher.

"Hey Maria, how can you be so upbeat this morning? Weren't you drunk last night too?"

"It doesn't take much for me to get drunk, and I took one of those hangover pills. So I'm doing all right, just a little tired. I mean, we didn't get to bed until three in the morning."

"Are you kidding me? I knew you were a planner, but making sure you woke up chipper while I have to rough it in the morning, not fair. I guess I can learn some new tricks. Can I call in sick today, boss?"

"You were good last night, but not good enough to call in sick. Just hop in the shower; you'll feel better."

"How am I supposed to take a shower with you in there, hogging all the hot water?"

"Strip and get in here with me. It looks like your shower is made for two people."

"Good point. I'll be in there in a minute."

"Meet you in there. Don't take too long."

Maybe my luck is changing because I'm going to die a very painful and scary death in the near future, and this is just God's way of saying sorry in advance. But enough worry about what's to come. For now I'm going to get in that shower and kick off this morning the best way I know how.

"Hey, are you coming or what? This offer won't be on the table much longer."

"I'm right behind you, calm down. So where did we leave off last night?"

Maria leaned in and gave me one of the most passionate kisses I've ever had. Did I mention she looked unbelievable just then, in the shower all covered with soap? I can't believe I'm doing this. I know I've said it a lot already, but shit, I feel like a kid whose prom night dreams have come true. I don't need to continue; the rest is self-explanatory. Suffice it to say that things will officially be extremely odd for the rest of the day. Not sure how we'll make it through without anyone noticing me acting like a prepubescent fourteen-year-old nerd stuck in a grown-up's body. I already struggled to act professionally around her. Now I'm definitely screwed.

Once we were out of the shower, Maria asked me for something to wear instead of the outfit she wore last night.

From a psychological standpoint, I assumed that Maria wanted to borrow some of my clothes so that she had another reason to come over, or for me to go over to her house. With wet hair and a pair of my sweats, I had to admit Maria looked quite amazing. But I know that only bad would come from a workplace affair with Maria, so I couldn't let this happen. I swear, it's just my luck; I actually meet a beautiful woman with the same interests as I have, and she's my chaperone at the bureau. I'm the kind of guy who would win the lotto, and on my way to cash in the ticket, I end up dying of a heart attack. I've given up on having that American Dream of a wife, two kids, a dog, and the perfect house. I just take what life gives me now and do my best with it. At my age—or any age, for that matter— that's all you can hope for.

"Thanks for helping to jog my memory of last night, not like I needed it, but I'll take it," I said with a big old grin on my face as she smiled back.

"Glad I could help. Do you see why I couldn't let you be left in the dark? We had too much fun last night."

"So where do we go from here?"

"I say we move on and enjoy the time we had. But we can't do this again. You know that, Neil."

"Better to have done it once than not at all, right?"

"I believe we did it four times, but who's counting? And I'm not saying it will never happen again. I'm just saying that right now we have to focus on the case, not each other."

"We probably shouldn't go into the office together. If anyone sees me there as early as you are, they'll know something is up."

"How about you stay here for a couple hours. I'll tell everyone at work that you're going to be in later because you want to listen to the CD that Cappelano left you and see if you can come up with anything."

"That sounds like a plan."

"You'd better use the time on the case and not to get some more sleep. If I have to be up all day on four hours of sleep, then you have to as well."

"After the shower wake-up call, I think I'll be wide awake for the day."

"All right, I need to drive home and put on some real clothes. I'm already running late as it is. Thanks for the much-needed good time and for the sweats. I'll get them back to you sometime outside of the office. Just keep me up to date on the CD and how it's going, all right?"

She was gone before I had a chance to kiss her good-bye, and just like that, I was alone again, like the whole thing had been a dream. Maria was right, though: Right now, all our focus should be on the case. Luckily, the night before had given me a lot to think about.

Why did Cappelano leave me a Frank Sinatra CD? Did it really contain some secret message, or was he just playing games with me? What really scared me was the possibility that

I might end up writing it off as a meaningless taunt when there was something genuinely significant hidden on it. I know that most FBI agents wouldn't tell you that they second-guess themselves or question their ability to figure out a case, but for me, it's quite the opposite. It is my constant questioning that helps me get to the bottom of cases; sometimes you have to question yourself to better yourself.

For some reason, the CD seems to be having trouble starting up in my stereo, which is getting older and might be on its last legs, or maybe the CD itself is a bum copy. I guess I'll have to take it to my new stereo in the bathroom that I just put in last month. Since I already showered this morning, all that's left is shaving and getting ready for the day, which shouldn't take too long. I'll just turn up the CD and get started on my morning routine. But before I can do anything, I'm going to have to answer my cell, which had just started buzzing in my pocket. Who would be calling me this early in the morning?

"Neil, did you get my gift? I knew you'd figure it out." Okay, last time I went a little crazy. Maybe I'll play it calmer this time.

"Frank, I know I rarely call you by your first name. But what can I say? I'm feeling nostalgic with the music you left me. But the CD doesn't seem to want to work. I guess I'll just have to listen to my copy from home unless you took this from there too."

"Neil, come now. You weren't even using that safe, it was in your garage unused for a while, we both know that. By the way, you seem to be in a much better mood today. It's nice to hear your voice. Just like old times . . ."

Maybe it's the conversations with Maria that have me more focused, or just being back in general, but I'm trying really hard not to lose it.

"Other than calling me to gloat, as usual, what can I do for you today? More importantly, you've never gone after bureau family before, so what's going on? Why Gracin? Why Ashley?"

"Neil, keep digging, not is all as it seems with them. You'll see they're not as innocent as you believe." CLICK.

Ah fuck, well, this should be fun to explain to my buddies at the bureau.

After getting the CD to load in my bathroom stereo, I noticed that every time the disc tried to go from track six to track seven, it skipped back to track three. There are no scratches on the disc, so my guess is Cappelano hid something under the music files. I've heard of a way you could hide other media files on a disc. I have no idea how it would be done, but I suppose it would be like hiding a safe behind a painting in your house. I'll have to swing by the warehouse and see if our digital forensics guy at CB, Inc., can figure it out.

As I've told Maria, it seems that Cappelano is always a step ahead; he always finds new ways to screw with me. Maybe he's put together a collection of files on his latest murders on this disc. Ones that haven't been properly credited to him, just as he did with that stack of case files he gave me back in Muncie years ago. I don't think he actually stopped killing for the past couple years; he just wasn't claiming responsibility for them until now. He believes that practice makes perfect. I know it's sick and twisted in the context of taking people's lives, but it's true. The more he kills, the easier it is for him to deal with it emotionally—as well as to clean up after he's done—because he has no connection to death anymore.

Tracking down a serial killer isn't as simple as it looks on television or in the movies. A lot of times they get away with it, at least at first. But eventually their egos start to hinder their ability to stay ahead of the cops. That's how they get caught; they *want* to be caught. It's the ultimate publicity for these guys to be on death row, exchanging fan mail with future serial killers. Take, for example, the man who's probably the most famous killer, maybe not in the media, but to people like myself: Dennis Rader. He went by the name BTK, which stands for "bind, torture, and kill." He called himself that for obvious reasons, but what really made him stand out was that he was so meticulous in his work when he killed his victims. It was impossible to track him. He killed people all over the country. The only reason we knew it was he half the time was that he would send the FBI and police letters mocking them for the fact that they had put the wrong person behind bars. To him, it was an insult that another man was getting credit for his kills, his work, his art. That's right, "art." To a serial killer, killing is an art form; it's an expression of self.

I have a guess that Cappelano has been working out of the country somewhere. The other possibility is that he's been killing off-pattern to keep us out of the loop. As I said, we may soon learn about a whole new string of killings he's been up to while he was off our radar, thanks to that CD. A puzzle for me to solve, something for the cat to chase while the mouse is at play. He enjoys the game to an immense level—designing it; implementing it; and, most importantly, watching it as it plays out.

Oh damn, I should really be getting to the warehouse; time just disappears. This is the kind of shit I'm talking about. I get lost in my thoughts and lose track of time. I just need to find my keys and my jacket. I already let the girls in, I have the Frank CD in my pocket, I have my cell phone, wallet, I think that's everything. I guess I'll just have to call Maria on the way to let her know what's going on. I was finally about to head out my front door when I noticed that Maria left her shoes last night in the entryway. She borrowed a pair of my sandals, which means I probably won't see those back along with the sweats, but that's okay, it was worth it. I tossed her shoes in the backseat of my car under a blanket in case someone notices them—someone like Mike, who would be able to put everything together pretty quickly.

In Metro Detroit, everything is about the drive, the ride, because our public transit is minimal. The commute from my place to the coffeehouse is somewhat depressing, with all the strip-mall shopping centers going up everywhere. They even fit one in behind a gas station and in front of an office complex, which is hilarious. There's barely any room for anything else anymore. I think it's the perfect example of how messed up Metro Detroit is—the city downtown is vacant and lacking, but the suburbs are squeezing in convenience stores and pharmacies wherever they have the square footage. I know I talk about Detroit negatively often, but that's because I want to see it succeed, prosper, and grow. The last thing I want is for it to continue to suffer. It's just like being self-deprecating; we're often hardest on the ones we love.

Now that I've had time to let my mind wander, it dawns on me that I'm almost to the warehouse and I haven't called Maria. I guess I should try her right now. She'd better pick up. I hate waiting on the phone for someone to pick up; even though it's just a few seconds, it always seems to drag on.

"Agent Garcia speaking," she said when she picked up, as professional as the day I met her.

"Maria, it's Neil. I'll have to come in a little later than planned. I've got to head back to my warehouse and check on a few things. Is that okay?"

"All right, just keep me posted. I've got you covered here at the office. Oh, by any chance, did I leave something at your house?"

"Yep, I found your shoes. I wrapped them up in a blanket in the back of my car to make sure no one sees them, and to make sure they don't get messed up. They looked expensive."

"They *are* expensive. They cost me seven hundred and fifty dollars."

"Holy shit, who makes shoes for that much money? And if they cost that much, I want to have you model them for me with nothing else on before I give them back. That's right, I'm holding your shoes hostage."

"They're Jimmy Choo, and they are worth every penny."

"Did you just say your seven-hundred-and-fifty-dollar pair of shoes are worth the money? I must be out of touch with reality or something. For that much cash, they'd better come with a little servant boy to rub my feet at the end of the night."

"You're an ass, Neil. But hey, those shoes got you into bed with me, didn't they?"

"I would say a few drinks and all that steamy Cappelano talk did that, and the fact that you're sexy as hell. Wait! That's sexual harassment. I'm sorry."

"After last night and this morning, you could harass me any time you want. As long as it's in private and you talk dirty to me."

"I'm just guessing, but you're not at the office, are you?"

"No, I'm actually on my way back. I just ran out for lunch. Have you had any luck with the CD?"

"I think I may have found something. I'll tell you about it later at the office. I have two long-shot hunches to play out. We'll see what I come up with."

"Sounds good. I need to get going, though. I'm pulling up to the office now. I'll see you later, my little Azzurri."

"I see you noticed the Italian soccer posters in my basement," I said, laughing. "I'll see you later, Maria."

It's hard to be driving around right now knowing that Cappelano has probably found his next victim and might be hunting them right now. Watching them, learning their patterns, breaking down how and when to make his move. Thoughts like this are probably the most difficult part of my job. You're trying to stop these people, and the whole time they're out there plotting their next kill. And each second that passes brings you closer and closer to that moment where you're looking at another dead body.

I arrived at the old warehouse, made my way around to the back, and began looking for my security card to gain access to the building. You need to have a security card that generates new access codes every six hours in conjunction with our high-tech security system. I pulled in and got ready to take the usual abuse from the guys, since I can afford to buy almost any car I want, and I still drive the same shitty beat-up Jeep that I've been driving for years. But then again, I love this car.

"Nice car, Baggio," Ken said. "When are you going to trade that piece of shit in?"

"Hey, don't take your jealousy out on me. You have to admit, Ken, this thing has come in handy on stakeouts. No one notices this junker."

"Neil, TJ is in the back ready for you. I got your text message saying you were in a hurry; we'll get you in and out in a jiffy. Need anything else while you're here?"

"No, I just got to head back to my place and check on something. That crazy asshole Cappelano stole my old-ass safe, the one that I reported stolen last month from my garage."

"That empty one. What the hell, is that what you guys and the USERT team were dealing with yesterday?"

"Yup. Now I have to figure out what's with this disc and why he put it in my safe."

"Neil, you know he likes to misdirect, so try not to focus on the obvious."

Ken made a great point. I ran to the back to find TJ and get him situated with the CD before I had to run over to my place and check on my music collection.

"Hey, TJ, how are you doing? Anything good going on in the tech department today?"

"Hey, Mr. Baggio, I didn't even hear you come in. It looks like you've got something for me."

"Call me Neil. None of that formal crap with me, you know that. And yes, I do have something for you to work on. This is the number one priority here. It's evidence from the case I'm working on for the FBI."

"Sure, Neil. What are we looking at?"

"It's a Frank Sinatra CD. On the disc, there seems to be a

glitch."

"Are you sure it's not just skipping?"

"No, I think the killer is hiding evidence under the music. When you are listening to the CD, and it's supposed to go from track six to track seven, it skips back to track three every time."

"Your killer would have to be pretty smart to pull off something like that. It might take me a while to dig into it, but I can probably crack it by tonight or early tomorrow. Is that going to be okay for you?"

"No problem, TJ. Just get it done ASAP, and don't worry about how many man-hours you need to use; the FBI is paying for this one, so work all the hours you need to on the clock."

"Thanks, Neil. I could use the extra cash, with the holidays coming up."

"Call me as soon as you find something one way or the other, all right? Thanks, TJ."

I damn near sprinted out of the warehouse and booked it back home to go through my music collection. Speeding as fast as I could, I got back to my place, pulled in, and ran inside without even greeting the girls. I began going through all my Frank Sinatra CDs one by one, opening them up, looking them over. Nothing was out of place; they're all here.

I decided to check all the booklets page by page, just to be safe, and after a good two hours of detailed searching, I found it. Cappelano left me a Post-it note on the inside of a matching Frank Sinatra's greatest hits album. I guess I'm heading back to the warehouse, because I'm afraid to load this up on one of my computers, to be honest. Or should I take it to the bureau?

Shit. Where to go?

Well, step one is to get in the car . . . or is it sitting at my computer?

Written on the note in Cappelano's immaculate handwriting was a file-sharing FTP site address. I can only imagine what's on there.

10

She hung up the phone while her messages were still playing, pushed me out of her office and down to mine.

There always seems to be the smell of fresh tar and sulfur in the air when you drive around downtown. I still can't believe Detroit is going to host the Super Bowl this year. I could imagine in a few years after a lot of cleaning up, but our mayor is too busy *acting* like the mayor than actually *being* mayor. Imagine having P. Diddy as the mayor of a major city; the sad thing is, I think he would do a better job than the guy they have in there. If you haven't figured it out yet, I've decided to head to the bureau to share my discovery with them—part of it, at least— and get to work on it ASAP. That's when I called the office to talk to TJ and Ken.

"Ken, I need you to head back to TJ's office real quick and put me on speakerphone. My hunch back at my place paid off— Cappelano left me an FTP address on a Post-it on a CD in my collection."

"Holy shit, Neil. Cappelano must have been in your house recently, since he wouldn't risk you finding that note too early. Where are you headed?"

"I'm on my way to the bureau to give them this info, pull up what we can, and get things started down there. But can you get it pulled up with TJ simultaneously?" As I finished talking, I could hear TJ in the background—well, mainly his music.

"Neil, we got you, all we need is the FTP site address and we can get to work."

I read them off the address, and TJ assured me he'd take some precautions before loading it onto a computer, then get back to me with anything he found. Shortly after I got off the phone with them, I pulled into the FBI's downtown field office. I'll tell you, the parking setup for the bureau is just as messed up as the city itself. If you're not there early or you don't get very lucky, you end up parking four blocks down the street and walking, and I'm not in the mood to walk right now. That's another problem with this city—even though there are vacant lots everywhere, for some reason there isn't any parking. Go figure. I guess that's how you know your city is crumbling down around you when you can't even use a vacant lot.

I don't have my credentials to get into the building yet, so hopefully George is still working the door; he was yesterday, and that's how I got in without them. George has been working the security entrance at the FBI building for as long as I can remember, and then some. Perfect—he's here: I won't have to wait.

"Hey George, how'd the grandkids treat you last night?"

"Not too bad, Neil, not bad at all. This is the fourth day in a row you've come in. One more and we have a full workweek.

Does this mean you're back?"

"For the time being, I am. They're trying to get me to come back in permanently, but we'll see. I just want to close this case once and for all, and then I'll decide."

"I can understand that. Do they have you working the Veritas case?"

"You and I both know that's the only reason they'd bring me back. I need to get going, though; I have to go grab my credentials from Agent Garcia and then go out to the lab. I'll see you tomorrow."

"Thanks for the chat, Neil. Have a good and safe day. It's great to have you back."

George is as good as they get; a retired military man, father of four, and grandfather to many. Whenever I have the time, I like to catch up with him and sift through the never-ending array of photos he keeps stuffed in his wallet. It's nice to see a man who takes great pride in his family. It's hard to come by men like that these days. More people seem to end up like Sheila and me than the way George's family worked out.

I got off the elevator at my floor and walked out to a smiling Jen at the front desk. She really is a sweetheart. I'm so glad that they finally took care of her. She's done more for this office than the field agents have.

"It's nice of you to join us this morning, Neil. Getting a late start, are we?"

"Your sarcasm is duly noted, Jen. I'll have you know I was

up around six this morning working, and then I ran something to get tested by the tech guy at my company because the bureau's lab couldn't come up with anything."

"You really have been working; I'm impressed. What's the occasion? It's not like you to get such an early start."

A very attractive burglar snuck into my house and started my coffeemaker against my will, I thought, trying to hide my smile. "I just couldn't sleep. Too much on my mind about the case. I need to get going, though. Is Garcia in her office?"

"Last I checked, she was. Oh yeah, she told me to tell you that your credentials are in your office. Everything you need to get around here is in there. And they just pulled your ID picture from the DMV, so don't worry about getting a new pic."

"Thanks, Jen, and I take it Garcia is ramping up the timelines on everything, isn't she? She moves pretty fast."

"We can't waste any time under the circumstances, you know that. Get going, I'll talk to you later, Neil."

"All right, Jen, sounds good. Talk to you later."

I headed to my office to grab my credentials and make my return to the bureau official. The last time I worked here, you needed a bunch of IDs and swipe cards to get you into the different buildings and wings. Yet, when I found the envelope that Maria had left on my desk, it contained only one card: my FBI ID. Maybe things have changed a bit around here, but if it meant I didn't have to carry around a bunch of different IDs anymore, it was a very welcome change.

With that bit of business out of the way, I thought I'd swing by Maria's office and see what she was up to. Her office is right down the hall from mine, which is hard to get used to because I'm in Bob's old office and she's in my old office. But I'm not going to complain because now I have more wall space to punch when I get mad. I made it to Garcia's office and found her chatting on the phone as usual.

"Come on in, Neil, I'm just listening to some messages that I missed while I was out at lunch. Any of your hunches pan out?"

"I guess we're about to find out. Cappelano left me a note with this FTP file-sharing site address. Let's load it up and see what's on it. Do you want to use your computer, or go to mine, since it's essentially empty at this point?"

"Neil, way to bury the lead, are you kidding? Get a move on, let's go." She hung up the phone while her messages were still playing, pushed me out of her office and down to mine, got on my computer, and asked for the FTP site credentials. I started to read them off. She repeated them back to me, then we stared at each other for a brief moment.

"Are you going to hit Enter, Maria, or do I need to do it?"

"You're the one who took forever getting over here in the first place. Now *I'm* taking too long?" She had a good point there. Maria clenched her teeth and hit Enter, and the files began to download. Case files, PDFs, and news clippings, dropping onto my computer for what felt like forever but was probably more like seven to ten minutes altogether.

Maria grabbed my desk phone and called up to Jen at the front desk.

"Jen, can you bring a couple of flash drives to Neil's office ASAP?"

Before I could even realize what was going on, Jen walked in and dropped off a handful of plain, black flash drives, and then Maria started making copies for me, Mike, and herself. She would also get the necessary copies to the field office's IT department to make sure it was okay to send it to other departments for scrubbing and researching.

"I guess we're heading over to Mike's office, unless you want to dig around in here first and see what we can find to present a better initial report to the boss," I said. Even though they told me I'm the lead on this case, I'm trying to learn how to play office politics between the two of them, mainly for the sake of teamwork and trust-building.

"We could simply call him and ask," Maria said, and started calling his office on speaker.

"Special Agent in Charge Ponecelli. What can I do for you?"

"Mike, it's Maria and Neil, we're in his office. Neil just got a great—well, what we *hope* is a great—lead from an FTP site download file that Cappelano left him. Do you want us to fill you in now, or should we learn as much as we can, then fill you in when the picture is clearer?"

"That's wonderful news, Maria. Tell you what: I'll give you

guys two hours to get started, while I finish up some briefings. Then I'll come see where you're at, and we'll go from there. Does that work?"

And like that, we were off and running on another wild goose chase with Cappelano.

Fortunately, the hard part of this case is already done—figuring out who is doing the killing and building a psychological profile of the person you're tracking down. Once you get into the mind-set of the killer, you can predict their tendencies in terms of where and how they might strike next, as well as their everyday activities. Since I already know the killer and have a psychological breakdown of him, I have a head start.

Having a good lead in the case allows us to run with the evidence as we get it, but it also makes the wait that much harder, because even though we know exactly who we need to catch, we have to find him. Plus, Cappelano *knows* we know his identity, which means he's a lot more careful than a killer who thinks they're still operating anonymously. We needed a new starting point to go off of. Currently we have to look at what's been given to us, but I know my general reluctance stems from years of Cappelano steering me where he wants to. The standard procedure is to sift through all the data, find any patterns, see if there is something we can find to help us track him down, see if we can find a new angle.

As Maria and I started to dig through the files, we noticed that there was a lot of overlap in case files we already had on

Cappelano. Murders already pinned to him; maybe this was his way of trying to confirm his kills. But there were two murders in there that didn't seem to fit his style, alleged drug cartel hits that fit my idea that he ran to Mexico. There were also a ton of files on Ashley and her father, Lawrence, but most files were on Lawrence's son Terry, Ashley's brother.

The files were organized neatly in folders and coded so that you can read them in sequential order. The first file was a news article about Terry Gracin's death, initially chalked up to a robbery gone wrong on the campus of Eastern Michigan University. The incident never made much sense to any of us when it happened because Terry went to the University of Michigan, which is very close to EMU. Oftentimes the U of M kids will wander over to the EMU campus to score harder drugs to find than weed and Adderall. The rumors were always that Terry was not just using, but also dealing, and at a pretty high level. At one point there was an internal investigation of his father because of it. Then Terry died, and it all went away.

The next big file is on Ashley herself, related to her being a witness to the murder of a local gang leader who was associated with the drug ring Terry was tied up with. I hadn't been privy to any of this information back then; now I wish I had been. Unformed thoughts were swimming in my head, trying to take shape.

"All right, gang, it's been a little over two hours. Where are we at?" Mike said, practically jogging into my office. "Maria, you go first."

Maria started going over all the case files that seemed to overlap and brought him up to speed on a few new details we picked up in the file dump Cappelano gave us. She even threw in the info about the cartel-related murders. There was no direct connection to Cappelano there, but it seems like that's what he was trying to tell us by including those files.

"Do you guys think there's a way to investigate the murders in Mexico?" Mike asked.

"Mike, you know there isn't. That's why Cappelano put them in there," I said. "Whether he did them or not, there's no way to get help from the Mexican government to help us look into old murders, which they don't care about."

"I have to agree with Neil on this one, Mike. We have to assume he did them but can't waste our energy on it. That being said, we should absolutely factor them into our searching grids, and expectations on where he might run to."

"Okay, so what's the other stack of files, and going old school paper files? Sometimes you just need to hold it and file it." Mike looked in agreement with our system.

"Good call: those are the Gracin files. Cappelano seems to have found a lot of dirty connections starting with Terry, working their way up to Lawrence. From what I can tell, Cappelano is either trying to infer or straight-up point at Gracin for being connected to the murder of a drug kingpin. The one who killed his son and used his daughter for false testimony."

"Wait a minute; that would mean this Ashley Gracin murder is less about attention and more about vengeance. Like he was cleaning up a dirty FBI agent?" Maria chimed in.

"Mike, I agree with Maria: that's what it looks like. Do you want us to get on the phone with the Internal Affairs office?"

"No, get me the file, and I'll send it to the head myself, but I want to have a conversation with Gracin first, give him a heads up. He's got to know this is coming. Hell, he just lost his daughter, buried his son a few years ago. This isn't good for anyone."

"So what's next?" I asked.

Mike hesitated. Whatever was on his mind, maybe he didn't feel like this was the right time to bring it up. "I'll take care of the Gracin stuff; you guys keep working the Cappelano trail, see if you can find where he's headed next." Mike left my office, visibly troubled by these new developments.

"Maria, if it's all right with you, I'm going to take this and some other old files back to the house and start trying to pattern this out. Between him breaking into my house twice and constantly upstaging me, I'm losing my patience. I already lost my life to this case once; I need this shit to be over."

Finally I can get out of here and do some real work. I'll plan to call Ken and have him put a few of our guys on a fact-finding expedition. That usually entails some of our investigators rustling up crackheads and drug dealers to get information. I hope Maria can pull something from the canvass this weekend;

we need all the help we can get. With the combination of the bureau using their influence and my people using theirs, we should be able to get something out of the neighborhood. I'm feeling especially confident about this case. Knowing I'll have my own men running an investigation alongside that of the bureau will allow me to do a lot more than I could four years ago.

"Sounds good, Neil. I'll give you a call later about swinging by to—"

"Yeah, Maria, that's fine. I can meet you halfway if you want."

"That's okay; I'm going to meet up with a friend of mine tonight. She lives on your side of town."

"Well then, I'll talk to you and maybe see you later. I'll be home most of the night reading case files."

"See you later, Neil."

I took some time to gather up some files scattered all over the field office while I had Jen pack me a few boxes full of anything and everything related to Cappelano over the past four years. It was amazing how many boxes we could fill between the files in my office and the building's archives. I'd need some major help getting this downstairs; otherwise I'd be making trips up and down the elevator all night. I'm sure I could get Jen and a couple of other people heading out to grab a box or two. It's a good thing I still drive the Jeep, since I was going to have that thing packed full. Speaking of getting help, I should call Ken before I start moving these boxes and talk to him about getting some of the boys involved in this case.

"Tony's Pizzeria, please hold," Ken said when he answered the phone. That man never misses an opportunity to bust my balls.

"Real nice, Ken, but this call is business. I need you to have some of the guys run down some information for me. I'll be emailing over some background about the plastic surgeons who did facial reconstructions for Cappelano over the years. We need to hunt down anyone and everyone he might run to, to try and see what he looks like today."

"All right, just send the files. I have a few guys who need some work. I have one in particular who will be good for this."

"That reminds me. Did you hear from Officer Johnson from the Detroit PD, inquiring about a job?"

"Yeah, I spoke to him earlier, he's going to come by this weekend and talk to me about doing some part-time work."

"Thanks, Ken. He really needs the work, and he's got experience. Two things we can always use at the warehouse."

"No problem. He's got a good background, and I know his supervisor; things should work out pretty easy. Just get me the info on those plastic surgeons, and I'll get the guys on it right away."

"All right, I'll send that over in a few. I'll have to send it from home, so give me a couple of hours."

"That sounds good. One last thing before you go. TJ said

you found the same info on the FTP site, and he's still trying to crack the CD. He's pretty certain that there's something there, but he's not holding his breath."

"How long are we talking? Days? Weeks?"

"He said he should have something to you by Monday; hopefully, Sunday. You know TJ, he won't sleep until he has this done."

"I know, he's a good kid. Tell him thanks for me, and I'll talk to you later, Ken."

"Can do. I'll talk to you later, Neil."

I'm glad to find out that there's something on the CD; now it's just a matter of finding out what it is. The anticipation is already killing me; I don't have a lot of patience for situations like this. When it comes to waiting for something to be done, or something like a stakeout, I'm horrible. I always need something to distract me. Now that I think of it, Hendrickson sent me on one stakeout, and after that, he never assigned me to another one, probably because no one would go with me. Everyone has strengths and weaknesses. My strengths are my inability to relax on a case and go at it with a vengeance mentally. I may seem like I'm just going about my day, but I'm constantly sifting through data and variables, searching for the next lead. But it's that strength that's also my weakness, because having an overactive mind can cause me to miss things along the way. That's where Ken and Maria come in.

I should probably tell Maria the good news about the disc

before I leave. I guess it wouldn't kill me to stop by her office on the way out, since it's only three doors down from my office. There's just something about her. Maybe it's because she shares the same interests as I do, maybe it's because she's gorgeous, but all I know is she drives me nuts. I feel like a freshman in high school with a crush on the head cheerleader. I know it's a cliché, but that's how I feel. I don't think there is anyone in my position who could control themselves around Maria.

"Hey Maria, good news about the disc we found."

"What's up? Did your guy find something already?"

"Yes and no. He said there is definitely something on the disc other than music. Still, it's encrypted extremely well, so it's going to take him a couple of days to crack it."

"Maybe our guys should look at it."

"I don't think so. TJ is an absolute killer when it comes to data encryption. If he says he can do it, he can do it. I lucked out with him; he studied at MIT until he got kicked out for giving a minor alcohol. It was bad for him but good for me."

"Well, at least you're helping him out. I assume you're taking care of him financially?"

"He makes a lot of money, mainly because he brings a lot of tech business our way. Having TJ on board allows us to do surveillance on people's computers. Big firms like to use him to check up on employees they think might be stealing or selling secrets to competitors."

"Sounds like you have a prosperous enterprise there."

"I do pretty well; I can't complain. And with the FBI helping out now, I should be able to finish remodeling my house. I still have to do the basement and the master bedroom; then I'm done with the inside."

"That's wonderful. But hey, I need to get going. I'll tell Mike about the disc, and I'll call you later."

"All right. Talk to you later, Maria. Drive safe tonight when you head out my way."

Needless to say, I haven't told Sheila about any of this yet. I can't wait for that conversation; it's going to be like Christmas morning. Sheila and I have an understanding that we won't be able to stay true to each other all the time, but all we ask is that we inform each other when we are messing around with someone else so that we know where we stand at any given moment.

At least I'm finally driving home. It's Thursday, and I'm going to pretty much have the weekend off to go through old files and just think about the case. Sometimes the best things come to me when I'm *not* thinking about a case; that's actually how I got into carpentry. It started when I needed a distraction from work, and a friend of mine was remodeling his house. It turns out I'm good with a saw. I learned pretty much everything from him when it comes to carpentry. I can't wait to get home, go out to the garage, and do some work with my hands. I'm finishing my basement, but I haven't gotten too far. I still have to get all the studs up and then put up drywall. Aside from all that, I'll be in my kitchen this weekend, looking over the files I'm bringing home.

A case as intense as this can be extremely slow in the beginning as you're building up evidence. Because of this, you'll have days with nothing going on except reviewing old files. By the end of the case, though, you're so tired from lack of sleep and constant moving that you miss the slow days. Just as I made the turn onto my street, I heard my cell phone go off; that ring means its Sheila. I guess now is as good a time as any to tell her what happened last night.

"Hey, Sheila. How are you doing?"

"Hey, Neil, I think I'm doing better than you. I passed by the house to check on the dogs, but I saw your car there, so I kept going. What were you doing home earlier? I know you wouldn't quit on this case no matter how much you hate the bureau."

"I had a long night last night—a *really* long night. I had the team over from the bureau to review the case for pizza and beer."

"It's not like you to mesh so quick, especially with people from the bureau. Why are you actually trying to make it work this time? Is Cappelano in the back of your mind this much?"

"Wow! You know me a little *too* well. Apparently I hooked up with the lady who brought me back into the bureau, Maria Garcia."

"You mean the one you talked to on Monday about coming

back to the bureau? You mentioned that she was young. She must be attractive, too."

"Very much so. Actually, the two of you have very similar features, just grew up different culturally."

"Interesting. Maybe we could have her join us. We'd have one hell of a night."

"If I didn't know better, I'd think you were being truthful, but I know you're just fucking with me."

"I don't know, I wouldn't mind experimenting with another girl, and if you say she's like me but Latina, that strikes my interest." Sheila likes to get a rise out of me, but more than anything, she knows a case like this can tear me up. She likes to give me mental rest to recharge.

"You really know how to push my buttons and get under my skin, don't you? But after the last couple of nights and no sleep, I'm not doing anything with anyone tonight."

"What's that supposed to mean? Do you want to see her again? You do, don't you? Aww, Neil has a crush on Maria."

"Of course not. You can't have a crush on someone you already slept with."

"Yes you can, because if she doesn't give it up again, you're screwed. You have a crush. You're so cute, you know that?"

"Shut up, you're driving me nuts. Plus I just pulled in the driveway, and I'm in major need of a shower and an aspirin."

"Does Neil have a headache to go along with his crush?"

"I'm getting off the phone with you. You're killing me."

"I'll talk to you later, Neil. Have a good night. Maybe your new friend will stop by and show you a good time."

"That's it, I'm done. I'll talk to you later, babe. Kiss Carol Lynn good night, will you? And I was thinking of stopping by tomorrow. Maybe the three of us can go out to brunch?"

"Sounds good, I'll tell Carol Lynn the good news."

"Night, Sheila."

I knew Sheila was going to give me a hard time; she can't help herself. Having her as an ex-wife is very similar to having a ten-year-old sister, at least when it comes to conversations about dating. Other than that, she's an amazing woman and an even better mother.

Finally I got all of the files and my things inside. I didn't even bother showering, I just changed into my grubby jeans and some work boots, threw on a sweatshirt, and made my way to the garage with the girls. I'll feed them in there, and just let them out the side door. They like being around me while I work, even when it's in the garage, though it helps that I have a nice bed made up for them in there. This weekend is going to be great—just me, Jackie, and Danielle. I need it after a long, hectic week. This case is going to drain me, I just know it is because I'm going to stop at nothing to get him. This time Cappelano isn't getting away.

11

I know I'm going to regret this later, but I don't have any choice; Cappelano will have to wait for a change.

The weekend was exactly what I needed, even if TJ didn't get the CD done yet. He said he should have it done by this morning. All I need to do is wait for his call, but I don't think I'll be able to wait around here much longer. This weekend I finished putting up all the studs and running electrical wire for the outlets. All that's left is to put up the drywall, and I'll have the walls all done in the basement. I think better when I'm doing something with my hands; it allows me to slow down mentally.

Especially after what happened Friday night with Maria when she came over to get her shoes. Let's just say that her shoes are still in the back of my car. I told you this was going to blow up in my face, I can feel it coming. Plus I had to spend all morning getting ribbed on by Sheila about the night before. She can always tell when I have sex. Hell, she was married to me for five years, and we dated for two years before that—not to mention the four years we've spent divorced—so she knows me better than anyone.

I remember when we first got divorced, all of my friends kept telling me that if Sheila and I didn't stop messing around, it would end horribly. That was four years ago, and we've both dated outside of our little messed-up situation since then. I went on a few dates with a district attorney, nothing serious, and Sheila dated a doctor on and off for about a year. He couldn't get used to the friendly relationship that Sheila and I still have, and he didn't even know we were still conjugating verbs on the side. Oh yeah, and there was that problem where he kept sleeping with every nurse who worked for him. He was a real keeper, one of those guys you bring home to Mom.

Just before I hopped in my car to head back to the FBI office, I heard my cell ringing.

"Neil Baggio speaking. Who may I ask is calling?" I said jokingly.

"Neil, it's Ken. Our guys tracked down something that might interest you, but you've got to head out right now."

"Did they find a witness to Ashley Gracin's murder?"

"Close; we have a couple of our informants keeping an eye out for suspicious activities. Well, one of them just called to tell me there's a guy eating breakfast at a diner not too far from the site where her body was found."

"It's about time you caught the breakfast diner bandit, Ken.

Did he not tip again? Come on, why did you call me with this?"

"Because the informant said he's almost positive it's the guy who dropped off the body in the river. You'd better get your ass going before he leaves."

"Tell our guy to keep an eye on him in case I can't get out there in time. I'm leaving right now."

"No problem, Neil. I'll text you the address of the diner when I hang up. Good luck and hit the gas pedal."

"You don't have to tell me that, Ken. I'll be there as fast as my car will let me."

Making my way toward the expressway, I witnessed an elderly lady drive through a red light. It wasn't like she was trying to beat a yellow light and lost, either, it was just solid red, and she blew right through it. Luckily she didn't get hit or hit anyone else. I ended up stopping at a red light a couple of minutes later and kept my line of sight up the road, where it looked like there was an accident. I got the green light and made my way toward the scene.

When I arrived, I saw that the same elderly lady had driven into the back of another car, catapulting herself through her windshield. Son of a bitch, this is a mess. Why is no one stopping to help? I don't have time for this right now, I've got to get downtown. I know I'm going to regret this later, but I don't have any choice; Cappelano will have to wait for a change. I grabbed my cell and sent Ken a text telling him what was up and asking him to send one of our guys to head to the diner where Cappelano was allegedly enjoying a nice breakfast and trail him if he went anywhere.

Pulling off the road and slamming on the brakes. I ran out of the car, leaving my keys in the ignition to check on the elderly lady. She was already dead; the accident had snapped her spinal cord in half, killing her instantly. Before I had time to take in what happened, I heard a woman screaming at the top of her lungs, "Help me, my daughter is stuck in the backseat!" I'm not happy I stopped, but right now I know why I'm here: I have a chance to save someone's life.

The accident had caused another car to buckle inward, crushing the backseat. The mother was pinned between the steering wheel and her seat. It looked as though her leg was snapped, but she kept screaming for someone to get her daughter out of the car. I pulled out my cell and called 911, telling them what happened and where to meet me. As I put my phone back in my pocket, a man asked me if I smelled gasoline. Now that he mentioned it, I did. I knew that time was of the essence, and there wasn't going to be more than a few minutes before the cars exploded. I directed the man and a few others to try and pry the lady out of the front seat. I was going to try and help her daughter.

What the mother had failed to mention was that her daughter was a newborn, maybe five months at the most. I started to squeeze myself into the car, sliding through the back window, which had been shattered from the crash. I couldn't get all the way in, but I could see around enough and move my arms somewhat freely. When I spotted the daughter strapped in her car seat, she looked as though she was knocked unconscious. As I worked to free her from the straps, I yelled through the broken back window for help. A woman who had been standing outside of her house came running over.

The thing that saved that little girl was her car seat, and the fact that she was so small. I was able to pass her right out of the back window and hand her off to the lady who had come over to assist me, but when I did that, I realized my arm was stuck. My shirt must have gotten caught between the caved-in roof and part of the driver's seat when I was moving the girl out of the car.

The bystanders who were trying to help the driver had just gotten the door off when the police and EMS showed up and started giving medical attention to the baby girl. Fortunately, her only injuries were a few shards of glass that had stuck into her leg, and they were easily attended to by paramedics. I kept trying to tug my arm free but was too afraid to cut myself, so I was doing my best to wriggle out, slowly and carefully. Not making much progress, I used my free hand to start searching my jacket pocket for a knife I could use to cut my shirt and free myself. Then I heard a phrase that changed everything.

"Everyone back away from the car, it's about to explode!" I have no idea who said it but was glad they did.

The men who had been trying to help the mother started to

run back from the car, leaving her behind to fend for herself. They were too worried that pulling her out through brute force would hurt her spine. That's when I lost it. I yanked my arm from the car, cutting it very deeply on a piece of jagged metal from the crushed roof. As I saw the blood running down my arm, the only thing I could think of was that mother in the front seat. Running to her side of the car, I looked at her and saw the fear in her eyes.

"Ma'am, those other men were afraid to pull you from the car because your back may get hurt. If I don't pull you out right now, you could die from the explosion," I said, trying to keep my voice calm even though my entire body was buzzing from the adrenaline.

"Well, what are you waiting for?" she said. "I want to be alive to see my daughter grow up, whether I can walk or not."

"Understood. Now listen, it's going to hurt really badly when I pull you out of here, but the more pain you feel, the better, because it means your spine isn't damaged. Okay?"

"Pain is good. Got it."

"On the count of three, I'm pulling you out."

"Okay, give me a second. All right, do it."

"One . . . two—"

Before I even finished counting, I pulled her from the car and threw her over my shoulder. As I ran with her for cover, the car suddenly exploded into flames, throwing shrapnel all over the streets. I stumbled from the blast on my way to the ambulance, and though she hadn't said a word since we had left the vehicle, right at that moment she started screaming in excruciating pain.

"It hurts. O my God, it hurts. This is good, right? FUCK!"

"This is very good. We're at the ambulance, I'm going to lay you on a gurney, and they are going to take care of you. I'll go check on your daughter. I'll be right back."

I ran over to the other ambulance and saw the woman's baby wrapped in a blanket, asleep in the arms of a female EMT. Before I could leave, one of the other EMTs spotted my bloodied arm and insisted on cleaning and dressing it. With the baby safe and my arm semi-intact, I turned my attention back to the mother. Running over to where she was being loaded into the ambulance, I asked her if she wanted me to call anyone for her. She gave me the number to her husband; that conversation was a nice change of pace for me. Normally when I have to call spouses, it's to give them the worst news possible, but though the accident was bad, his wife was alive. I found out that the ambulance was taking her to St. John's of Macomb on Twelve Mile and Hoover. I told her husband what happened, that I worked for the FBI, and that I happened to be there after the accident. Although he had asked me to ride with his wife, I had to inform him that she had already been taken to the hospital but that I was following behind in my car on the way there.

Despite the EMT's best efforts, my arm wouldn't stop

bleeding during the drive to the hospital. I figured since I had followed the woman over there, the least I could do is stay and tell her husband what happened. Oftentimes, first responders are trained to give little to no information to anyone claiming to be a family member or friend. I know, I used to do it. As I pulled up to the hospital, I was told to stay in the waiting room, which will be fine as long as Christina from Channel 4 News doesn't show up. A story about an exploding car with a young child inside seems like just the thing that would lure Christina out from underneath her rock, but the last thing this family needs is reporters all over them. For now, I just need to sit down and relax. It was at that moment that a nurse noticed my arm.

"Sir, are you okay? Your arm is bleeding pretty badly."

"I'll be all right. I had an EMT take a look at it already."

"Sir, let me bring you to a room and clean this up better for you."

"I can't leave here. The husband of a woman who was just brought in is supposed to meet me in the waiting room."

"I'll have the receptionist tell him where you and his wife are. He probably won't be able to see his wife for a while, so I'll have her send him to us. Okay?"

"All right, I guess that sounds fine. But let's make this quick."

As the nurse led the way to a room, I noticed that she hadn't even taken the time to admit me officially and file paperwork. She must be doing this off the books and out of the goodness of her heart. It's not common practice for a nurse or any hospital employee to do anything to anyone in a hospital without taking their medical information, mainly their insurance. The nurse kept trying to make small talk, but I was short with my answers, thinking of what had just happened with the car accident and the chance I might have just lost to catch Cappelano. I know it wasn't the best thing to do for the case, but I wouldn't be able to live with myself if I drove past that accident and not helped, especially knowing now that a young child could have lost her life.

"Can I get you anything for pain?" the nurse asked me. "I need to put in a few stitches to close up these wounds. Some of them are pretty big."

"No, I don't like pain meds. Just put the stitches in and grab me a bag of ice, I've got enough calls and texts to catch up on. They'll distract me."

I have a few missed calls from Ken. I need to sift through all this stuff as quickly as I can and get back to what I was doing before this whole shit show happened in front of me. The crazy part is the possibility that somehow Cappelano had something to do with this crash. There's no evidence for that, and I know it's just me being paranoid and overanalyzing everything, but I have good reason to. I've learned over the years that Cappelano is capable of virtually anything.

"Whatever you say," the nurse said, "but this is going to hurt really badly."

"I know it will; I've had stitches put in before. But I don't have the time to waste; if I cloud my judgment with meds, it will take more time out of my day than I can spare."

I swear she was more uncomfortable than I was during the whole process, but that's the norm for me when I'm at the hospital. I don't like pain medication at all. I think it's a control issue for me. I don't like relying on pills to function, so when it comes to pain, I just deal with it.

"All right, it looks like you're all set. Don't worry about the paperwork."

"What do you mean? I have good insurance. Hell, I work for the government, it's not a big deal."

"One of the nurses told me what you did. I'm not going to bother with it."

"Thanks, I guess. Well, I'm going to head back out to the waiting room. Can I just get a bag of ice first?"

As she left to get me a bag of ice, I began calling Ken and walking out of the room. Distracted, as usual, looking for the husband as well as any sign of those news vultures, and that's when I saw the Channel 4 News van pulling into the ER lot. Then I heard Ken yelling at me through the phone.

"Neil, where the hell are you, and what is going on? NEIL! Are you okay? At least say something."

"Ken, I'm fine, I'm at the hospital. Something happened. I came upon an accident and—"

"Neil, you're not making any sense right now. Which hospital? I'm going to have TJ track you and see where you're at."

"Ken, seriously, I'm fine. I'll call you back in like five minutes. Everything will be back on track, I promise. Sorry for worrying you."

I traversed from my room to the front as if I were riding the walkway at an airport. The nurse handed me a bag of ice. I saw what looked like a very distraught man about to get bombarded by a camera crew and my least favorite TV journalist. I had to get in there and break this up before he suffered a nervous breakdown on camera. And then I needed to get on my way and figure out if my next stop is the warehouse or the bureau, and quick. I'd already wasted enough time.

"Hey, are you Adam, the husband from the phone?"

"Yes, I am. Are you the guy who called me about my wife?"

"Yeah, my name's Neil. I was there when everything happened. Your daughter is okay. I talked to the doctors, and she will be fine. Just a few cuts and bruises."

"What about my wife? How is she doing? No one will tell me anything right now."

"It's hard to tell. She was trapped between the steering wheel and her seat. From what the paramedics said, I know she broke her leg for sure, but she was alert and in good spirits when they put her in the ambulance, and the staff here is fantastic. She's in great hands."

"Thank you for everything, Neil, you've really done more than you needed to."

All of a sudden my vision started to blur, and I felt my legs get all tingly. Too much excitement for one day. "I need to sit down, I'm sorry," I said. "It's just been a long morning."

"I understand. Could you tell me who helped pull my family from the car? I want to thank them."

"There were a lot of people who helped, I don't know anyone's name. Sorry, but I was getting caught up on everything. Can you excuse me? I need to make a call."

"Yeah, that's fine. Thanks again for everything."

I hated to cut out, but I needed to call the office and tell Maria I was running late; I decided that the bureau was the place to be right now. I didn't want her to think I was still in bed, ignoring the fact that we had a meeting scheduled this morning. I know it seems odd that I wouldn't tell Adam that I had pulled his wife and daughter from the car, but I really don't want any press. When it comes to megalomaniac serial killers, you have to do your best to manage the media. I just hope Maria believes me when I call her and tell her what's going on. I also hope she isn't pissed when she finds out I might have missed a chance with Cappelano. Then again, maybe I don't have to tell her about the Cappelano part.

"Hey Maria, how you doing? It's Neil."

"Neil, where are you at? The meeting is in ten minutes."

"Well, something came up. I can't talk about it now, but if you turn on any of the local news channels, you should get the gist of it. I'll fill you in on the rest when I get there."

"Wait. What? Are you okay?

"I'll be fine; I should be there within the hour. I'm at St. John's Macomb right now, not that far from the office. But I have to go. I'll talk to you later."

I didn't want to hang up on her, but I have to get out of here before my face ends up all over the news. Plus, the fewer cameras I have following me, the easier my job will be. Well, it looks like I spoke too soon, because running in my direction here comes Christina from Channel 4 News, the last person I want to talk to right now. If I get stuck talking to her and people piece together what happened, I'm going to be the night's lead story, and not just locally. I don't have time for this shit; I just want to get out of here. I know it would be good publicity for the bureau if I got in front of the cameras and played the hero, but I want to focus on the case, not interviews.

"Hi, this is Christina Moore with Channel 4 News reporting live from St. John's Hospital on Twelve Mile and Hoover. Bringing you an interview with Neil Baggio, the FBI agent who saved not only the life of a baby girl but also the life of her mother. Neil, can we get a minute of your time?"

"I'm really busy right now, Christina, I really don't have time for this. I need to get back to work. I'm sorry, but I need to get going."

"Neil, just a few questions for us, please? It will only take a minute."

Quickly moving from the lobby of the hospital to the parking lot, I saw Christina Moore and her cameraman running after me, still trying to get their story. One would think after all the years she's dealt with me that she would get it through her head that I'm not giving her an interview, not now, not ever. By the time I made it to my car, I noticed that she wasn't behind me anymore. I'm hoping she gave up, but I know better; she probably ran to the news van to tail me. Luckily I have some good friends who still work for the Detroit PD. I got on the phone and called Officer Johnson from the Ashley Gracin murder scene to see if he could help me out with my current problem.

"Hey, Officer Johnson, are you working right now?"

"Yeah. What's up, Neil? By the way, thanks again for helping me out. I appreciate it."

"No problem. Listen, I have a fucking news van that's tailing me and won't get off my ass. I can't have my face on the news right now, not if I'm going to catch Cappelano." I know what you're thinking: Cappelano already knows you're on the case; hell, he *wants* you on the case. Think of our relationship like two professional poker players who have sat at the final table a few different times. The problem is, I can't seem to beat Cappelano; he keeps beating me. I need to try and control as much information at the poker table as I can.

"Is this about the car wreck? I heard what happened. Nice job, Baggio."

"Thank you. I'm glad it turned out all right, though I'm not interested in becoming a feel-good story on Channel 4 News tonight. Can you have someone pull the van over and get them off me so I can get to work in peace?"

"Got ya covered, Neil; I'll put the call out right now. One of our officers will pull them over and maybe take an extra- ong time running the driver's license. That should give you enough time to get away."

"Thanks, man. I owe you one."

"Call it even. You got me the job with your company. You have no idea how much that means to me."

"No problem with the job, and thanks for helping me."

"I'll let you go, Neil, so I can make the call and get you some help. I'll talk to you later."

About two minutes later, I saw a pair of police cruisers pull onto the road, one in front of the van and one behind, flashing their lights to get the van to pull over. That made my day. At least now I can get to the office without any more hassles. By the way, my arm is still killing me. I didn't realize how badly I had cut myself until the adrenaline started to subside. I almost forgot I needed to call Ken and see if our guy got to the diner in time to tail Cappelano. I still can't believe all of this happened on my way out to catch who I presumed was either Cappelano himself or at least someone who might know where he is.

"Ken, its Neil. What happened with the diner?"

"Sorry, Neil, the guy got away. He left before our guy could get out there. And the informant doesn't have a car, so he couldn't tail him."

"Did the informant at least get a look at his car? Anything we can go on?"

"Nope, he said he turned away for a minute, and the next thing he knew, the guy was gone from the diner and nowhere to be seen."

"Son of a bitch. I really don't have any time to be pissed right now, I'm heading to the office from the hospital. I'll call you later tonight."

"What? Why were you at the hospital?"

"I can't talk right now. Just turn on Channel 4 News; they should be covering what happened. But I have to go."

"'Bye, Neil. I'll talk to you later."

I eventually made it to the office and walked Maria through everything that had happened. More importantly, I got my blood sugar back up and started to refocus on the case. To give you an idea of the kind of power Cappelano has on a case like this, more than one agent asked if it was possible Cappelano played a role in the crash that threw my day off. The truth is that I don't know, but it's highly possible. He's motivated, capable, and batshit crazy.

As for my time at the field office, we got to work organizing a game plan for the days ahead. We had some leads on where Cappelano might be working out of. Narrowed down to a few different city blocks based on the data he gave us, as well as data on unsolved homicides that don't follow normal crime patterns, etc. We are using every tool in the bag and even trying to invent a few along the way; there are whosits and whatsits galore.   For those of you without daughters, that's a Little Mermaid reference. We're going to have to get creative if we're going to catch a break in this case. Add some intense hard work and immense man-hours and we might actually have a shot.

12

I sat in my chair . . . drifting into and out of consciousness, which is how I do some of my best thinking sometimes.

It's Friday morning, following one of the longest weeks of my career. It wasn't the most exciting week, but it was filled with the kind of procedural grunt work necessary for gathering information and building a case file. We utilized multiple teams working around the clock, knocking off sections of the city. Following leads, looking into old cases, and tracking down any information we thought might be connected to Gracin or Cappelano. Starting on Monday afternoon with a strong talk, stronger coffee, and a Braveheart-esque speech by Mike. The troops were fired up to conquer the grid he had drawn up to systematically narrow the field. Though they hadn't found anything Monday or Tuesday, we had made huge headway on cutting down chunks of the city where Cappelano wasn't.

I know what you're thinking: isn't that about as positive as describing a poop Popsicle as not that bad? When you're looking for a needle in the haystack, you'll be happy with cutting down the amount of hay you need to sift through. By Wednesday we felt like we were getting close. Because the chatter and information we were getting from people in the communities we were searching was starting to match Cappelano's MO. But by late Thursday night, we hit the jackpot, at least what felt like a jackpot. Remember, if you've been playing slots for three days and you win a fifty-dollar jackpot, you might forget about the five hundred dollars you lost all week, at least for a little bit.

Maria and I had what felt like three great leads going into Thursday night and sent teams of agents to canvass and investigate what we thought were hideouts or staging areas for Cappelano murders. Late that night, we lucked out and found a staging area for one murder. Being able to connect it to Cappelano is another case altogether, but when you already have ten life sentences you can put around a man's neck, you're more concerned with getting them than building the next case.

The staging area we found was near a run-down neighborhood off Chalmers in Detroit. It was in a crumbling two-story house that looked like an old crack house judging by all the needles. It was surrounded by vacant lots, high grass, and a fence that allowed some semblance of privacy. Inside the house, we found plastic, blood, and remnants of body tissue that the lab will try to connect to current murders, solved or unsolved.

Most of the week's canvassing ended up as strikeouts, leading us to little or no information, at least pertaining to the Cappelano case. We did find a group of young women who were being held captive by a pair of small-time human traffickers, selling slave labor or worse. We got the women to safety and "accidentally" knocked out a few of the suspects' teeth before shipping them off to jail. When you end up knocking on a couple of thousand doors that are not normally knocked on, you can occasionally get lucky. Maybe even save a few lives, even if it's not for the purpose you intended.

And that's where we are now. We have teams canvassing in plainclothes all over Detroit looking into the Gracin connections. We looked closer at an uptick in gang violence, and when we revisited some old interviews, community leaders kept describing a "White Devil" killing in the ghetto. And from looking at the information Cappelano gave us, the information we got from the Detroit PD and the gang members themselves. It looks like Cappelano was trying to build a case against Gracin and was coming at it from every angle he could find.

"Maria, this has been one of the longest weeks of my life. Can we please get some sleep?" Maria and I were taking a much-needed break at my place. Sure, we were still staring at case files, but at least we were doing it in front of the fire listening to some Frank in my study, relaxing.

"Neil, first of all, you had plenty of time to sleep, but you kept opting out of sleep, and insisted that you would be fine. I told you that you're getting too old for this lifestyle," she said with a huge grin on her face.

"Okay, fair enough, burning the candle at both ends is probably not the best idea, but hey, I didn't have a single drink all week."

"You're saying that like you should be proud of not drinking for three days."

She has a great point, but then again, Cappelano has me on such an edge that I've been a shell of myself the past couple of years. I have my best friends, family, and ex-wife constantly worried about me. Shit, I can even tell that my dogs are worried sometimes. But this week was the first time it felt like we got into the game, which is what Cappelano wanted. He got my attention, but Maria has my focus, and she has me running strong. I feel like the last time I was running an obstacle course trying to get to Cappelano, and this time I have someone supporting me, pushing me, and I just have to get out of my own way. As I was getting through that last thought, I saw TJ was calling me.

"Hey Neil, good news, bad news. I got the files off the CD, and it's a lot of duplicate case files from what I can tell. I wanted to wait before I called you because I know you guys have been swamped. So I cross-referenced all the files and ran a few programs to see what stood out, and it looks like there are about forty percent new files on this disk compared to the FTP site."

"Since that FTP site is a simple file-sharing page, would you be able to upload and share those new files?" I asked. "Shit, they're *his* files at this point, but it'll show him that we have them, maybe strike his interest. But I need you to do me a favor before you do that. I'm going to email you a photo; I need you to upload it to that site along with the other files."

"Sure, boss, no problem. I'll look out for that email."

"It'll be a case file; just make sure and rename it so that it sits at the top of the file stream."

"I can do that, no problem; it'll be pretty simple with the system he has set up in there."

"Thanks, TJ. And make sure you get copies of everything over to the bureau. I'll text you Jen's number; she can help you coordinate everything."

"Got it, boss."

Maybe it's the progress we made this week, maybe it's Maria, maybe it's the twenty gallons of coffee pumping through my veins sans alcohol that have me hyperfocused. I'm about to have a little fun with Cappelano. Right then, Maria chimed in, between overhearing me on the phone and seeing that devilish look on my face.

"Neil, what do you have in mind? Are you going to leave him a note in there, something to draw him out?"

"I've had this theory for years that he started killing when he was still at the bureau, right before he started to groom me, and there's one case in particular that has always stood out. I'm going to place it there. It's a crapshoot, but at this point I'll take anything. It was a homeless man that we ended up looking into because he turned out to be a former government agent, military hero, and all-around good guy. Someone up the flagpole asked us to look into it. Or so I was told."

"Not a bad idea. At this point, *no* idea is a bad idea."

Well, my first thought may have been a bad idea. I wanted to take a picture of myself flipping the bird, then name it "Cappelano FBI File" and upload it for him. That's probably a bad idea, but who's keeping track? The case of the homeless man always stuck with me, though, because it never made sense when we looked into it. I felt he was using the murder as a dumb reason to train me; now I know he was doing it to show off, or so I think. *"Look, I killed this guy, and you can't tell."* It was the beginning of our twisted-ass relationship. I just want to wring his neck. Come to think of it, I want to beat him to within an inch of his life and nurse him back to health, only to beat his ass again.

"Hey Neil, you daydreaming about beating Cappelano's ass again? You've got that Cappelano on your brain face."

"Yeah, you got me. It's that, and the feeling that we're treading water, going nowhere, no matter how much we do. We spent all week running all over town, spent countless man-hours canvassing neighborhoods, and where did we end up? Back where we started, just with more piles of paperwork.

Enough back and forth; call me when you get home and settled. Otherwise I'll see you at the office tomorrow."

And like that, she left, and I sat in my chair, surrounded by case files, going over what TJ had sent me, drifting into and out of consciousness, which is how I do some of my best thinking sometimes. It's getting late, and my arm is still throbbing; it's been starting to swell pretty bad, but thanks to a few bags of ice, the pain isn't bothering me too much.

The one thing that *is* driving me nuts is all of the files I've had to sort through. I've been working on these files for more than four hours, and I'm about to slam my head into the wall. Screw it! As my head starts to reach out and touch the wall, the girls look up at me, their heads tilted to the side with a look of confusion—a look similar to the one I'm giving my computer. Hours of going through files and the end is still not in sight. I don't know how I'm going to finish this, but I'll think of something.

I had one of the guys from the bureau tuck a big-ass map of the United States in one of the boxes I grabbed from Jen earlier, about the size you would find in a classroom. That way I can pin and date the murders that I come across and eventually make some sense of everything. So far I've been able to find a pattern that shows a series of murders progressing from the upper Midwest to the Southwest, as if Cappelano were making his way to Mexico. I know it sounds like a cliché to make a run to Mexico, but that seems to be what he was doing, at least from what I could make of the files he sent me.

Over the next couple of days, everything should start to piece together for me. This way, I can have a definitive pattern to work off of, which will get me to narrow a grid. Even when humans think they're acting randomly, they are still following some form of a pattern. We just don't realize it. But now it's 10:15 p.m., and I think I'm going to call it a night. I wonder if Sheila is up; I could really use someone to take my mind off this case, just talking about anything other than these files. Hmm, I guess not. She didn't answer her phone, and the only time she doesn't answer is when she's asleep or at work. I could always call Maria. I'm sure she's up; at least I hope she is.

At the last second, I realized it's a shit thing to do to keep calling people and dropping my crap on them at two in the morning. Whether it's Sheila, Father Roberts, or now Maria, I'm just going to sweat it out and go from there. I guess this is what they call "personal growth."

The basement is still under construction, but I have a little setup with some dumbbells and a punching bag; it really helps on late nights like tonight. I bought the heavy bag during my divorce, and it was the best investment I've made in a long time. There's nothing quite like unleashing my doubts and fears on a heavy bag for an hour or so to relieve some stress. That, and it keeps me from taking out those frustrations on innocent bystanders to my bad moods. I had to stop in my room before heading downstairs to plug in my cell phone and grab my MP3 player, so I don't wake up the neighbors with extremely loud music. When I work out, I like to blast the music, so I feel the bass pulsating around me, but when it's almost 3:00 a.m., I try to be considerate and just throw on headphones.

Lost in the music, I start to do my routine on the bag, jab, cross, hook, and uppercut. I repeat that series over and over, followed by a series of fifty reps on each punch, with each arm. Before my divorce, I used to box as an amateur for the bureau. We had boxing tournaments every six months, and I won several times, although there was no actual prize other than bragging rights and a little extra pride. When dealing with a bunch of men whose egos have begun to consume themselves, it helps to let them beat the living daylights out of each other every couple of months. It keeps everyone's workplace aggression to a minimum; at least that's my theory. Without a healthy outlet for aggression, eventually someone will go postal. Hitting the bag, especially after the injury I received earlier this week during the accident, is probably not a good thing for me to be doing, but I couldn't care less right now. I'm in major need of a good sweat, and I hate running, so I might as well hit the bag. I might be able to get some sleep tonight if I go upstairs right now and take a shower, but I decided I might as well do some sit-ups before I get ready to go to bed. Mind you, when I do sit-ups, I usually do five or six sets of a hundred, if not more. I'm kind of a workout nut, although I don't take care of my body as well as I should when it comes to my diet.

I know it's late as usual when I call, but I could really use a good talk with Father Roberts. I need to clear my head, bounce some ideas off of him, and get the usual mental ass-kicking an old friend can give you from time to time.

"Father, I know you're used to me calling between the hours of two and four in the morning; I hope this is okay." I know he's still up; he usually goes to bed at about 10:30 p.m.; I probably caught him doing his late-night prayers before bed.

"Neil, you know you caught me doing my prayers before bed. What can I do for you?" Told ya.

"I just need to talk for a bit, get your brutal honesty, the kind only you can give me, the kind that I'll take only from you, especially these days. We caught a couple of breaks in the case, and I can't help but wonder if Cappelano placed them there for us to catch. I don't want to mess it up."

"You know there's always that possibility with him; you just need to keep yourself measured and controlled. Make sure you don't get carried away or too aggressive, keep your responses level, and ensure that you control the outgoing message that he receives. I'm not telling you anything you don't already know."

He's right, and he's also correct on giving me my own advice. We've had these conversations so many times over the years; he's just regurgitating advice back to me. The difference is when he says it, he has a flare to it, a way to get it to set a fire in me. If I were drawing up a comic and needed a sidekick to my hero, he's exactly what I'd ask for; he just wears a clerical collar instead of a cape. Some might argue that the collar carries more weight and more cachet. Just don't tell him I said that; he'd never let it go.

"Father, you're right on many fronts, but the biggest concern at this point is also the way the bureau is handling this. I think it's time I really start leaning on my own team and keeping the bureau out of some items. I get the feeling that the suits at the field office are rooting for me publicly but setting me up to take the fall if anything goes wrong, and Maria with me. I need to make sure for both our sakes that she's insulated. She deserves that much."

"Neil, I know you can think of yourself as selfish sometimes, but you often act selflessly, especially on a case. If you think it's the best course of action to protect yourself and others you care about during this case, you need to do what you feel is right."

Father Roberts has a way of saying the words that are echoing in my head. We've been friends for so long I can remember the first time he had to pull me aside and give me a talking to. We were in high school, and my father and I had gotten into a big argument over a girl I was seeing. I remember Father Roberts had literally grabbed me as I was walking down the hallway between classes. Threw me into the lockers, and told me to stop acting like an asshole and just apologize to my dad. He's always been the angel on my shoulder, with Balboa's jab-cross combo to back him up.

"I know, I just needed to hear it from someone else to help me get over the hump. Thanks for helping me, as always."

"Neil, just get that bastard, and not for the obvious reasons. Put this demon to rest. It's time for me to finish my prayers and you to get some rest. Good night, Neil."

"'Night, Father."

Time to get in the shower. It's a little after midnight, and I have a lot of work to do tomorrow—scratch that, make that today. I've never been much of a bath person, although when I get into a brawl that leaves my body a little too beaten up, I'll pick up a couple of bags of ice. Then fill my bathtub with cold water, throw the ice in, turn on the jets, slam a few shots of Jack, and hop in. The first few minutes suck in an ice bath, but once you get past the initial freeze, it is quite soothing. Just ask any professional athlete, especially football players; they'll back me up on it.

For some reason I can't seem to shake the idea that Cappelano is trying to lead me to where he's been hiding for the past couple of years. Most of the murders I have covered on the disc were very quick, one after the other. In a couple of days I should have a better grasp of everything going on with Cappelano's last four years. If I'm lucky it will lead me to where he might have been hanging out, where other people might have actually seen him. That reminds me: I wonder if Ken's guy has made any headway on tracking down plastic surgeons who work for cash and don't ask any questions. It's quite hard to find them; it's not as if they advertise on every street corner or radio station. The steam is starting to build up in the shower as I make my way in.

13

The two of us spent the whole night nursing one or two drinks and talking . . . about a homeless man who was found dead in an abandoned building.

As the water hits me, I'm taken back to that fateful day in 1996 when I first met Frank at the bureau before all of this happened. Cappelano was known for having guile, knowing what suspects were thinking, and getting inside their heads. He was also known as being that guy you hated. Let's be honest: the bureau and most investigative branches are full of the kind of assholes you couldn't stand in high school. The ones with the great physique, high intelligence, and that magnetic personality. You look for any fault you can find so you can talk shit behind their backs. Then they invite you to their high school party and even try to set you up with a girl you might have a shot with. Cappelano was one of those guys. He had the look, the suave nature, and the overall self-awareness that allowed him to read a room almost instantly.

It was this attitude that drew me and others to him. He came off as though he cared and didn't care at the same time. It looks weird when you type it, read it, or say it, but when you meet someone who pulls it off, you know exactly what I'm talking about. He was our Fonzie, the coolest kid in town.

"Neil Baggio, I presume, judging by the way everyone is keeping away from you. I wanted to come over and introduce myself: Special Agent Frank Cappelano."

"I know who you are. I think we all know who you are, Mr. Cappelano," I said. "I'm a little surprised you know who *I* am." I wasn't just being modest—why would a senior special agent know who I am, a fresh recruit so green I might as well be the Jolly Green Giant?

"Now that we got that out of the way, I heard about how you've been crushing it lately, and I'm looking for some young, aggressive, talented agents to bring on my team. Are you interested in a once-in-a-lifetime opportunity? Chances are your colleagues will despise you, as if they don't already."

"Will I get any more information on what the job entails? Or do I have to take the offer on faith, that a senior officer with a great track record is going to have my best interests at heart— not just his own career, like most bureau agents?" Any other recruit in my position would probably say "yes sir!" without a second thought. But despite the flattery of being noticed by one of the bureau's top dogs, I had no interest in agreeing to an assignment without knowing what exactly I was signing up for. Plus I'm a pain in the ass by nature, but you already knew that.

"Fair enough. Tell ya what, let's go catch the Red Wings

game tonight and grab a beer, get to know each other, and enjoy some of that rocking Detroit atmosphere."

Already he was speaking my language. The Red Wings were one of the hottest tickets in town. Though Joe Louis Arena can often smell like a huge locker stuffed with dirty socks, it has a loud, wild ambience that screams Detroit sports scene. Granted, half of the festive atmosphere is due to the fact that they keep winning.

"Sounds good, Frank. Want to meet up at the Village Idiot, downtown on Mac, and head over from there?

"Perfect. See you then."

A simple enough evening, one would think, but the two of us spent the whole night nursing one or two drinks and talking about a case that he was asked to take on involving a homeless man who was found dead in an abandoned building; signs pointed toward homicide. The reason Cappelano was asked to look into the case is that a higher-up at the bureau was bunkmates in Vietnam with the homeless man. They said that for a time, the victim even worked in the government after he served several military tours.

"I'm a little confused about why you asked me to come on board," I said. "You build me up, say you're looking for an aggressive investigator to help you with some cases, then hand me a whodunit on a beaten-down bum? I'm not trying to speak ill of the homeless, especially someone who served as much as this guy did, but what do you expect me to do, interview the

Fisher King?"

"Neil, I picked you because I didn't think you would treat one case differently than any other. Whether it's a homeless victim or some high-profile case with a lot of media coverage, why should you change your approach? It's a lesson to be learned quickly and early in your career."

"Of course, that makes sense. Everyone deserves justice, right? If that's the reason, then I'm on board. I'll just have to come at it a different way."

"It will definitely be outside of your comfort zone. Working around the homeless and their reality can be like going to another country."

"I can only imagine the way they see the world. What it looks like from the outside, looking in."

"What do you mean, 'outside'? Just because they're living outside, on the streets?"

"No, I mean they don't operate with the same constraints the average person does. They don't have to be concerned with what time it is, appointments on the calendar, or whatever else distracts us daily."

"Okay, that I understand. Maybe you'll get a better view once you get into the case."

We spent the rest of the night enjoying the hockey game, getting to know each other, and formulating a game plan for the next day. Little did I know what was in front of me with this case. What seemed like a test from a veteran led to learning the amazing story of Sarge and what it means to serve your fellow man. For someone in his twenties learning about life, what it means to be more than a self-centered consumer is huge; some people never learn it. I would have to get outside of my comfort zone for sure, but early in my career, this was exactly the kind of lesson I needed.

It was going to be a cold, long week—or longer—full of interviewing witnesses and canvassing the area trying to find people who knew the victim and his routine. That would mean long hours, lots of conversations with people who don't trust anyone resembling law enforcement. Perhaps sleeping in the streets, visiting shelters, and simply integrating myself in the network that Sarge was a part of. I remember watching an investigative piece on one of the news networks about the homeless recently. Not just focusing on the national epidemic that it is, but also the world they live in, the alternate reality they operate in compared to our own. The different perspective that circumstance can create is hard to overstate. When your life is a daily fight for survival, it affects everything from your daily routine to how you interact with the people around you—and how they treat you, of course.

I remember interviewing a priest and his assistant at St. Patrick's Church downtown near Fox Theater, asking them about the victim. I started there because a business card for their shelter was found in his pocket after his body was discovered. That's where I first learned that people always referred to him as Sarge, and the impact he had on so many in the community, even though he was homeless and struggling.

As I entered St. Patrick's Church, it wasn't hard to be enamored with the history within the walls. Old Catholic churches have a way about them; you can feel the history in the pews, the stained-glass windows, and the high, arched ceilings covered in detailed artwork. The beautiful exterior of the church in the decaying neighborhood is a sad reminder on how the city has changed over the decades. How the church has been a cherished staple in the community despite it all.

"Father Duffy, thank you for taking the time to meet with me. You said on the phone that you knew Sarge and that he frequented your shelter?"

Father Duffy was everything your imagination is expecting. He was an old Irish Catholic priest, with a thick beard and hair a mixture of red and silver, as if someone had handpicked which strands to change. Though he stood nearly half a foot shorter than I am, he carried himself with a sense of kindness and warmth that made him look six feet tall.

Father Duffy wasn't one to mince words or get into small talk; he knew why I was here, and he wanted to get right into the meat and potatoes of it. Not only was he a busy man running a parish and being a pillar in the community, he also wanted to get me back on the street and on the trail of the person who would hurt Sarge.

"Yes, Sarge was here often. He was great at finding new

people on the streets and bringing them in, getting them out of the cold. He saved many lives, in fact. Anyone on the street who was struggling, he would tend to. He was one of a kind. I can't believe anyone would kill him. Even if someone were mad at him, he would go out of his way to fix it, find a way to solve it. I pray this person is found before they can harm someone else."

It was a very priestly thing to say; most people would say they wanted vengeance on the person who killed their friend. I could have talked to Father Duffy all day, but we had to try and keep the conversation focused on the important facts about Sarge. We ended up speaking just shy of an hour. The stories he told described a military man fighting the demons of what he had done in combat but who had service of others in his heart. After a week on the streets and more than forty witnesses interviewed, I couldn't find a single person who spoke ill of Sarge, which made finding a motive for his murder even harder. The easiest explanation for a homeless killing is usually drug use or a fight for survival—heat, food, etc. I remember this was the first time that Cappelano got on me hard, pushed me to dig, and broke me down as an investigator.

"Neil, after a week of investigating and a few hundred pages of notes, all I have is a great eulogy for this man, but nothing that helps me solve his murder. What the hell am I supposed to tell my superior who is up my ass about this shit?"

"Cappelano, you act like I'm out there dicking around. I've

been turning over every rock trying to find something to connect Sarge to anything negative. By all accounts, he was a saint. Would you prefer that I make shit up so that you and you're superior can sleep better at night?"

We argued until we both came to a point where we wanted a resolution, but there just didn't seem to be one. We continued to work the case for almost a month, grueling hours, early mornings, late nights—you would think it was a movie star who had been killed. I could only imagine the pressure Cappelano was getting from his superior. I'd never seen a case like this, with pressure coming directly from the top brass, or at least that's what I was being told. The thing is, I never personally saw anyone else pushing us, but I was the new kid, and he was the star. If this is what he said needed to be done, I didn't have much choice but to follow suit.

Eventually we ended up leaving the case unsolved, but only because another high-profile case came through, which took tons of man-hours and all hands on deck from the top teams in our office. Otherwise, who knows how long we would have been searching for Sarge's killer?

It was that very case, though, that bonded me and Cappelano and our careers. As time passed, I came to realize that there never *was* a superior who was putting pressure on Cappelano to take that case. He had committed that murder himself and was grooming me the whole time. Testing me to see if I had the skill and intelligence to figure it out, getting a depraved thrill out of how close I was to the truth.

Unfortunately, I was just a little too green back then to crack the case. But I also believe my inexperience saved my life. Because if I had started to suspect Cappelano was responsible for Sarge's senseless murder, my new mentor would have killed me too, without giving it a second thought.

14

His ego has driven him even farther down the path of a

madman.

That's interesting; judging by these dates, it looks as though Cappelano did a bit of backtracking before he made his run down South. The tally of murders that are mentioned on this disc has reached sixteen. I don't know if he's trying to challenge me to figure out which of them he committed, if any, or if he really was on a silent multistate rampage that no one knew about. I use the term "silent" in that no one was aware that it was Cappelano. Normally he would take credit for a murder, but in this instance he was trying to hide it, and it seems he succeeded in doing so.

In a sense, I think these murders were a way for Cappelano to vent his frustrations; he was upset with the way the FBI handled me. He believed—and still does believe—that he is training me to become the greatest investigator ever. His ego has driven him even farther down the path of a madman because the FBI kept him from fulfilling his destiny in completing his training program for me.

I need to call Mike at the office and see if he can track down case files on these murders. All he'd have to do is contact the closest FBI field office to each murder and have them track down the information for us. Then fax everything over, or better yet, just email it all out.

"Mike Ponecelli speaking. Who may I ask is calling?"

"Mike, it's Neil. Can you do me a huge favor? I've got a list of murders that I need case information on. I need to determine if these murders were, in fact, done by Cappelano. I'll email you the list and some details on each one. Can you have someone track down the case files for me?"

"Yeah, that won't be a problem. It might take a while to get everything together, but I'll have one of my office assistants track everything down for you. Got anything else to report?"

"Yeah, from what I can tell, Cappelano made his way through the Midwest down South. It looks as though he was making a run to Mexico within his first year of disappearing. All the murders on this disc are from 2001. I haven't found anything since then."

"That would explain a lot if he did hide out in Mexico, or maybe in Central America. It would have been very hard to find him down there. He could have even been working there for all we know."

"That's exactly my point. We should contact the Mexican ambassador and see if they have any information that might help us."

"I'll look into it for you, Neil. Just keep working your way through that disc and keep us posted. I have to let you go, though."

"No problem; I'll email you the information right now. Talk to you later, Mike."

The nice thing about being back at the bureau is that Mike can assign a team to do the grunt work. Like tracking down case files, talking to the ambassador of Mexico, and anything else I'd need that would save me some time. I have to admit, it feels kind of nice to be back in; I think I made the right choice. Wait a minute. What's this? This document is in Spanish. It looks like a newspaper article from some Latin country. However, the story is a mystery because I don't speak Spanish. It looks like I'll be saving these for later, when Maria comes over. She's fluent in four different dialects of Spanish, as well as in Italian and French. She's a smart kid, to say the least.

As for now, I'll just copy the files in Spanish to my desktop so I can save them on a disc for Maria to read when she comes over. I asked her to bring her laptop, which shouldn't be a problem, since she keeps it with her at all times because she never knows where she's going to end up working for the day. Ahh, the glamorous life of an FBI agent. This is going to be one hell of a night. I think I'm going to take a nap this afternoon so I'll be refreshed mentally. If I don't get a nap today, I know I'll crash later when Maria is here, and it's time to get some work done.

It's almost three in the afternoon and I've been working on these files since early this morning. I'm going to grab the girls and take them to the park for a breather, and then a nap. They love going up to the park. Whenever I get a chance, I get them out to either Dodge Park or Metro Beach. I'll probably take them to Dodge Park today because I don't feel like paying three dollars to get into a park my taxes already pay for. If the state isn't screwing you one way, they'll always find another. I told you I hate politics. I'm not for anarchy, don't get me wrong, although it *would* be fun to visit a place without laws for a couple of days. I think I'd be able to kick some major ass in a situation like that. It'd be like feudal Japan back in the days of the samurai.

I know it's a little off-subject, but I'm really fascinated by the Far East, China, Korea, Japan, and the tenets of Buddhism. I've always wanted to sit down with the Dalai Lama and just talk to him. I was lucky enough to meet him very briefly at a conference in New York at the UN building, years ago. I spoke to him for only a minute, but he had an amazing presence about him. It was very humbling to talk to someone whose life is dedicated to peace no matter what, nonviolence, and love. During the few moments we talked, he said something that has stuck with me all these years. I remember our conversation like it was yesterday.

"Good afternoon, my son. How are you today?"

"It is an honor to meet you, Your Holiness . . . I mean, Dalai—"

"Shh . . . calm down, young man. What is it that's pressing

you?"

"I have the utmost respect for someone who can live a violence-free life. You really are an inspiration."

"Judging by the cut of your coat, I would say you are law enforcement of some kind, and judging by your soul, I would say you've had to use violence many times in your life. Don't forget, we may want peace, but sometimes peace is not ready for us. Even Catholics believe in St. Michael of the Sword. Go with peace, my son."

I didn't know what to say after that; I was speechless. The rest of that day, I just walked around the conference in silence, lost in thought about anything and everything. It's amazing that an encounter with one man, for one minute, can change your outlook on so many things. Speaking of change, it's starting to rain at the park, and the girls are about to play in the mud, which means it's time to head home. I called the girls to come and get in the car, and they started tackling each other back and forth as they headed over; the two of them really are a stitch. I had to put Danielle in the back because she was covered in mud from Jackie drilling her into a puddle. Plus if they aren't separated in the car, they'll tear everything up fighting for room.

As the three of us began cleaning off, I noticed Maria's car turning onto the road. I thought she wasn't going to come over until later, not to mention she said she'd call me before coming over. Let me check my phone—oops, three missed calls from her. Oh well, she's here, might as well get to work. I got the girls cleaned up and let them in the house so they didn't tear Maria up. After two visits, Jackie and Danielle were ready to adopt Maria as their mom, which is odd because they're usually very protective of me. They must see the same things I do in Maria.

"Hey Maria, sorry I missed your calls. I left my phone in the car when I was at the park with the girls."

"No problem. I figured you were still in bed."

"Very funny. I've actually been up since six, working on the disc. I needed a break, though. My brain is pretty fried."

"I was out on your side of town tracking down a witness, but that didn't work out, so I figured I'd take a shot and see if you were home. And I was right."

"Let's get out of the rain."

"I was waiting for you to say something. How's everything coming along with the disc?"

"Not bad; there's just a lot of information on it. I actually found a few cases in Spanish. I was hoping you could go through them for me."

"What?! You don't know Spanish? *Qué lástima.* I'm saddened by your lack of language versatility. I can take a look; I'd be happy to help."

"Thanks, Maria. I was just about to take a shower and a quick nap. You're more than welcome to work in the kitchen while I'm sleeping."

"Sounds like a plan. I'll be there when you wake up."

"Great. I won't be asleep long, I just need an hour or so."

"No problem. I might putz around in the kitchen and make some dinner if that's okay with you."

"It would be more than just okay. Waking up to dinner on the table has been a fantasy of mine for quite some time."

"It's your fantasy to take a nap and wake up to dinner being ready? You are one crazy boy."

"Shut it. I'm going to hop in the shower and pass out for a bit. I'll see ya in a few."

"Enjoy the nap. Like I said, I'll be here when you wake up."

I'd be lying if I said I didn't wish Maria would surprise me in the shower right now, but then again, we've done enough messing around as it is. We don't need to get into any more trouble, not now, not with the case finally showing some signs of forward motion. Some of it might just be timing. Maria was engaged for almost two years, but it fell apart about a year ago, and she hasn't really met anyone since then. As for me, you know my story. It's complicated, but who knows? Maria is aware of my situation with Sheila and my daughter Carol Lynn and is all right with everything. I mean, it would be hard not to notice that I have a daughter and an ex-wife, considering there are pictures of the three of us all over my house. I like family pictures, no matter how dysfunctional we are.

Sheila and I may no longer be married, we may no longer live together, but we still love each other and our daughter very much, and that's what matters. It's nice to know Maria isn't intimidated by that; it helps that she's a very self-sufficient girl.

If I remember correctly, she said her independence is what ended her engagement. Her fiancé just couldn't handle the fact that she wasn't a needy or clingy girlfriend. That she had her own set of obligations that didn't always involve him. I understand where she's coming from because I'm the same way. I like my privacy, and I don't like relationships getting in the way of my work.

I got out of the shower and dried off, grabbed a pair of sweats to throw on, crawled into bed, and before I could even finish a thought, I passed out into dreamland. Even in a nice deep sleep, I couldn't help but dream about the case. Mexico keeps coming up over and over again. I have a suspicion that I'll end up there at some point. Eventually my eyes opened again. Time to rejoin the land of the living.

"Hey, sunshine, good to see you're up. I couldn't find anything to cook, so I ordered Chinese. It should be here in a few minutes. I got you cashew chicken from the Green Dragon restaurant. You had it circled on your takeout menu, so I figured you liked it."

"Impressive deduction, Sherlock. What shall be your next trick? I'm just messing; thanks for ordering."

"No problem. How was the nap? You didn't sleep long, only about forty-five minutes."

"That's all I needed, just some time to rest my eyes and quiet down the internal chaos. Or at least slow it down for a while."

"You know, you really need to go grocery shopping. You have half of every recipe. You're short on just enough ingredients that you can't really do anything with them."

"I know, I've been busy with the case and working on my basement. I haven't taken the time to go shopping."

"Sounds like the Chinese food is here. I'll go get it. Why don't you go throw a shirt on or something and meet me at the table when you're a little more presentable."

"Sounds good to me. Be back in a minute."

Dinner hit the spot. The cashew chicken was perfect, and Maria also ordered wonton soup, egg rolls, and some chicken and pea pod dish, which I'd never had before, but it was damn good. Now that our bellies are full, I guess it's time to get back to the case files. This is going to be a long night. Maria got started on the couple of files in Spanish that I put on a disc for her, while I continued to make my way through the journey that was this disc. If the amount of information it contained was a road trip from New York to Los Angeles, then I would be somewhere between Ohio and Missouri. In other words, I'm not even halfway through it all, and I've been at this for two days now. But with Maria's help, things should go a little faster.

"Any luck with that first article, Maria?"

"Yeah, it looks like there was a rash of murders in Mexico City that they first believed to be the work of Zapatistas. The chief investigator said the murders were too clean to be rebels."

"Sounds like somebody we know. I have Mike tracking down

the Mexican ambassador in hopes that we can find some more recent information about Cappelano's movements."

"Judging by this article, I wouldn't be surprised if there are more articles and maybe a video or two on that disc that you haven't come across yet. Keep your eyes open."

"Mexico City is one busy town. It wouldn't be very hard to get lost there, would it?"

"Not at all, and it would be perfect for someone like Cappelano," Maria said. "He's already got a dark complexion from being southern Italian. On top of that, there are a lot of unlicensed physicians down there. He could get plastic surgery and no one would be the wiser."

"This could be a good thing or a bad thing. If that's where he went, we could try and track down info on him. But Americans in a town like that? Not a good mix."

"Luckily, you have a sexy Latin lady working with you. I'll be able to get a lot out of the locals down there. Get back to reading for now. We have a lot of work ahead of us."

"I don't have a map of Mexico to pin and mark the cases you find. But I think I have an atlas around here somewhere."

"I'll go look for it. Where would it be?"

"If I had one, it would be in my front hall closet. There's a box full of maps and atlases from all the cases I've looked at over the years."

"I see the box; I'll go through it. Get back to work; don't worry about me."

"All right. If you need help, just let me know."

"I'll be okay. I think I can handle it."

Maria had a point; it's not like I was asking her to do a difficult task. She found a few different maps of Mexico in the box, and luckily one was just of Mexico City. That would come in handy, since we found mention of seven different murders in Mexico City alone. By now we had a running total of twenty-one dead across thirteen murder scenes. The only good news was that almost all of the files we were finding were articles or videos of news coverage on murders we had already pinned and marked. It looks as though the number will stand at thirteen cases and twenty-one dead over the course of eighteen months.

"Neil? How many files do we have left? It's almost three o'clock."

"Holy shit, are you kidding me?! We've been at this for almost eight straight hours. I guess time flies when you're having fun."

"I know, tell me about it, although I have a migraine the size of . . . well, my whole head. It's killing me."

"Why don't you go take a bath? I have that big garden tub with all the jets. It's very relaxing."

"You sure? You won't mind me taking a bath here? If I take a bath, can I just crash here, since we're probably going to do this in the morning again anyway?"

"You know you can stay here. This time how about you use

my room, and I'll stay in Carol Lynn's room, since she's not using it."

"No, I can't stay in your room. I'm a lot smaller than you, I'll stay in Carol Lynn's room. You sleep in your bed."

"Fine with me. I'll start the tub for you. Can you put the girls out for me?"

"Yep, I'm on it."

The garden tub is really nice because it doesn't operate like an old faucet tub with hot and cold knobs. Instead, it runs digitally with a thermostat. You just set your temperature and it takes care of the rest, keeping the water at a consistent temperature for you. The one reason I hate baths so much is because the water always ends up getting cold. Not with this baby. I never would have put something like this in my house. Thank goodness for the previous owners and their remodeling.

"Hey Maria, it's all set. The tub is full, and I threw in some bubble bath for you. I figured you'd like vanilla?"

"Thanks, Neil. For being a hard ass most of the time, you really are a sweetheart. I appreciate it."

"No problem; I even lit a few candles for you and put on a jazz CD to help you relax. Try to keep your head above the water. We wouldn't want you falling asleep."

"I just might."

As Maria went into the bathroom, I fell straight into bed, looking forward to at least five good hours of looking at nothing but the back of my eyelids. After a couple of minutes I heard

Maria start saying something, but I couldn't make it out through the door. I really don't feel like getting out of bed, but she keeps calling for me, asking me something. I guess I'll get up and crack the door, see what she wants.

"What's up, Maria? I couldn't hear you through the door."

"I was just saying this tub is huge. Thanks for the candles and the music. If I didn't know any better, I'd think you were trying to seduce me."

"Sorry, I wasn't trying to. I just wanted to help you relax after a really long day."

"Well, it's working. My head feels better already. You know what? You should hop on in and join me; this feels really good."

"I don't know if that would be the best thing to do. You sure you want to go down this road again?"

"What road? It's just a bath. Nothing major. Calm down."

"All right, I'm coming in."

I stripped down and slid in behind Maria so that she was between my legs. Believe it or not, all we did was sit there and talk. I ran a sponge up and down her neck and arms and started giving her a massage. After a good twenty minutes of talking and about ten minutes of massage, Maria started to fall asleep on me, so I woke her up, drained the tub, and we got out and dried off.

"Hey Neil, do you have something I can sleep in? Maybe just a shirt."

"Sure, help yourself to the top left drawer of my dresser."

"Thanks. Well, I'm going to bed. I'll see you in the morning."

"Have a good night, Maria. Do you need me to set an alarm?"

"No, I'll be all right. I have my cell phone to wake up to. Thanks, though. Good night, Neil."

15

Let's go into the family room; less breakable things in there.

There seems to be a pattern with Maria whenever she stays the night, even if we don't do anything. For starters, she's an early riser like I've never seen before. I don't know if this case is making her restless, or she may just be a Type A personality. Judging by what I know about her past and her will to succeed, the latter is probably a safe bet. It isn't uncommon for FBI agents to be Type A, since one common trait that goes along with that is a relentless motivation to complete a task they've started. There's something about follow-through for most bureau agents that makes us stand out. Most of your successful businessmen and -women fit that personality type; it's what makes them successful. I'm not sure which type most fits me. One thing I do know is that when I get a task on my mind, it's extremely hard to get me off it until it's completed.

"Morning, Neil. How did you sleep last night?"

"You're lucky you're cute or I'd kick your ass for waking me up this early."

"Try me. I bet you ten bucks that you can't pin my back to the ground."

"Is that a challenge? Don't be playing. Just because you're a girl doesn't mean I won't drop you. You don't have to punch someone to get them down."

"I'm well aware. So, bring it, big fella. Let's see what you've got."

"All right, it's on. Let's go into the family room; less breakable things in there."

Wrestling like two kids who won't admit they like each other, Maria slammed her foot in my stomach and flipped me over. As I tried to catch my breath, she climbed on top of me, pinning my shoulders to the floor. I don't know if it's my ego giving me excuses for what happened, but my guess is that it didn't help that I just rolled out of bed, and Maria has been up for God knows how long. Luckily, I don't have to worry about her telling anyone at the office. Because anyone she tells will be more interested in the part where she woke up at my house.

"It looks like I won, I pinned you first. You're a big fat loser." Maria pegged me good.

"I don't know if I'd say that, because right now I've got a beautiful woman straddling me in nothing more than my T-shirt and boxers. I'd say it was a win-win situation."

"Look at you, Mr. Smooth. What do you plan on doing now that you've got me where you want me?"

"Just this!"

I locked eyes with her, leaned in, and kissed her. I don't know why, I just did, and it turned out to be a damn good decision. We laid there just kissing for the next ten or so minutes, and eventually we ended up tearing each other's clothes off on the couch—well, sort of on the couch. It looks like I'm going to have to replace a lamp that we knocked over in our little tussle.

"Well, wasn't that a nice surprise. I'm used to a good run in the morning, but I guess that will do me just fine."

"Sorry about that, Maria. Once I saw that smile and those eyes, I couldn't help myself. Well, I could, I just didn't want to."

"You're so cute after sex, you know that? You've become the rambling man, but it's okay. We're two consenting adults who have a strong attraction mixed with a shared high-stress environment. It's going to happen." Maria has a way of staying in control and on top of the situation.

"That's an understatement, Maria. But as much as I love rolling around with you, we should really try and keep it to a minimum so it doesn't get in the way of the case and working together. Is that cool with you?" If Maria was fine with keeping things casual, then so was I.

"Fine with me, Neil. We mess around, I don't worry about it. I just enjoy the time that we do. It doesn't hurt that you're one hell of a kisser." Maria has a way of calling my bluff. I can't tell if she knows I'm falling for her, or if she's really that measured in everything she does.

"Thanks. You're not so bad yourself. Now that we're all sweaty, how about we use the double shower head in . . . well, my shower?"

"I'll get started cleaning up; you start the shower. And sorry about the lamp. Let me replace it; it's the least I can do for you. Plus you could use a nice lamp around here."

"Dig taken. Thanks, Maria. We were both responsible for it. I'll pick up a new one later today when I go grocery shopping. It wasn't anything fancy." Which was her point in the first place.

"If you say so. I'll meet you in the shower. Don't take too long. I don't want to use up all the hot water."

"Don't worry, I'll be there in a flash."

While I was cleaning up the lamp, I remembered that we don't need to worry about the hot water because last year I put in one of those hot water systems that don't use a tank. It uses a system of heating pipes that heat the water as it's being sent to the device you're using—shower, bath, etc. It's nice, especially for someone like me who's in the shower all the time, not to mention someone who takes showers as long as I do. I know it isn't anything truly important, but my mind seems to drift for a few moments after sex; I'm a man; what can I say? As a famous comedian once said, God gave man two brains and only enough blood to run one at a time.

"Are you coming, Neil?"

"What are you talking about? I'm right here. Turn around."

"I didn't see you there. When did you get in the bathroom?"

"I don't know, like a minute ago. Now move over and let me get in."

"Pushy . . . pushy, aren't we? Get your cute tight butt in here and wash my back."

"Yes, ma'am. Private shower buddy here at your service."

"Quit messing around and scrub. All this work has me getting hungry. How about you? I can make some breakfast as soon as you're done with your duties."

"Aww, we're done already. I guess I took a little too long cleaning up out there. Breakfast does sound good."

"It's okay, we did make a little bit of a mess, between wrestling and messing around. I'm sure a few things got knocked around besides the lamp."

"If you're cooking breakfast, I like my eggs over easy, scrambled, or as an omelet. Surprise me."

"Sounds good. I'm going to get out of here. I'll see you in the kitchen for some grub. Don't take too long again."

"I won't. I'll be out in a few minutes."

As the water put me into a trance and my memory rebooted and revisited the events of the previous weeks, it hit me all at once. Maria, Cappelano, and Bob Hendrickson getting moved to DC; there's just so much to think about right now. For instance, Maria and I are almost certain that Cappelano was hiding out in Mexico City or another nearby place. I never realized all of the national parks that are in or near Mexico City, not to mention all of the small towns within the city. As Maria told me yesterday, it would be extremely easy to get lost in Mexico—that's what it's famous for, at least to criminals on the run. I really don't want to get out of the shower just yet, but I'm done, and the only thing I'm doing is letting the hot water run over my head. On top of it, breakfast smells good, and I'm hungry after a morning full of working out; sex and wrestling always work up an appetite.

"That smells wonderful. What are you making?"

"It's an old treat my mom used to make on Sunday mornings after church. You sauté some diced tomato and fresh spinach with a little olive oil. Then you melt some shredded cheese on it—all I could find in your fridge was shredded Parmesan—and then you throw a couple of eggs on top, cover it, and let the eggs cook."

"Damn! She's hot, she's smart, and she can cook! What are the odds?"

"Coffee is on the table, along with your creamer. Just grab a seat. It's almost done."

"I have to say I'm very impressed. I was expecting to come out here and see toast and cereal."

"I can keep the eggs to myself if you want to have toast and cereal instead."

"Bring that over here, and let's chow down. Wow! That looks good."

I'll have to remember that recipe for myself; it really hit the spot. Sheila and Carol Lynn would love it too. Even though she's young, Carol Lynn is very adventurous when it comes to trying new foods. I still can't believe how good that was. Every day I spend with Maria I think I fall for her more and more, but I can't let her know that, not now. Someday I'll share with her how I feel, but right now I need to concentrate on the case. It may seem I say that a lot, but sometimes I have to remind myself or my mind will stray, especially early in a case when it's more of a waiting game than anything else. I just hope the leads we have will help turn something up.

The thing about my mind is that I function like a six-lane freeway. Most people operate with two to three max, it seems. It doesn't mean I'm not giving the other things attention. It just means I can process more things at once. And let's be honest, not everything deserves full attention 24/7. Even when you're racing the clock, something will take precedence. I can prove it, too. Eventually you will have to go to the bathroom and sit on a toilet. It will take precedence over everything else you have to do for the day, even if just for a moment.

"Hey Maria, I need to make a couple of phone calls. How about you call Mike and fill him in on our headway with all these files and see if he's gotten any of the case files we asked for."

"No problem. Let me clean up here, and I'll get right on it."

"All right, I'll be right back."

I stepped away to the bedroom and closed my door to get changed. That, and I didn't want Maria to hear me talking to Ken about the case. I'm going to see how the guys are doing trying to find a plastic surgeon who did work on Cappelano. I don't know for sure that he had work done, but trust me, he did.

He wouldn't risk being seen or recognized after four years; he knows better than that. It's not the best move to be hiding information from Maria right now, but I'm still a little gun-shy when it comes to trusting the bureau after everything that happened. I need to hold my cards close to my chest a little while longer.

"Hey, Ken, what's up? I know it's early, but I have some information to share with you."

"Early for you, maybe, but you know I'm always up by five every morning. How can I be of service, Neil?"

"A little bit of a break in the case. Have your guy who's searching for the surgeon head down to Mexico City with another one of our guys, preferably someone who speaks Spanish. Have them try and track down any information they can on Cappelano down there."

"I'm on it, Neil. By the way, who's going to foot the bill for everything? The bureau?"

"No, the bureau doesn't know what's going on. I'm just going to use the pay I'm earning from the FBI to pay for everything the guys do. So we're covered."

"All right, I'll get the guys together and have them jet out by the end of the day."

"Thanks for everything, Ken. And make sure TJ knows that the FBI was impressed with him."

"Can do. But I need to get going, I'm at the gym. I'll talk to you later when everything is all set."

"Thanks again. I'll talk to you later."

This is going to be perfect. If I can get two guys down in Mexico doing some recon work this early in the case, I might be able to catch a break later. The nice thing about Mexico is it's cheap. The guys know they aren't going to be staying in the Ritz, they'll be staying in small motels. I might even buy a small cruddy place down there since they might be down there a while. I know it's asking a lot for them to be able to find anything concrete on Cappelano, but if they take their time and get to know some of the locals, they might be able to get some much-needed information. I hope Ken sends Tony and Carl; they are both fantastic investigators who speak a couple of different languages, including Spanish. Plus Carl is half Mexican and half Cuban, so he should be able to blend in quite easily. One thing I've learned about Mexico—or any country, for that matter—is that if you're not a local, it's really hard to find anyone who will talk to you, especially about an old murder. That's just the way it is. People are very protective of their home turf and distrustful of outsiders.

Wait a minute, I have an idea. I need to call Mike on this one; the bureau would be able to get more on something like this than my guys would. It's almost 9:00 a.m., so Mike should be in his office. If not, I'll call his cell.

"Neil, how are you this morning? I just talked to Maria. She filled me in on everything, said you guys worked late and that she's going back to your place today to work on the files some more. Good work, guys."

"Hey Mike, I have something. It's a long shot, but I think it's worth the time. I need you to get someone to grab a few photos of Cappelano from before his first surgery, as well as pictures from after his other two reconstructions."

"Sure, but I don't see where this is going. Want to fill me in?"

"I remember watching this special on plastic surgery, and the thing is that after so many surgeries, your choices start to become limited. If we had an agent track down one of the top plastic surgeons, then have them come up with the three most likely reconstructions that could be done with Cappelano's latest face, we might be able to catch a break and narrow down what he might look like now."

"Brilliant, Neil. How did you come up with that one?"

"Don't call me brilliant yet; we don't know if it's going to work. And I came up with it the same way I get all my other great ideas: I took a shower."

"You never cease to surprise me, Neil. Keep working on the files. I'll have an agent drop off all the material we get on the murders before the end of the day."

"Thanks, Mike. I like working out of my house; it's where I do my best work."

"No problem. Just keep it up. If you need anything else, remember to give me a call. You're not in this alone, we're here for you."

"I'll talk to you later, Mike. Keep me posted on everything."

"You got it, Neil. I'll talk to you later."

I hope this works with the plastic surgeon; having some photos to work with would really help my guys when they get to Mexico City. Not to mention we'll be able to get a decent facial composite to all the local authorities, so they can keep an eye out for anyone who shows a resemblance to the pictures we come up with. If we get a few pictures that are detailed enough to where we could put them on the wire, I might even have our guys leave them with a few businesses where I know Cappelano might show up. Could you imagine what a break in the case it would be if we got a hit on a facial composite? I'm getting excited just thinking about it, but I shouldn't get ahead of myself. Either way, I need to fill in Maria on the long shot I'm having Mike look into. I'd like to tell her about my guys in Mexico, but she's still a little too "by the book." If I tell her, she'll tell me I don't need to go outside of the bureau for help. But the reality is, the FBI will need to secure clearance from the Mexican government to go into Mexico, and all the political crap will slow down the investigation. My guys can get in there with no questions asked, and snoop around without any worries about international relations between the United States and Mexico. Don't laugh; crap like that slows down intercountry investigations.

I tracked down Maria in the bathroom, blow-drying her hair. I know what you're thinking: where did she get a hair dryer? Well, believe it or not, I own a hair dryer. I also have a daughter who's getting to be that age where she likes to look good. With hair as long as hers, I need a hair dryer around the house. I filled Maria in on everything that's going on, and about my hopes that this long shot will pay dividends for us in the form of witnesses who've seen Cappelano around town. Chances are he's somewhere in Detroit at the moment, and he's not going anywhere until he finishes what he started back in 1998. This game of teacher-student is starting to get old, because I know if I don't catch him soon, he'll keep killing. And when I do catch him, all he's going to do is take credit for me catching him, saying it was his tutelage that gave me the ability to track him down. He might even say that he *let* me catch him because he grew bored with the game. It's a bad situation for me either way.

"So what do you think, Maria? Is there any chance we can get something from a surgeon that we can actually use?"

"I definitely think there's a chance. If he's had his face changed twice before, he's got to be running out of options. The bones break down, and you start to lose facial structure, so eventually, his face will look like a doll, won't it? Kind of like that pop singer from the '80s."

"Exactly what I was thinking. I mean, you can only butter bread so many different times before you destroy it."

"What if Cappelano's just learned the art of disguise, with latex and facial prosthetics?"

"If that's the case, then we're screwed because he could change his appearance whenever he wants to," I said.

"Let's hope he went the route of surgery and not disguises. I'll cross my fingers; you should do the same."

"It's not a good sign if we're already resorting to crossing our fingers this early in the investigation."

"I don't know how early it is. Technically we've been chasing him for the better part of seven years."

"Point taken; I guess it has been a while. Hey, listen, I need to go run some errands, grocery shopping and things like that. How about you stay and try to narrow the search area for Mexico, just in case it comes down to that."

"All right, sounds good. While you're out, can you pick up a few things for your place in case I end up here again?"

"Of course. What do you need?"

"I already added them to your list. I saw it on the fridge. Sorry."

Looks like she's moving in already, I thought. Not that I'd be upset about it. "No problem. I'll be back in an hour or so."

"I'll be here with bells on."

With my shopping list in hand—half of it written in my chicken-scratch scrawl and the other half in Maria's nearly immaculate penmanship—I set off to do my grocery shopping, one of my least favorite activities next to picking up dog poop. The funny thing about that is, I found a service that comes out and picks up your dog poop for eight dollars a week. I was like, hell, I'll give up eight bucks for not having to pick up after my dogs. There's a job out there for everyone. The messed-up thing is the guy who does it drives a nicer car than I do, a Ford F-150 that couldn't be more than two years old.

Hopefully, by the time I get back, Maria will have a good idea of where to look for Cappelano in Mexico, so that I can send the information to Ken before he sends our guys out. The hardest part of some of these investigations, especially for someone like me, is filling in the gaps, filling the time in between. You work, you grind, and you look for leads, then you wait. It's not as glamorous as TV or the movies make it out to be. My inner dialogue is what keeps me sane and allows me to multitask. Oftentimes you see agents get overly focused, hyperdriven, then not know how to disconnect, so they turn to other things, such as alcohol or even drugs. There's a lot riding on this long shot, but I think it's what's going to give us the edge we need. Without it, we're going to be sitting on the SS Waiting Game a lot longer.

16

When we try to act randomly, we are consciously aware that we are trying to do so, and that contradicts the idea of randomness.

Maria and I sat in the kitchen, trying to figure out some sort of pattern to these murders. If we could find a connection, we could narrow the search area in Mexico. The girls have joined us for this morning's session; actually, they've joined Maria. They seem to have found a liking to Miss Maria Garcia similar to myself.

Serial killers are very consistent. They stick to a pattern without even realizing it, even when they are trying to be random. The hard part is trying to find that pattern. We might have to go to the mathematicians on this one. Finding sequences and patterns is a major role for the FBI mathematicians, and they have formulas for a lot of these very problems. The amazing thing about randomness is we as humans cannot create it no matter how hard we try. When we try to act randomly, we are consciously aware that we are trying to do so, and that contradicts the idea of randomness.

"Hey Neil, what if we send all this data over to the math guys at the bureau? Let's see if they can find a pattern or an underlying sequence."

"I was thinking the same thing. It's worth a shot. We don't have much more to go on, so let's use the bureau's resources as best we can. Plus we're just waiting around for the files for more insight anyway."

"What about the murders in Mexico. Any luck with those?"

"Mike said they're still having trouble getting Mexico's government to cooperate. They are asking for something in return for the case files, and our government doesn't want to do it."

"What are they asking for?"

"I don't know, probably money, or weapons for their military. It usually comes down to weapons, tanks, things like that."

"I can't believe we might have to trade a tank for some murder files. That's ridiculous."

"Don't look at me. If I could do something about it, I would."

I could tell Maria was upset because she knew if we got our hands on those files, we could be certain that Mexico would be getting some early Christmas presents from the US military. War, it's what makes the world go round. I remember working on a case my first or second year with the bureau where our perp had run off to Cuba, and there was nothing we could do about it. We knew he had killed seven people, the Cuban government knew, but they didn't care, so they granted him protection just to piss off the United States. It's sad when international politics can get in the way of bringing a killer to justice, but that's just the world we live in.

Maria decided that she needed to get going and head home, at least for tonight. She said she'd be back first thing in the morning and that she'd remember to pack a duffel bag this time so if she spends the night, she'll have a change of clothes. This reminds me: her shoes are *still* in the back of my car, but it's a little too late now, since I just watched her pull out of the driveway. I really don't feel like running after her, and my cell phone is in the bedroom, so I guess she can get them tomorrow.

It's almost 6:00 p.m., and Mike said the agent he sent should be here around seven o'clock. That should give me an hour without anything really to worry about. I think I might set up a workstation downstairs—a command center of sorts in the comfort of my own home. Or maybe I'll just take the night off from reading files and put up drywall instead. I might even lay the carpet I have laying around down there. It's just one room, so it shouldn't take me too long. In case Mike's delivery guy gets here early, I'll do some cleaning up around the house before I go downstairs. And it's a good thing I waited because I can see through the front window that the delivery guy is here with my case files. He's carrying only one box; that's not too bad. I also see that it's starting to rain again. I guess I should let him in so he and the files don't get drenched.

"Hey buddy, Mike said you'd be coming by tonight to drop off the files for me."

"Neil? Neil Baggio? It's an honor to meet you."

"I don't know if I would go that far, but thanks anyway. So is this the only box?"

"Sorry, no. I have six others just like it in my trunk, and I'll be dropping off a couple more boxes tomorrow. We haven't quite gotten everything together yet for all of the files you needed. But I'll be here with them no later than noon tomorrow."

"Well, let me help you carry these in. We'll just set them right inside the door here. I'll move them later."

"Thanks for the help. You have a pretty nice house here, Mr. Baggio."

"Thanks, kid. So let me ask you, how do you know about me? Just call it a little curiosity."

"To be honest with you, I first heard about you when I was going through training. You and your old mentor hold most of the records in all the training exercises. Eventually I found out a little bit about . . . well, everything that's been going on. So do you think you'll be able to catch him this time?"

"I sure do; I don't have much choice. If I don't get him this time, I don't think I ever will."

"Well, that's all of them. I need to get going. Like I said, I'll be by tomorrow around noon to drop off the other boxes."

"Thanks."

"I'll see you tomorrow."

The rest of the night was a blur. Once I start working, especially when I'm building something or working with my hands, time just flies by. I finished putting up the drywall along with a coat of primer, and I even laid the carpet down. It was 3:00 a.m. before I finished everything, but it was done, and it looked halfway decent. I'll have to call somebody at CB, Inc., tomorrow to bring by a couple of desks and chairs. We have a bunch of office furniture just sitting in a room from an office building that closed down a couple of months ago. You never know when you need office furniture, and for how cheap it was, we figured we could use it for home offices for our field investigators.

The office furniture was brought out on Friday, along with the rest of the case files. Maria and I spent the rest of the day organizing everything in the filing cabinets I bought. The office I built was starting to come together; we had all the case files put away and organized, maps up on the wall, and we were set up to fly through the weekend.

Saturday and Sunday kicked into high gear because we had a team of people over at the house. Maria was there, along with Mike, and a few interns to help with the filing and errand running; mainly they just kept us full of caffeine and kept the place clean. Mike gave me a hard time because I turned my basement into an office when I had one of the biggest office spaces in the McNamara Building. Oh well, I don't want to be driving around downtown knowing Christina Moore and her camera crew will be looking for me, not to mention Cappelano. This will keep things a little more on the down low. To be specific, it will make it easier for me to keep the FBI out of the loop on what my guys from CB, Inc., are doing.

Ken told me the guys are having trouble getting information in Mexico City, but they have had a few breaks on plastic surgeons. Mike told me that we're getting closer to a definitive answer about the facial reconstruction. Mike said the agent he put on it was tops in his class. He went to four different surgeons, and three of them were on the up and up while the fourth was a guy famous for doing cash jobs, similar to the one Cappelano had done. By Monday we should have a good idea of what Cappelano might look like today.

As for the latest round of canvassing, it came up empty for witnesses on Ashley Gracin's murder, and we haven't found a crime scene yet, at least for the place where she was killed and not just dumped. But I'm getting close, I can just taste it. Victory is in the air. All settled into the newly formed command center in my basement, I can feel things coming together. I know I could just as easily do this out of the FBI office, but I want to make sure everything runs through me this time, and this is the best way for me to maintain control of the case.

VERITAS

17

On top of that, I'm afraid of someone leaking the picture to the press. If somebody does, we're toast.

Normally I hate Mondays, but not today; today feels like a sign of good things to come. Maria and I are supposed to meet up with an agent later who's been looking into Cappelano's facial reconstruction and what he might look like today. He said that all four of the surgeons he interviewed came back with very similar ideas. That will help a lot if I can get a photo to my guys in Mexico who are trying to track down any bit of information on Cappelano. Ken had told me they were making good headway. They found a bartender who remembers a man who looked similar to the last picture we have of Cappelano from 2001. But the bartender said he only saw him for a couple of months, then he just disappeared. It's more likely that Cappelano had the surgery done and was laying low for a couple of months while he healed, and then made his way back to his usual spots.

If we have three good composites to work with, we can

present them as three buddies when we ask if anyone has seen them, and no one will know that it's the same man. It's better than saying we think a man may look like one of these three photos. I've learned through my studies and just through experience that you have to ask the right question to get the right information. It won't come freely for you, it's all in how you approach the situation. Think of questioning someone as if you were hitting on a woman. The key is not to be blunt about what you want. If you start the conversation by asking, "Will you go home with me?" or "What's your phone number?" you're not likely to get a positive response. If you warm her up with small talk and hint at the information you would like, a lot of times she will give the information without you even having to ask the straightforward question. Isn't this a nice surprise, Sheila's calling me while I'm driving downtown.

"Hey, Sheila, how are you?"

"I'm doing really well. I just wanted to call and say thank you for yesterday."

"What do you mean? It was no big deal."

"It was to Carol Lynn and me. We both know you're very busy with the case, and it was sweet of you to surprise us in the morning by cooking breakfast for us. You're a real sweetheart, you know that?"

"It was nothing. I needed to get out of the house anyway. There have been so many people in and out of that place, but it's better than being downtown all day."

"I can imagine, plus it saves you money on gas. I just called to say thanks again. Before I let you go, how are things with Maria?"

"Well . . . we're colleagues who have an attraction to each other. We both know it's nothing of substance; things are just too complicated for it to become anything more. We're just enjoying the ride while it lasts. Before you know it, I'll be all yours again, trust me."

"I'm not worried about that. I actually met a cute younger guy at the bar the other night. Carol Lynn was at a sleepover, and I went out with some ladies from work."

"You didn't tell me you met someone. How old is this younger man, exactly?"

"Don't laugh at me when I tell you. He's only twenty-four. But he is sexy as hell, and a real sweetheart."

"Well, I'm guessing he doesn't know you're thirty, does he? Are you still telling guys that you're twenty-seven? You could pass for even younger, by the way."

"Shut up! I hate that number thirty! It just sounds so vulgar to a lady. I didn't tell him I was twenty-seven; I told him I was twenty-six."

Even after all these years, Sheila can still make me laugh like nobody else in the world. "Women are amazing creatures. But hey, Sheila, I need to get going. I'm at the office, and I have a meeting in a few minutes. Give Carol Lynn a hug for me tonight. I don't think I'll be around."

"No problem, Neil. Have a good day, and be safe."

I got off the phone as I was making my way to the front door of the building, almost falling on my ass in the process. It's extremely icy outside, and apparently we're last on the list for salting. You'd think that government buildings would be a number one priority, but they aren't, especially in Detroit. Exiting the elevator, I was expecting to see that big smile Jen greets me with in the morning, but I wasn't lucky enough. Jen was busy getting the conference room ready for the meeting I was supposed to be at in five minutes. Mike is having the agent who tracked down the plastic surgeons do a presentation on the renderings the surgeons came up with, showing what Cappelano might look like today if he had additional surgeries. The doctors based their renderings on patterns from old surgeries as well as what was left of Cappelano's face to be reconstructed. After a while your face starts to lose all the distinguishing features it used to have and becomes one that no one can remember or notice.

"Good morning, Neil," Mike said as I entered the conference room. "Maria should be with us in a minute. She just ran to the bathroom. How are you doing this morning?"

"Not bad, after this weekend. I'm hoping this week will generate some really good results. How about you?"

"I'm doing all right. Just a little tired. Here she comes."

"Sorry for making you wait, guys. Let's get started. The sooner we get this over with, the sooner we can get these photos out on the wire."

"All right. Neil and Maria, this is Agent Phillips; he'll be walking us through today's presentation. You can start whenever you're ready, Agent Phillips."

"Thank you, Mr. Ponecelli. Let's get started. As you can see . . ."

Over the next hour, we talked to Agent Phillips and went over each surgeon's renderings. Surprisingly, two of the doctors had almost identical renderings, and the other two surgeons came back with very similar renderings as well. We essentially ended up with only two different pictures to work with. The two different compositions were also very similar to each other. We could present the two photos as brothers when questioning people if they had seen either one, which will aid in their capacity for memory recall. If we were to ask, "Have you seen this man, he may have looked like either one of these pictures?" the brain has a tendency to focus on only one, and because people like to help, they will say they saw one or the other just to say they helped, even if they hadn't seen a man having any resemblance to either photo.

Agent Phillips was trying tremendously hard to impress us, probably because it was his first assignment of this nature on a high-profile case. After the presentation, he handed out packets that had high-resolution glossy photos of the renderings and a disc with the photos in digital format for further use. I have to say, the kid came prepared. Better to be overprepared than under-, I always say—okay, I don't really say that, but it's good advice. The digital format will help me because I can have Ken send the pictures to our guys in Mexico, either to their PDA phones or to an email account they can access down there. Either way it will speed up the process exponentially. If you haven't caught on already, Ken and I really do like our toys. If it's a new gadget and we can use it, we need to have it. Luckily our business allows us to buy some of the coolest tech equipment around and write it off as business expenses. Just recently, we bought PDA phones for everyone on the team so we could share information quickly and easily with everyone.

It helps a lot when you're out on a stakeout and you need information on a person you just took a picture of. You can pull the memory card from the camera, load it into your laptop, transfer the photo to your phone, and send it to somebody at the office. They can look up the photo with our facial recognition software. That has to be my favorite toy of all; that program is unbelievable. It can analyze a picture, read several points on the face, and then search a database to find a match to those data points; it speeds up the identification process tenfold.

Back at my office, I began to upload the pictures Agent Phillips gave us onto my phone, so I would be able to send them out to Ken. I would love to send him the photos from my computer because it would be a lot easier, but the tech geeks at the bureau trace all emails outgoing and incoming to keep track of information such as these pictures. Ken should be able to get the pictures to our guys in Mexico before the day is out, and hopefully we'll get some hits on them. That reminds me: I need to talk to Maria about our plans for the rest of the day. It's Monday, and I'm working as if it were the middle of the week. Usually I don't get very much done on Mondays— or Tuesdays, for that matter; I don't know why. It's probably all those years working in the bar business; your weekend is Monday and Tuesday because those are the slow days for that particular industry. I would just walk down to Maria's office, but that would require a level of motivation I'm not ready to use just yet. I guess I'll just call her on the office line.

"Maria, hey, it's Neil. What's the plan of attack for today?"

"I'm not sure yet. You're the lead investigator on this case; it's your call. After this weekend, there's not much we can do other than getting the photos out on the wire."

"We need to be careful about those pics. If the media gets their hands on them, we'll be screwed because Cappelano will lose that arrogance he has, especially about being seen in public."

"But the more people who know what he looks like, the better chance we have of catching him."

"True, but if he's one of them, he won't go out without a disguise on. And Cappelano loves to talk to people who he knows should know who he is, but don't know what he looks like now. He gets off on that crap; it's all ego."

"All right, then how should we get the word out to people

about the pictures?"

"For now let's hide the file in an email that seems harmless in case Cappelano has access to one of our email accounts. You never know, the guy is slick."

"All right, I know just the thing. I'll attach it to a bogus birthday announcement. Most people will look at it, but someone such as Cappelano couldn't care less about something like that."

"Wonderful. Get to work on it; I need to take care of some things today. Keep me up to date on anything you guys come up with."

"Where are you headed off to? Want someone to come along for the ride? I can have some first- or second-year agent take care of the email."

"No, I want you to take care of it personally to make sure it gets done right. Also, don't send it to more than ten people at a time, and try and keep the emails grouped by department. If it's a mass email to everyone, Cappelano could pick up on it."

"You got it, Neil. I'll talk to you later. This is going to take me a while, so I need to get going on it."

"Thanks, Maria. I'll talk to you later."

I don't think that Cappelano has an insider in the FBI field office, but you never know. On top of that, I'm afraid of someone leaking the picture to the press. If somebody does, we're toast. I should call Maria back; I have an idea.

"Maria. It's Neil again."

"What's up, Neil?"

"Instead of sending the new Cappelano composites out, find pictures of someone in our database who looks similar to Cappelano but different enough that if it makes the news. Cappelano will laugh when he sees that the pictures look nothing like him. I guarantee we have a leak in here somewhere."

"Anything else?"

"Yeah, have the tech guys keep an eye out for people forwarding the pictures to outside emails. And make sure they encrypt the files so they can't be saved to a disc, for obvious reasons."

"Got it, Neil. Look at you, mister bright idea."

"Quit messing around. I need to get going. Thanks for doing this, Maria."

"No problem, Neil. I'll talk to you later."

I have a feeling we can kill two birds with one stone doing it this way. If we have a leak, we'll find out soon enough, and I'm actually banking on the fact that someone will leak the photos. If Cappelano thinks we are off the beaten path, he'll be a little laxer in his daily activities. Not to mention he'll be tempted to try and talk to me, and not over the phone, but in person. He'll think I won't know who he is, but that's the fun part, I *do* know what he looks like. And this isn't something Cappelano taught me; this is understanding how to manipulate someone's oversized ego through psychology.

I should call Ken and let him know what's going on so that he doesn't wonder when he sees the picture all over the news why the photos I sent him look different than the ones that went out to the rest of the country. I'll have to get out of the office before I make the call; I don't want to take the chance that someone hears me. Just to be safe, I should drive out to the warehouse and just talk to him one on one. I'll send him a text message first to make sure he's there. I made my way through the office, down the elevators, and passed George without small talk, which was a feat in and of itself. I felt my phone vibrating—it's Ken.

"Ken, what's up? Did you get my text message a minute ago?"

"No, I haven't gotten it yet. I have a message waiting to download, but it won't seem to come through. Can you send it again?"

"I'll do you one better: I'll show it to you in person. Are you at the warehouse? I'm heading there right now; I need to talk to you about a few things."

"Yeah, I'm out here. I'll see you in a few minutes, then."

"Sounds good, Ken. See you in a few minutes."

I guess it's a good thing that I'm making my way to the warehouse, since the message got lost in the wind somewhere. The file sizes of the pictures were probably too big; I should have converted them to smaller jpeg files. Think of it like trying to cram a foot-long sub into a sandwich bag; it's not going to happen, no matter how hard you try. The problem is I didn't realize how big the sandwich was until it was too late. I'm almost to the warehouse, and I'll be face-to-face with Ken anyway. As I pulled around the back, the bay door was open, which is odd for this time of day. Maybe Tony has seen Ken or at least knows why the bay is open. Tony is one of our investigators and an ex-marine, but don't call him that. He'll just scream back that "a marine is a marine for life!" Marines are crazy sons of bitches; I'm just glad they're on our side. Tony's a good guy and a hell of an investigator, especially on stakeouts. He spent most of his career in the marines as a sniper, which means the guy has patience that I could only dream about.

"Hey Tony, have you seen Ken around?"

"Yeah, he's in his office. I think he's waiting for you."

"Yeah, he is. Can you answer me something?"

"I can try. What's going on?"

"Why's the bay door open?"

"Oh, sorry about that, I opened the door to air out the smell."

"What smell? I don't smell anything."

"Keep going, you'll smell it in a little bit," Tony said. "One of the guys thought it would be funny to put a couple of hard-boiled eggs in the ventilation system of the van I was using for a stakeout. If that wasn't bad enough, they boiled the eggs in vinegar. Needless to say, those jokers are at the wash bay cleaning the van from head to toe. I told them not to come back until the smell is gone, but it was too late for the warehouse; it reeks."

"Whoever it was, make sure they pay for everything they use to clean it out, and if they don't, just take it from their pay."

"That's harsh, but I'm already on it. I told them this is on their dime, not ours."

"I appreciate it, Tony. We just don't have time for this frat-house bullshit right now. I need to go talk to Ken. I'll see you later."

"See ya, Neil. And good luck on that case you're working on."

"Thanks."

He wasn't kidding, the warehouse stinks of vinegar and rotten eggs. Those guys should get their butts fired; the smell is just horrendous. Don't get me wrong, there's nothing wrong with a good practical joke—hell, I'm the one pulling off most of them—but when you make the whole warehouse smell, that's just crossing the line. Speaking of jokes, there was one night about a year ago when Ken and I were working late. We decided to turn the heat off in the warehouse and pack the vents with confetti, so when they came in and cranked the heat, there was confetti blowing all over the warehouse. Ken and I didn't care because we both had the next week off. It was classic because we had left Tony in charge, and we made it look like one of the other guys did it. Things got a little out of hand, though, because one of the guys who took the blame was so pissed about getting blamed that he almost quit. It was all in good fun, though. I know you're probably thinking, "you guys are assholes," but you have to remember it's the bunker mentality. Many if not most of us have done stakeouts with each other for days, sometimes weeks, and you get a different kind of trust. Tony said it took almost two whole days to get the warehouse warmed back up. He wasn't kidding; our electric bill was through the roof that month from trying to reheat a freezing cold building.

"Ken, what's up? Other than the nasty smell in here."

"Hey, Neil. Yeah, a couple of the guys tried to get Tony back for that prank he pulled last month. Remember?"

"Oh yeah, that was great; setting a greased pig loose through the building was classic. That thing caused so much damage, but it was still funny as hell."

"I still have the videotape. I'm having TJ make it into a DVD so I can give them out as Christmas presents."

"You're a cheap ass, you know that? Funny, but a cheap ass."

"Hey, I love spending money when it's something for the company or for my enjoyment, not for these guys. We give them bonuses anyway."

"True. Before we get carried away on pointless conversations, let's get down to business." I pulled up the photos on my laptop of the renderings we compiled. "We had four plastic surgeons come up with what they think Cappelano would look like today if he had more work done. There were two different renderings among the four of them, so we're feeling confident about the photos."

"We'll have to give TJ the disc so he can copy it for me. Let me call him in here real quick."

Ken got on the phone and called TJ to his office so he could make a copy of the disc and send the images down to our guys in Mexico. In the meantime, I sent a message to Sheila, asking her if she would be up for dinner at her place. I was in the mood to cook for her and Carol Lynn tonight. Here comes TJ; I should get off my phone.

"Hey TJ, how are you doing today? Have a good weekend?"

"Yeah, it was pretty relaxing compared to last weekend with that disc. What do you have for me today?"

"Another disc, but this one won't take as much work, I promise. Copy this disc right now and bring it back, then send the files out to the guys."

"No problem; I'll be back in a few minutes."

It took TJ about twenty minutes to make the copy, and while I was waiting, I explained to Ken what I had, Maria will try and find a leak as well as throw off Cappelano. He agreed with me that there had to be a leak somewhere at the bureau; there's almost always a leak, it's just a matter of how bad a leak it is. But like usual, we ended up off subject talking about shit that didn't matter, mainly my situation with Maria right now. Just as Ken and I were finishing up, TJ came back into the room.

"Did I hear that right, Neil? Are you dating Maria? That ten from the office I met last week?"

"Sort of, it's complicated. It's definitely none of your concern. In other words, if you tell a soul, I'll track you down and kill you."

"Damn, man, I was just wondering. No problem, I won't tell anyone. Maybe someday you can show me how to pick up babes like her."

"If I knew how I did it, I would have written a book a long time ago. So did you get the photos sent out?"

"All done; I even encrypted them in case they land into the hands of the wrong people. Only our guys and a handful of geeks like myself should be able to access the photos."

"Nice work. But I need to get out of here. I have to run to the grocery store."

"What for, Neil?" Ken asked. "Didn't you run to the store yesterday?"

"Yes, I did, but I'm going to cook dinner for Sheila and Carol Lynn tonight, so I need to pick up a few things from the market."

"Look at you, Mr. Player, juggling two women at one time. I'm just giving you a hard time. Have a good night. I'll keep you updated with the guys in Mexico."

"Thanks, Ken. I'll talk to you guys tomorrow. And try to keep the warehouse from stinking up, please?"

"I'll try, but you know it's hard to keep these guys under control. They're like a bunch of teenagers around this time of year."

Finally, I got away from that smell. It was just wrong in so many different ways. It was one of those smells that go through your nostrils up to your brain and right down your spine, causing you to gag a little bit. At least tonight will be relaxing after a long week and an even longer weekend. I know I told Sheila this morning that I wasn't going to be able to stop by today, but since things are slow tonight, I want to spend any time I can with her and Carol Lynn. What can I say? I still love the two of them very much.

The market was really busy tonight; I have no idea why maybe there was a sale or something going on. I was making my way back from the market to Sheila's house when my phone started vibrating. I hoped it was Ken or Maria giving me good news, but I was way off. It wasn't anyone I'd expected.

"Hey, Neil. How are you doing tonight?"

"Frank, is that you? What are you doing calling me again?"

"I just wanted to let you know I'm taking care of a problem for you. You won't be bothered anymore."

"What are you talking about? If you even put one finger on my family, so help me God!"

"Calm down, Neil. You know I would never hurt you or your family. This is someone who deserves it. If it weren't for him, you would have been able to do your job the first time around, and I wouldn't have to keep killing."

"You could stop killing whenever you feel like it. Don't make this about me. This is all you."

"No need to thank me, Neil. You'll know soon enough. I have to go." CLICK

I pulled off the road and slammed the car into park. I needed to call Maria. Why isn't she answering her phone? She always answers her cell. *"Hello. This is Maria Garcia, sorry I missed your call, but if you leave me your name . . ."* Just then I saw that Maria was calling me on the other line.

"Maria! Where is Bob Hendrickson?"

"Why do you care? What—"

"No time for this. Where is he? Is he still in Detroit?"

"No. He's in DC unpacking from his move. What's this about?"

"Cappelano just called me; he's going to kill Bob. He said he was going to take care of the problem that kept me from catching him last time."

"Okay, I'm calling DC right now. I'll call you later, Neil. Meet me at the office."

"I'll be there in twenty minutes. I'll call Mike; just get ahold of DC right now. They need to track Bob down." CLICK

I have to get Mike on the phone, but judging by all the ringing, survey says, nope! DAMN IT! I need to call Sheila too and give her the bad news; I was really looking forward to a quiet night with the people I love. The phone's ringing; Mike had better pick up.

"Neil, how's it going? What are you—"

"Mike, just listen! Cappelano just called me. He has Bob, and he's going to kill him. Get on the phone and call everyone and anyone you know. We need to get to DC right now. Meet Maria and me at the office as soon as you can."

"What?! I'm on it. I'll set everything up. I'll see you at the office in a few minutes."

"See you there. And hurry your ass up."

I can't believe this is happening right now. We were getting so close, and now Cappelano is going to kill another person with ties to the FBI. If Ashley Gracin wasn't bad enough, now he's going to kill Bob? Don't get me wrong, I hate Bob Hendrickson, but he doesn't deserve to die. I mean, he has a family, and a life is a life. I'm not going to sleep until Cappelano is in custody or in a casket. I know I shouldn't say that, but I don't care—this has got to stop.

Sheila understood why I had to cancel dinner. I knew she would, but it's Carol Lynn I'm worried about. I don't want her thinking I can't keep a promise because of my job. She was just starting to get used to me being around when I said I would be. Over the past year with CB, Inc., I had total control of my schedule, so I could keep regular days with my daughter. It was nice for a change. This is going to kill her, I just know it, but I don't have a choice.

When I got to the office, I didn't even bother parking in a spot, I just pulled alongside the curb and took off running into the building. Security didn't try to stop me; I'm guessing Maria warned them that we'd be running in, so if you know us, just get out of the way. Riding up the elevator, my cell phone went off. It was Ken.

"Neil, what's going on? I saw you driving down the highway like a bat out of hell. You just passed me on the road a few minutes ago. I've been trying to get through."

"Cappelano called me. He's got Bob."

"Hendrickson? Oh shit. This isn't good, I know he's a prick, but nobody deserves death at the hands of Cappelano, that crazy fuck. If you need anything, just let me know."

"Actually, can you call some of our military contacts and see if you can get Maria, Mike, and me a flight down to DC ASAP?"

"No problem. Give me like ten minutes, I'll call my buddy at the base out here. I'll call you back."

"Thanks, I have to get going. Talk to you in a few."

I came running off the elevator when I noticed that Jen was still here. She must be helping Maria, since it's pretty late for her to be around.

"Neil, Maria is in the conference room with some other agents; they're setting up shop in there."

"Thanks, Jen. Can you grab me a cup of coffee and a duffel bag? I need to pack some things. We're going on a trip real soon."

"No problem; I'll bring the coffee to you, and the bag to your office."

"Thanks."

It was a madhouse in the conference room. People were surprisingly fast in their efforts to get organized on such short notice. Then again, these are extenuating circumstances. I saw Maria on the phone, along with another handful of agents.

"Can someone catch me up on what's going on?" I asked.

"Maria is on the phone with the DC police, and we have agents trying to get ahold of anyone they can to track down Bob. "The DC office said that Hendrickson isn't answering his phone, and no one has heard from him for almost twelve hours." Jen was all over it, as usual. Keeping the office dialed in, the duffel bag was in a cabinet in the hallway between her office and mine. Coffee, and bag in hand in under a minute—now, that's service.

"This isn't good. Tell Maria to come to my office. We need to make plans to get to DC."

"Can do. Can I get you anything else?"

"I'm okay. Jen's grabbing me what I need; just talk to Maria."

"No problem."

Rushing out of the office, I almost ran over Jen, who was holding my coffee. She said she'd have a duffel bag for me in a minute; she's having someone run three of them up as we speak, just in case Maria and Mike need one as well. It's a good thing most of us are prepared for something like this. I'm sure Maria is, but I'm not sure about Mike, although he was at his house and he'll probably pack something up quickly before he heads out to the office. As for me, I have three changes of clothes stored away in my office, plus one suit, a change of shoes, and a shaving kit full of anything else I might need—deodorant, and things like that. As for underwear and socks, I'll just have to stop when we get to DC.

"Hey Jen, thanks for the bags. Put one in Maria's office and one in Mike's, please. We need to get everything together and get out to DC as soon as we can."

"What's going on? Why DC?"

"Cappelano has Bob. He's going to kill him."

"What?! He can't, not Bob. What about his wife and kids?"

"Cappelano doesn't care about them. He thinks he's doing me a favor. But I need to get some calls done. Grab Maria for me; I need to take this call."

It's Ken, hopefully bringing some good news. Ken's a pro at getting things on short notice, especially when it comes to transportation. My guess is Mike is setting up commercial plane tickets as we speak, and Ken already has us a ride on a cargo plane from the military base.

"Ken. Give me good news."

"Get out to the air base. I told my boys the FBI needs a lift and they said they'd love to help. They're taking you guys in a cargo jet. I should be able to get you there in less than two hours. Good enough for ya?"

"Thanks, Ken, the FBI owes you one. If you ever need anything, just let me know. I'll get it taken care of."

"Thanks, man. I know you're good for it. Just catch this

fucking bastard. Oh yeah, I got some other good news. The guys called from Mexico City; they found the surgeon who did Cappelano's last facial reconstruction. They should have pictures for us within a couple of hours. When I get them, I'll send them to your phone."

"Thanks, Ken, you always got my six, much appreciated."

"No problem, that's what I'm here for. Good luck, and be careful."

It's only 7:30 p.m., which means Maria, Mike, and I should be able to get out to the base by 9:00 p.m. and get out to DC around 11:00 p.m. or so. I can hear Mike coming down the hallway right now.

"Neil, I just got off the phone with the airport. We can get out of here at 10:15 p.m. on a direct flight to DC. I tried calling the base, but I couldn't get through to anyone."

"Don't worry about it; I had an old friend call in a favor. I got us a ride out of the base on a cargo plane, departing as soon as we show up. They'll be waiting for us."

"Damn, you must have a pretty influential friend. Would I know him?"

"We'll talk about it on the plane. For now, get your shit together—we're heading out of here in a little bit. Have you seen Maria yet?"

"I saw her packing in her office on my way through. Meet you outside?"

"Thanks, I was in a little rush. Yes, I'll meet you outside as soon as I'm done."

All three of us are here, and we should be ready to go momentarily. I had a feeling that things were going to take a turn for the worse. Even though a man's life is at stake, I got the familiar rush of adrenaline that comes when a big case takes a turn, whether it's good or bad. When the case takes on a life of its own, and you're right in the middle of it, you get a rush like you're on a roller coaster. As for what the future holds, only time will tell. For now, the three of us need to get to the base, and as soon as possible.

18

Nowadays, the only safe place in any government building is a bathroom stall.

The team that met us at the base was extremely helpful; if we had to take a commercial flight, there's no way we would have gotten off the ground. They just warned us ahead of time that there'd be a fair amount of turbulence, and we were off flying through a blizzard—you have to love it. Mike and I were getting a kick out of it, though Maria wasn't too happy with the situation. It was pretty rough for the first twenty minutes or so, but once the pilots took the plane above the storm, it was smooth sailing—except for the landing, which was pretty rough, too. During the flight, Mike and I kept joking around with some of the crew while one of the soldiers was nice enough to keep Maria calm; I think he had a little thing for Maria. I can't fault the kid for trying; she's one amazing woman.

We had spent the two-hour flight talking about Bob Hendrickson and how unbelievable it was that Cappelano tracked him down and grabbed him. Bob's an asshole, but he's still a pretty sharp guy. If Cappelano really has him on a table somewhere, I just hope he makes it quick and painless. But if I know Cappelano as well as I think I do, then Bob has gone through or is still going through unimaginable torture and is preparing himself for death. I hope we can save him in time, but I have to be realistic. Chances are, we'll be too late. As my grandmother used to say, you can be hopeful, but prepare for the worst, so you're not surprised if it comes.

The guys at the base back in Michigan gave us some nice winter coats to keep us warm, both on the flight and when we got to DC. Somehow it was even colder in DC than it was in Detroit. I don't know what to expect when we get to the DC office, but I'm not looking forward to it in the least. The next couple of days are going to be crucial to the case and our ability to find Cappelano. I wonder what's on everyone else's minds.

"Hey Maria, how you holding up? Are you going to be okay?"

"I just can't believe that he's gone. If we're even lucky enough to find what's left of him, I don't think I'll be able to handle myself around his body." You could see Maria was trying to put on a brave face, but she was clearly rattled. She had spent much of her time at the bureau working for Hendrickson and was taking his likely death like a punch to the gut.

"Hey Neil, what's the game plan while we're down here?" Mike said, trying to get us on task, feeling the awkwardness in the air.

"Well, we need to hope Cappelano left us something in DC; otherwise we're lost all over again."

"Hey guys, they're waving us over to our ride. Let's get going," Maria said. "We can talk about it more when we get in the car."

"Anyone know how long a drive it is?" I asked.

"Yeah, it's about an hour or so drive, but in this weather, we're talking closer to an hour and a half, if not more. Luckily these Humvees can drive through almost anything," our driver said, trying to make us feel calm. Not sure it worked.

"I guess we might as well try and get some rest," I said, "because we aren't going to get any when we get there, at least not until early in the morning."

We spent the ride dozing into and out of sleep, not saying much more to each other than small talk. All of us knew what was ahead of us, at least in general. Once someone like Hendrickson gets kidnapped and probably killed, it really puts everyone on notice. Cappelano knows we're coming after him in full force now. Then again, he's still banking on the fact that no one knows what he looks like, but for right now, we have a good idea, and soon I might have more than that from my guys in Mexico. Now, that's what I call timing: I'm getting a call from Ken.

"Hey Ken, what's up? Thanks again for getting us the lift. By the way, everyone has been awesome."

"No problem. Why are you whispering?"

"Maria and Mike are asleep in front of me in the Humvee. Anyway, what's the latest? Shit, I'll take a fucking haiku at this point. Just give me something of substance."

"The guys just sent me a photo of Cappelano as he looks today. They also said that the surgeon mentioned something about a house out there. In the mountains outside of Mexico City. They're going to look into it. From the way the surgeon was talking, it seems like Cappelano's been operating out of there for quite some time."

"Thanks, Ken. Tell the guys, great job for me. When should I expect the photo?"

"You should be getting it within the hour. TJ has to tweak the photo format a little bit so we can send it to you with no problems."

"Thanks again, Ken. I'll call you later when I learn more about what's going on here in DC."

"No problem. We're here for you. I'll have the guys keep digging up information on Cappelano. Now that they have his photo, they might be able to get more out of the locals."

"'Night, Ken. Thanks again."

This is awesome; I'll have a photo of Cappelano, not a rendering. Our guys are going to get some fat bonuses for helping me out on this one. It's kind of sad that my independent investigators pulled more information than the FBI could. Last I checked, the FBI was still working with the Mexican ambassador to get us approval to look for information on Cappelano. Meanwhile, my guys have been moving around free from the watchful eye of the Mexican government.

"Hey Neil, who were you talking to just then? Anyone important?"

"No one important, Maria, just an old friend. He was the one who arranged the transportation for us."

"Make sure and tell him thanks for us. If it weren't for him, we'd still be in Detroit."

"I'll make sure to the next time I talk to him. For now, why don't you go back to sleep? You're going to need all the rest you can get."

"What about you? Aren't you going to get some sleep?"

"I'm used to going days without sleep. Plus I've got a few phone calls and emails to take care of while I have the chance."

For the remainder of the ride, I pondered the fact that eventually I would have to tell the bureau that I've had guys working outside of the investigation. Not to mention that I have a photograph, not a rendering, of Cappelano. This is going to be huge. If I show them now, though, I have a feeling the picture will end up plastered all over the press, and I don't need that, at least not yet. For now, I need to feel out what's going on here in DC and get as much information as I can on the death of Bob Hendrickson—well, the soon-to-be-confirmed death.

"We're almost here, Mr. Baggio. If you want to wake up your companions, you should do so now."

"Thanks, Lieutenant, I'll let them know. Hey guys, it's time to get up. We're almost here. Get your stuff together."

"Wow! We're already here?" Mike said. "We made good time. Did you get any sleep, Neil? Every time I opened my eyes, I saw you were awake."

"No, I didn't get any sleep, but it's hard for me to relax right now. I've got too much on my mind."

Making our way from the Humvee, we could feel the cold air cutting through our jackets as if we were walking shirtless through the cold winter night. It was almost one in the morning now, and we were just making our way through the doors to the bureau's building here in DC. It really is a beautiful building. Not necessarily in terms of aesthetics, but just the history the building has. This is the headquarters for the entire bureau; it all starts and ends here.

Once through the doors, the three of us were met by an agent who was probably assigned to chauffeur us while we're down here. The amazing thing about law enforcement personnel is that we're not too keen on escorting out-of-town agents. It just seems to put a damper on our usual routine as well as making us glorified babysitters. We didn't work our butts off to get this far and have to fetch some other officer's coffee.

"Agents Baggio, Garcia, and Ponecelli, I presume? I'm Agent Dickerson. Follow me this way, please. How was your trip down here through the blizzard?"

"It wasn't too bad, actually. I have a newfound faith in our flyboys. Those guys are amazing, flying through a storm like that." Maria is always keen to praise.

"Agent Dickerson, what's the latest word on Agent Hendrickson?" I asked.

"We'll get to that soon enough. Just follow me; all will be answered shortly."

We got off on some umpteenth floor; I wasn't paying attention because I could feel my phone vibrating, and I knew it was the photo of Cappelano, but I didn't want to look at it with agents and cameras around. As soon as I have the opportunity, I'll have to excuse myself to the bathroom so I can get a good look at it. Nowadays, the only safe place in any government building is a bathroom stall. No one is going to watch or listen in on you taking a shit these days. Security is a top priority, and Uncle Sam will infringe on your privacy virtually anywhere to ensure it.

Agent Dickerson is an older man, probably in his mid-to-late forties. He has a shaved head with a goatee, and I'd guess he's about five-eleven and weighs about 185 or so. One thing is for sure: he walks extremely fast. Then again, that could be because of the situation's urgency. Just as I was about to ask where we were headed, Agent Dickerson told us to put our bags down in his office, then to continue following him to the war room, where all the action is going on. Their war room doesn't double as a conference room similar to ours back in Detroit. It's twice the size, with screens on every wall, computer terminals lining the table in the center of the room, and more cables and connections than a Best Buy Geek Squad.

"Hey Neil, do you have any idea what's going on?"

"No, Maria, but I can tell you we're about to have the longest night of our lives."

"At least I got a little bit of sleep. Will you be all right?"

" As long as I keep the coffee pumping through these veins, I'll be fine. On a case like this, you need to take the old 'sleep is the enemy' approach."

Maria and I joked around for a few moments while Mike and Agent Dickerson had a sidebar, probably about the fact that I had just gotten my security clearance days ago, and my past of going off the cuff. The boys down here in DC don't like to do anything unless it's by the book; the only time I use the book is when I'm hitting someone with it.

"Agent Baggio? Sorry we had to meet in such circumstances. Let me get you caught up."

"What did you guys find at Hendrickson's hotel room? Were there any signs of a struggle?"

"No. But the hotel computer said his room's door hadn't been opened since early this morning. Our guess is he was grabbed outside of the hotel."

"Have you tracked down his car? Cappelano has had extensive facial reconstruction, which means Hendrickson wouldn't have recognized him. Not to mention Hendrickson is in a new town, in a hotel . . . he was probably at a bar. Was there a bar in the hotel or close by?"

"There is a bar in the hotel, as well as a few within the same city block. We're checking them against his credit card records right now."

"Good; I'll make sure and check them out tomorrow. I know how Cappelano works—he likes to slip something into his victims' drinks while befriending them. It makes it easier to overpower them later. People just think he's a friend helping out another friend who's had too much to drink. They don't know that Cappelano is probably going to kill the guy he's carrying out the door."

"It seems we have a lot to talk about," Mike said. "How about we get together a group meeting where we can go over the information we all have. The hotel that you guys will be staying at is just down the road. I'll have Agent Dickerson take you guys there to get your things in order and maybe grab something to eat on the way, and we'll meet back in the conference room in an hour."

"Sounds good, Mike. We'll see you then."

Now I have to debate with myself if I'm going to share the new photo of Cappelano I've acquired with everyone or keep it to myself. I think I'm going to keep it to myself for now and see how far we can get without it. Sometimes people have a tendency to stop thinking when an easy opportunity arises. Without a photo to focus on, the other agents will have to think outside the box and work hard to figure out how to track down

Cappelano.

Over the next couple of hours, we shared as much information as we could to form a basic plan of action. I found out that Bob Hendrickson's credit cards were used at two different bars for substantial-size tabs. That will give me a centralized area to start with, and if I show the picture to a few bartenders, I'll have a good chance of finding someone who saw both Bob and Cappelano in the same bar recently.

It's about 6:00 a.m. now. Maria and Mike went back to the hotel a couple of hours ago while I stayed around working with Agent Dickerson on tracking down Hendrickson's activity the past couple of days. If I can find the same pattern that Cappelano noticed, then there's a good chance I can find the exact location where Cappelano took Hendrickson. It's very common for Cappelano to set up a temporary base of operations in close proximity to his victim so that he can follow his prey while integrating himself into the community. Cappelano takes every kill very seriously. He is a perfectionist in everything he does, from stalking his targets to fading like a morning fog.

19

If there is one thing I've learned about the bar scene, it's that information always has a price.

The phone kept ringing in my room, and it was beginning to annoy me. It had better be something important. If it's just some stupid wake-up call, I'll go nuts. My guess is that it's Mike or Maria trying to get ahold of me. They can't get to me through my cell because I've turned it off so I can charge it. I should probably turn it on and answer this ringing phone before I smash it. I rolled over in bed, grabbed the phone, and put it to my ear, all without opening my eyes or taking my head from the pillow. I know I'm smooth, aren't I?

"I didn't order any fries, and when did room service start doing cold calls?"

"Neil! It's Maria. What are you still doing in bed? It's almost two in the afternoon."

"What am I doing? I didn't even get back to my room until after six this morning, then I took a shower, had a drink, and relaxed, and by that time it was almost eight o'clock. So I'm sleeping, that's what I'm doing. I know I talked a big game earlier about going without sleep, but that's when I forgot I'm not twenty anymore. Plus I won't be able to get anything done before four or five this afternoon. Why? What's up?"

"We've been running around with the guys here at the D.C. office, and we keep hitting dead ends. Any ideas?"

"Yeah, stop calling me and let me sleep. I'll call you when I get out of bed, and I'll fill you in then. Or you could just call Agent Dickerson; he was with me last night, so he can catch you up. There are a couple bars I'm going to tonight, to talk to the help and see if anyone saw Hendrickson with anyone matching the photos we came up with."

"All right, Neil, get a little more sleep. You're annoying when you're tired anyway. I'll call Agent Dickerson to see what's up. I'll talk to you later."

"Thanks, Maria. Talk to you in a few hours." I know it seems odd for me to sleep past noon on a day like this, but my intention was to offset Maria and Mike. If I work while they sleep and vice versa, we cover more ground. Not to mention I want to avoid burning myself out to the point where my brain starts playing tricks on me.

I could tell Maria had no idea what I was talking about, but it didn't matter. I had given her an avenue to go down and move forward with, which should keep her and Mike busy for at least a couple of hours and allow me to get some more sleep. Plus she knows I can be a big crank-ass when I'm not rested. To be honest with you, I haven't actually slept much since I crashed this morning. I guess that's the price you pay for being dedicated to something wholeheartedly. No rest for the crazy. Luckily for Maria, I fell back asleep for a couple more hours, and it was quite restful. It must have been REM sleep; that's the deepest sleep one will get at any point while sleeping. It's when your brain is doing the most work, and usually when dreams occur. Come to think of it, I did have a pretty messed-up dream—a little racy, even for my taste—but I can't lie, it was a great time. I just never imagined Sheila and Maria were that kinky, not even in my dreams.

As for tonight, I'm going to have to do a lot of bribing to get information. If there's one thing I've learned about the bar scene, it's that information always has a price. Bartenders and servers are in the business of making money; if you give them a little bread to eat with, you'd be surprised what you can get in return. A twenty-dollar bill might not be that much money, but to the right person it can mean a meal, a bill, money toward rent, or money toward their next fix. Either way, it's a good way to get what you need.

It's almost four in the afternoon, and I finally pull myself to the edge of the bed. Sitting up, I began to rub my eyes, trying to defeat the fatigue gods, knowing that once I'm in the shower, I'll be good to go. I used to date this girl in college—it was a short relationship, maybe three months—and every morning she had her routine. If she didn't follow it as planned, then her entire day would be thrown out of whack. My morning routine— or should I say "getting my butt out of bed" routine— is almost complete. All that's left are a few more sit-ups, and I'll be good to go for the night. I know tonight is probably going to last until 6:00 a.m. all over again.

Anyway, back to what's important. This case is driving me nuts, making me scatterbrained. I worry about the case so much that I start to lose track of where my mind was going in the first place, but I usually end up where I need to be when it counts. Time to call Maria and see what she and Mike have been up to the past couple of hours. I'm too lazy to call her from my phone; I'll just use the hotel line.

"Hey Maria, it's Neil. Can you meet me in the lobby in thirty minutes?"

"I don't see why not. Do you know something we don't know?"

"I'll fill you in when I see you. I need to find my toothbrush. Meet you in the lobby in thirty!"

"Like I said, no problem. We'll see you there."

I guess it's time that I shed a little light on the case to Maria and Mike. I'm not sure about the DC guys yet; if you haven't noticed, I have trust issues. But Maria and Mike need to see the picture, if for no other reason than they can help me canvass at a faster pace. Three people can get more done than one; it's simple arithmetic. Then again, if they show this photo to anyone else, I'm screwed—everything will be messed up. I need the release of the photo to be just right. I can't take any chances of tipping off Cappelano; there just isn't any room for error. As for my wardrobe for the day, I don't want to look too professional because I know that Maria and Mike will be in the usual agent suit and jacket. I'm going for something more friendly: a pair of torn jeans, a gray T-shirt, my brown suede jacket, brown work boots, and my favorite camouflage Detroit Tigers hat. In thirty minutes flat I was ready and waiting for Maria and Mike.

"Neil don't dress up on our account," Maria said, clearly displeased with my outfit choice. "At least Mike put a suit on; you just look casual."

"That's the point. If I'm going to get any information out of these bar employees, we'll have to blend in a little bit. Otherwise they'll smell 'Fed' on us a mile away."

"What the hell are you talking about? Are you drinking on the job?"

"Very funny. What I mean is, Mike will have the suit look going for him, you'll have the sexy but assertive female thing going for you, and I'll have the laid-back casual look going. It will allow us to divide and conquer, depending on who we meet while we're out."

"Whatever you say, Neil. Anyway, we canvassed all afternoon, and there wasn't anyone who's seen either Bob or Cappelano."

"See, you gave me shit for sleeping, and now you're the one

who's slow to catch up. For starters, the people you talked to were probably off the clock too early to have seen or met either of them. On top of that, you didn't have this." I flipped open my phone and showed them the picture of Cappelano. Nearly every part of the man's face had changed in some way, but his eyes were still unmistakable.

"Holy shit! Where did you get this?" Maria said. "Is this who I think it is?"

"Yes, it's a picture taken of Cappelano after his last surgery had healed. And those bad-lookin' hombres he's posing with are from a couple of the local drug cartels in Mexico. I have the full picture back in my room, but for now all we need is the part of the photo that has Cappelano in it."

"We need to get this to the other agents," Mike said. "They'll be able to help with the search. Don't you think so, Maria?"

"Yeah, Neil, we should get this out on the wire to see if anyone in the area has seen him. That's the basic procedure for this kind of case."

"Well, Cappelano isn't a basic case, now is he? You told me I would lead this case, and I say no, not yet. We'll release the photo when I want the photo to be out there. For now we need to find out where he's been and what he's been up to. Knowing Cappelano, he's probably still here in town watching us and laughing, but what he doesn't know is that we know his face now."

"All right, Neil, have it your way," Mike said, "but if we get in trouble for this shit, it's all on you."

"And what if it works out and we catch him? Is that all on me too?"

"I didn't say that," Mike barked back

"You're an ass, Mike, but it's okay. Let's just catch this bastard. I could care less who gets credit when we get him. If you guys got the credit, Cappelano would go nuts. It might actually be fun."

"Anyway, what's the plan?!" asked Maria, jumping between Mike and me going at it.

I forwarded the photo to Mike and Maria's PDAs so they could show it to the people they would be interviewing today. I laid out a game plan for the next couple of hours; I informed them that as far as the rest of the FBI knew, they were taking the night off, and I was working solo since I had slept through the morning. We couldn't let on that we had information that no one else did. After last night—or early this morning, for that matter—Agent Dickerson and I finally realized we were stuck. It was a stalemate; we had no move. Our only option was to sit back and wait to see what Cappelano's next move was going to be. Of course, Agent Dickerson didn't know I had a photo of Cappelano that showed us what he looked like right now, giving us an upper hand over our target.

Think of my choice not to share the photo with the DC office, like playing a game of poker. Imagine there is one player who leads all players with the most chips. You're a distant second, but what the leader doesn't know is that you have a pair of pocket aces in your hand. You don't want to let that on to the other people around you, because the main player you are going after would back out and fold, not allowing you the move you wanted. But if you hold back and bluff a little bit, the rest of the players will play accordingly, building the pot, as well as pulling more chips in from the leader. Now all you have to do is time it right to make your big move to get the other guy to call on you, and if he does, then you have it hook, line, and sinker. That's all I'm doing with this photograph, just trying to get Cappelano to fall for the bluff. I guess that would make Dickerson one of the other poor schmucks at the table, holding only enough chips to fuck up the plan.

After hours of searching bars where Hendrickson had spent money, according to his credit card records, we had come up empty. We were about to give up, but we had one last bar to check, so we figured if this one didn't work out, we could just sit down for a bit, have a few drinks, and call it a night. As they say, you always find what you're looking for in the last place you look—but then again, why look after you found what you're looking for? As we turned the corner, we realized we were standing in front of our first stop, a bar called Tini's. It's a martini bar, go figure; martini bars always seem to have the corniest names. It was almost midnight, and the weekday night crowd was pretty thin. Tini's looked more like a weekend hot spot than a weekday chill bar, but oh well, it's the last bar that we knew

Bob had been to, at least from his charge accounts.

"Hey Mike, go talk to the manager over there, fill him in on what we're doing, and see if he's seen Cappelano or Hendrickson. Maria, I want you to go up to that surfer boy–looking bartender over there, and please don't be afraid to flirt; we need to get his attention."

"You want me to flirt? Who do you think I am?"

"An agent willing to do whatever it takes to track down a psychopathic killer—even some harmless and shameless flirting. Unless you're too chicken to do it."

"Oh, don't go down that road, we both know that's not the case. I'll see you guys in thirty minutes or so. Meet you back by the bathrooms."

"Neil, who are you going to talk to?"

"See that angry-looking girl sitting over there in the back smoking a cigarette? She's holding her paycheck and just came out of the back. I guarantee she's a bartender who can help. Meet you guys in thirty minutes."

I made my way over to a corner booth that looked like the general employee hangout for the moment and made my move on the girl. This is going to take a little bit of precision; since there are other people around, I might be able to get the group to help me out.

"Hey guys, can I ask you for a few minutes of your time? It won't take long; I'm just trying to track down a couple of old friends who have been in the DC area the past couple of weeks."

"Depends on who's doing the asking. If it's that fine brunette you came in with, I'll tell you anything."

"Shawn, shut up! Sorry for the guys. They are helpless dogs. What can we do for you? By the way, my name's Nyla."

"Thanks, Nyla. For the inquiring minds, I work for the FBI out of Detroit, and I'm trying to track down a couple of friends who are missing."

"When you say 'friends,' are you using that term loosely? I'm just guessing."

"Very perceptive, Nyla. It's Nyla, right?"

"Yeah. We'd be happy to help you out. What do these friends look like?"

"Here's a picture of one of them; his name is Bob. Anyone seen him in here?"

"Yeah, he's been here a few times in the past week. I remember him because he was hitting on me, and he didn't even have the decency to take off his wedding ring. His name was Henderson or Hendricks?"

"Close. Bob Hendrickson. How'd you know his last name?"

"He always had a tab, and it would get pretty big. You get used to knowing big spenders' names. It makes them feel special. What about your other friend?"

"Here's a photo of him. All I have is this picture on my phone. It's pretty clear, though."

"I haven't seen him in here. How about any of you guys?

Come on, speak up. You watch the door; you should see everyone that comes through here."

The hound dog previously referred to as Shawn took a reluctant glance at the photo. Then he squinted at it, looking closer. "Yeah, I saw that guy in here the other night, at the same time as your boy. They never sat together, but this guy was keeping a very watchful eye on Bob. I remember because this fine young lady was trying to get him to buy her a drink, and he wouldn't even acknowledge her, and I've never seen a guy ignore that girl. When guys ignore girls like that, it usually means trouble, so I made sure we had a guy watching him the rest of the night."

"Do you remember who you had watching him? It could really help me."

"Yeah, his name is 'Bear.' Well, at least that's what we call him. He's in the back cleaning out the keg cooler. I'll go grab him for you."

"Thanks, man."

I spent the next ten minutes talking to everyone at Tini's trying to get any other information I could get, but only Nyla and Shawn had something for me. I hope this "Bear" guy works out; I need to get a timeline for Cappelano watching Hendrickson, to figure out what his next move might have been. Timing is everything in this business; you could have the right tools for the job but be using them at the wrong time. I'm starting to notice Nyla's help is turning into blatant and obvious flirting.

Still, I'm kind of enjoying it right now. Hey, everyone loves it when their ego gets a little push every now and then. Just as we started to get into the conversation, Shawn came back with his buddy "Bear."

"I see why they call you Bear. Damn, you're a big fucker, aren't you? Where'd you play football?"

"How'd you know I played football? I played defensive tackle at West Virginia, but I grew up around here."

"Nice. You must have been a beast on the football field. Before I get off track anymore, can you tell me when this guy was in the bar, the night Shawn said you were watching him?"

"Yeah, that was four nights ago. But that wasn't the last time I saw the two of them in here at the same time. They were here again the very next night, and again two nights ago."

"Is there anything else you can remember, anything at all? Did they ever talk?"

"Yeah, but only the last time I saw them in here, so that would be two nights ago. The guy I was watching started to approach this Bob guy, and as I made my move to step in, he just walked up behind Bob and patted him on the back like they were friends. But by that point Bob was pretty wasted, so he probably didn't know who he was talking to. After that, the two of them started drinking together. They eventually called a cab and got out of there. I just thought they were a couple of gay guys. We get a lot of them out here, and I didn't think anything of it; you see it once, you've seen it a thousand times. I figured the guy I was watching was just trying to work up the nerve to start a conversation with that Bob guy."

"Thanks, man. Do you remember which way you saw the cab go, or what time?"

"No, not really, but I remember the cab company, and I know they take credit cards, if that helps."

"What's the name of the company?"

"DC Taxi. They're around here all the time. I can get you their number if you want."

"Thanks, Bear, that would be perfect. Here's my card. If you guys can think of anything else, just call me. Or if you get in a little trouble and you need a favor, all you have to do is hand this to the officer and you should be good to go."

"I appreciate that. Here's the phone number. Their central dispatch station is downtown."

"Thanks, guys. I'll be getting back to you later."

I struck gold; it's time to see how Maria and Mike are doing. From the looks of it, both of them are carrying on pretty decent conversations. Let's hope we can get matching stories to make sure everything pans out. I remember working in the bar scene, and a lot of the nights can blur into one; it becomes really hard to remember exact dates and times. Seeing that I finished up with my group, Mike started making his way toward me. Maria still looked to be pretty locked up with the surfer boy.

"How'd it go, Mike? Did you get anything?"

"Not a lot of details, but the manager remembers Bob

coming here every couple of nights since he moved down here."

"Anything about Cappelano?"

"He said he thinks that Bob left with him two nights ago and they got into a cab together. He wasn't positive, though. How about you? Any luck?"

"As a matter of fact, I have a bouncer that can put both Bob and Cappelano here on a couple of nights. He also said that it looked like Cappelano was watching Bob, getting ready to make a move. That's why he was keeping an eye on Cappelano; he was told to watch him by the head of security."

"Nice, so we have two people who can put Bob and Cappelano together and leave in a cab. The manager said it was a cab company called—"

"DC Taxi?"

"Yeah. I take it, that's what your guy said, too. Here comes Maria. Let's see what she got from model boy over there." Maria joined our huddle, looking like she'd aged an entire year in the past half hour. "So Maria, I was talking with Neil here, and we got some pretty good info. How about you? Did you get anything?"

"I couldn't get that guy to stop talking about having sex with me. Thanks for that, Neil, you jackass."

"Hey, don't blame me. I didn't know he would be worthless to us. Okay, well, maybe I had a feeling he might not be able to help us."

"Did you get the laugh you wanted? I hope you're happy. It took me thirty minutes to get away from that idiot. I mean, I've met some self-centered guys before, but that one took the cake."

"Well, sorry to hear about your luck, Maria, but Mike and I did get something worthwhile. The manager and one of the bouncers have Bob getting into a cab with Cappelano two nights ago. They said Bob was pretty drunk."

"Did you guys get anything else while I was over there in hell?"

"Mike didn't, but the bouncer I talked to said Cappelano had been keeping an eye on Hendrickson for a couple of nights. The head bouncer made him tail Cappelano because they were afraid he was going to start trouble. The bouncer thought that Cappelano was hitting on Bob and that he was trying to get him home with him. He was close, just wrong about Cappelano's intentions."

"Do you think Cappelano would simply play off flirtation with Bob to make it seem normal? Or maybe he did take Bob home for a little late-night romp before he killed him."

"Nice. Thanks for that image, Maria. Let's get out of here and call a cab from DC Taxi. We'll have the cab take us to their dispatch station so we can try and track down where Cappelano and Bob got dropped off."

"You lead and we'll follow," Mike said.

"Hey Neil, I just realized you never told us how you came by that photo of Cappelano."

"No, I didn't, Maria, and I don't plan on telling you just yet. I'll worry about it; for now, let's just try and find him."

Mike called us a cab as we waited outside the bar, and it didn't take much longer than a few minutes before it pulled up to the curb in front of us.

"Hi there. Can you take us to your central station?" I said.

"You mean the central train station?"

"No, take us to where your dispatch offices are."

"Sorry, buddy, I can't take anyone there. My boss will kill me if I'm not out making money."

"I don't think you understand," I said, flashing my ID. "We're with the FBI, and you need to drive us there. Got it?"

"Sir, yes, sir. Why didn't you just say so?"

The drive was a quick one, and the cabdriver didn't sit around and wait for us to pay him. He dropped us off across the street, told us where to go and who to talk to, and took off. He was genuinely scared about being around the office while on the clock; I can't wait to see what kind of lowlife asshole we'll be dealing with inside. This case is finally starting to pick up. Let's hope that we keep things rolling for the rest of the night.

20

*Son of a bitch, now I have all this information about
Cappelano, but none of it points me in any direction.*

The building was nothing more than an enclosed parking
garage with a few mechanic bays for the cabdrivers to tune up
and clean out their cars. It doesn't look like DC Taxi does
anything for their drivers except give them a place to store their
cabs and take a piece of the money they earn. As we made our
way toward the dispatch office, I noticed that it's just a few
computers and desks surrounded by a cage. It reminded me of
that TV show back in the day, I wish I could remember the name
of it. The other thing I noticed was that it was freezing inside.
The only heat seemed to be coming from the cage where the
manager was. They must really care about their employees if
they're only willing to heat the manager's cage. Can you sense
the sarcasm?

"Not what I expected, but then again, what is? Maria, you
and Mike go talk to the manager and see if you can track down
Bob's credit card. Let's hope it was used to pay the cab fare. If
not, go through all the records between one and two o'clock

that night. That's when the bouncer said the two of them left together."

"What are you going to do?"

"I'm going to talk to some of the guys around the garage. To find out if any of them have seen either Bob or Cappelano in their cabs." I'm trying to keep Maria and Mike at bay as long as possible because of all the issues that happened last time. I'm not going to settle for failure, but if I do fail, I don't want to look at someone else as the reason why.

"Okay. Just call us if you need anything, and we'll do the same."

The two of them made their way toward the cage to see what they could get out of the night supervisor, while I decided to call Ken to see what our boys have come up with since we last talked. Usually, when you get something like this photo, a lot more intel starts to find its way toward you. When it rains, it pours, as the old saying goes. Looks like I can't get a signal in here. I guess I'll have to make my way outside to make the call, and it's so freaking cold out there. Oh well, I'm a big boy.

"Ken, what's up? It's Neil. Any word from the guys in Mexico?"

"Yeah, they said they're working on something right now. It seems that Cappelano was doing some contract work for the drug cartels in Mexico, as a hit man. He made a big sum of money, from what they said. Now they're trying to track down a house or apartment that Cappelano might be keeping. I'll keep you posted. How's your search going?"

"Good. Thanks for the pictures. How much money are we talking about here?"

"Let's just say it looks like he was pretty busy. They said it's up in the tens of millions. He loves to kill, and now he's doing it for money."

"Son of a bitch. My phone's starting to die. I'll call you later when I get back to the hotel."

"No problem. Good luck, Neil."

If the guys in Mexico are able to find a place that Cappelano is keeping, that would be perfect; there's a good chance he'd return there if he felt threatened. If I have to, I know just the way to scare him up and get him to run for the border, for lack of a better phrase. I'll just keep my fingers crossed and hope the guys can find something. As for the moment, I should get back inside and do some digging around to see if anyone recognizes Cappelano's picture. I know it's a long shot, but so far that's all we have to work with.

I had to shut my phone off since my battery is almost dead. Lucky for me, I have another copy of Cappelano's photo in my pocket; I had time to print one-off in the business room at the hotel. It's not the best picture since it's on plain white paper, and the printer wasn't the greatest, but it's better than nothing. It looks empty in the DC Taxi garage, but I can hear some noise coming from one of the mechanic bays. It looks like there's someone here, though all I can see are a pair of legs in a jumpsuit sticking out from under a car.

"Excuse me. Can I ask you a few questions? I won't take too much of your time."

"Who's asking?"

A man in his late fifties slid out from under the car with a look that made me realize this wasn't going to be easy. At least I can try; I have to wait for Maria and Mike to finish up with the night supervisor anyway. The man had a face that had clearly seen some tough times, Judging by cuts and bruises on his knuckles, he was probably working two different jobs as a mechanic to help pay his bills, maybe for himself or maybe to help his kids get an education. Either way, he didn't look like much of a talker. The other thing I noticed was his shyness to say anything as I approached. There's a good chance he's not from around here, if you catch my drift.

"Agent Baggio, but you can just call me Neil. I'm not immigration, so don't worry, that's not why I'm here."

"I'm a US citizen, so I don't know what you're talking about. If you're not with the INS, who do you work for?"

"I work for the FBI, out of Detroit. I'm trying to track someone down, and I have witnesses that place the guy I'm looking for in one of this company's cabs."

"We pick up a lot of people, and we have a lot of cabs. Sorry, bro, but you're pretty much screwed unless you have every single driver from that night come in and talk to you, and even then, you probably won't get anything."

"I'll tell you what. A couple of my friends are working with your boss to see who picked our guy up and where they dropped him off. All I need to know is if you've ever seen this guy, the one here in the middle."

"He looks familiar, but I've seen a lot of faces, bro. Sorry, but that's all I got. I hope everything works out for you, but I can't tell you anything about him."

"All right, but it would be a damn shame if the next time you're out driving, you get pulled over, again and again, until your ass is in jail because I can do that if I feel like it. Perks of the job."

"That's fucking harassment. You can't do that."

"Watch me. Now would you like to rethink your answer? I know you've met this guy on more than one occasion, judging by the way you looked at the photo. I didn't even have to tell you which one he was in the photo since you were already focused on the middle guy. That's another thing about me—I can tell when assholes are trying to put one over on me. Now let's try this again."

The old grease monkey looked like he just bit into a lemon. Poor guy. He didn't want to talk, but he was going to. "All right, I met the guy a couple of times. But I haven't driven him in almost a week. He got in my cab at the airport and had me drive him around for two days following some guy around town. He paid me a lot of money, so I didn't say anything about it. For all I knew, he was working for the government."

"Do you remember where you picked him up? An address?"

"He had me pick him up on Capitol Hill every time, but it was always a different place. That's why I figured he worked for you guys."

"Thank you. If you think of anything else, here's my card."

Wow! I didn't think he was going to say anything else. I was just playing because I had some time to kill. All that stuff about harassing him with tickets. No one really does that, and besides, I have more important shit to worry about right now than messing with a cabbie just because he wouldn't talk. Usually, civilians come clean pretty fast when they're holding information. They don't like pissing off guys with a government badge. I can understand why. I mean, if you tick off a local cop, you can always move to a new town, but if you end up on the wrong side of a government official, it tends to be a little harder to get away from them. At least that's the perception.

Mike and Maria should be finishing up soon. I'll make a couple more passes around the garage and see what I can find, but it's likely I won't find anything else. I was lucky enough to get something out of the first guy I saw that almost never happens. If you get lucky enough to find something quickly, you might as well stop for the day, because chances are you're not going to get anything after that; that's just the way it works. An hour has gone by, and I haven't heard from Maria and Mike. Then again my phone's been off, so that could be why. As for the garage, there doesn't seem to be anyone else around to talk to. I'll just make my way down toward the cage and see if the guys are down there still. The garage is pretty eerie at night, with no one around and no lights on. Good thing I have my Glock on me and a flashlight so I can look around; both might come in handy. I can see the light of the cage through the dark garage, and from what I can tell, it looks like the guys are still there.

"Neil, where the hell have you been?" Mike shouted through the chain-link. "We've been trying to call you. Maria and I got something here—the name of the driver and where he dropped them off. He's on his way back to the station as we speak. He should be here shortly."

"Nice job, guys. I got a little bit of information myself. As for my phone, the battery is dying, so I had to turn it off. How'd you guys track down the driver?"

"They have a pretty decent system here," Maria said. "The drivers have to record the time and location of every pickup and drop-off. And there was only one pickup from one of their drivers at Tini's. Lucky for us."

That really *is* lucky for us. In fact, it seems too easy. I'm normally not this paranoid, but it's surprising that Cappelano would get a cab and leave a witness to him following Hendrickson around, and on top of it, use the same cab company to pick him up from the bar the night he grabbed Hendrickson. It's just not like him unless he was doing it on purpose, leaving me clues to find him. My honest opinion is that his ego is starting to consume itself, and he doesn't think he can ever get captured. To him, this is all a game that he's already won.

Just then, a cab pulled into the garage. I saw the night manager nod at Mike, as if to say *there's your guy.* As the driver shut off his lights and opened his door, I could start to see an outline of his features. He wasn't more than 150 pounds, barely standing five-five, a small man probably in his late forties.

"Hi. I take it you guys are the ones from the FBI? What can I do for you three?"

"Nice to meet you. My name's Neil; this is Maria and Mike. We'd like to ask you a few questions about the other night when you picked up this man and our colleague from Tini's. Is that all right with you?"

"No problem, I have a really good memory. Ask away, I'll help as much as I can."

I figured I would get basic answers from the cabdriver telling me he remembered picking them up and dropping them off, nothing more. But the driver wasn't kidding, he had an amazing memory. He described Cappelano perfectly, down to his physical mannerisms. He told us what we expected about Bob, saying that he was pretty much knocked out, fading into and out of consciousness.

"Is there anything else you can remember from that night? Anything you think might help that we haven't asked you about?"

"Actually, there was something kind of odd. The drunken guy—Bob, I think you said his name was—he was really drunk, but that's not the odd thing. What struck me as odd was that his friend pulled out what looked like a prescription bottle, shook out a pill, and told Bob to take it, saying it was aspirin. And last time I checked; you don't need a prescription to get aspirin."

"Can you describe what the pill looked like by any chance?"

"Sorry, I didn't get a look at the pill, just the bottle. And one more thing. I dropped them off at the hotel, like it says on my sheet. What it doesn't say is that I stayed out front of the hotel hoping to pick up another fare, and while I was there, I saw your two friends come back out minutes later."

"What do you mean, 'come back out'? I thought you said Bob was pretty much passed out."

"He was, but the other guy was helping him to a car that the valet guy pulled around. He threw Bob into the car and drove off. They headed toward Capitol Hill from the hotel."

"Thanks. Do you remember what kind of car it was?"

"It looked like your government-issue Crown Vic; I figured one of them worked for the government; that's usually the case around here. I really can't think of anything else."

"Thanks; you have no idea how much you helped. If you do think of anything else, here's my card. Thanks again for everything."

Son of a bitch, now I have all this information about Cappelano, but none of it points me in any direction. It just tells me what I already know: Cappelano has Hendrickson, and we're waiting to find out where his body is going to show up, if at all. The three of us asked the driver for a ride back to our hotel, seeing as he was heading back out. On the way there, the three of us sat quietly, trying to think of the next step, where we might go from here. As for now, we need to get to our rooms and catch some sleep so we can start tomorrow anew.

"All right, guys, it looks like we're here," Maria said. "I'm going up to my room to pass out."

"I second that, Maria. I'm exhausted," Mike said. "We weren't lucky enough to stay in bed until two in the afternoon, like someone we know."

"Shut up, guys. I didn't get to bed until seven in the morning, so I guess it's an even trade. Go get some sleep, I'm going to change and go for a swim to clear my head."

We said our good nights and went our separate ways. Maria and Mike are probably going to fall asleep pretty fast. As for me, I'm going to talk to the head of security here at the hotel. Since this is where Hendrickson was staying, I don't have too far to go—lucky for me, since I don't have a car. Before I head back out, I need to grab my backup cell battery in my room and charge my other one. It's not uncommon for me to go days without having a chance to charge my phone, so I always have a couple of backup batteries with me when I travel. Hopefully I can get something that will pay off and not just information that reaffirms what we already know.

21

Even though I ended up in the emergency room and had to get a tetanus shot in my ribs . . . I was the lucky one.

You'd be surprised how much you can get done in the middle of the night. There are no lines, nothing really going on, you can get to and from anywhere pretty fast. That, and nocturnal people are usually too tired to care if what they are telling you could get them in trouble.

The stylish girl at the front desk called the hotel's head of security for me; apparently he's a late-night guy just like I am. I'm hoping his surveillance tapes go back a week so I can try and catch Cappelano and Hendrickson in the hotel the other night, and maybe even get the license plate of the car they left in. I've had luck so far on the first two hunches, so why not go for the hat trick? It's almost three o'clock early Wednesday morning, and I'm waiting for this guy to show up. I hope he doesn't give me any shit about getting my hands on those tapes. I don't need another "by the book" idiot on my hands.

Just then I noticed a woman in business attire walking at a pretty swift pace toward me. It's a little late to be dressed for work unless you're working right now.

"Hi, my name is Angela Strong. You must be Neil. Come this way."

"Good to meet you, Angela. I was wondering how long you guys hold your surveillance tapes."

"We hold them for a month. The files are kept on a computer; all of our surveillance is digital, not taped. It helps us to keep more video on backup."

"Is there any chance I can look at them? I'm trying to track the movements of a colleague."

"I know who you are and what you're doing in DC. I've already been contacted by Agent Dickerson. I uploaded the last two weeks' worth of surveillance onto ten discs. I was told you have a laptop with you. You should be able to review them in your room."

"Then where are we going, if you don't mind me asking?"

"We're going to the hotel bar. I need a drink, and since you called me at three a.m., I'm guessing you could use something to take the edge off."

"Isn't the bar closed by now?"

"Yes it is, but that's one perk of being the head of security— I can open it. I heard you were never one for the rules. Did I hear wrong?"

"Glad to hear my reputation precedes me."

Angela is what you would expect from a head of security in DC, even at a hotel. She was ex-military, for starters. She gave me a brief history of her tours and how her family has been in security or the military for generations. I can assume this isn't the job she dreamed of, but it pays well, and the stress is low. Compared to dodging rockets in Baghdad, at least.

"Give me a second to light a couple of candles. Turning on the lights will make people think there's someone in here. I don't want my people thinking they can slack off because I'm here with you."

"I understand completely. So how long have you been working here at such a fancy place?"

"Before we start talking, what are you drinking tonight?"

"Jack on the rocks, with a lemon. Please."

"A whiskey man; I like that. I'm a fan of Johnny more than Jack. But I won't hold that against you."

"Red or Black Label?"

"Is there really a choice? I mean, come on. To answer your question, I've been working at the hotel for about two years now. It's not what I saw myself doing for a living, but the money is good, and it's in the right town."

"Right town? Do you have aspirations to do more than work in hotels?"

"What do you think? Of course I do. I'd love to run the security for one of the government buildings. It's really hard, though."

"Why? Because you're not military anymore? Or because you're not working for the government already?"

"No. Because I'm not a man. It's sad that in 2005, I still have that being held against me."

"Plus you're attractive. I'm sure that makes some people underestimate their abilities as a security specialist. It's sad but true."

"I never thought my looks would hinder my ability to do a job. But my whole life I've been told I can't do things because I have a pretty face. It's really annoying."

"Yeah, I can only imagine. So are you from the DC area originally, or just here for the career?"

"Both, actually. I grew up just over the state line in Arlington, Virginia. And I've always had a liking for the DC area; that's why I chose the field I'm in. At least that's one of the reasons."

"Cool; so you're pretty much a local girl. Do you know your way around the city? I could use a guide while I'm here to help me with this case. And you could use helping the FBI as a reference."

"I think I could do that for you. I've got the next two days off. Before I forget, here's my card. It has my personal cell phone number on it. Just give me a call tomorrow afternoon. I'll be glad to help."

"Don't worry, I won't call too early. I'll probably be up all night again, more than likely going through the surveillance files."

"That reminds me. Let me make a call. I'll just have one of

the security guys run the discs up to your room so you don't have to worry about it."

"Thanks for everything. You've been a gracious host."

While Angela was on the radio with one of her guys, I couldn't help but think where this case is going and how it's changing me. I'm becoming self-destructive at times, trying to keep people at bay so that when this all falls around me, I'll have no one to blame. There were moments during my time visiting with Angela that I caught myself flirting, trying to distract myself from a failure I felt was coming. Then it started to hit me—all my self-sabotaging behavior, this pattern of working tirelessly, then playing it loose almost as a defense mechanism. The conversation with her and her knowledge of the area have been great, but I need to get to work and focus.

"Sorry about that. My guys said they'll have it up there within the hour when they're on their rounds. So I guess we've got at least an hour to kill. Do you have anywhere to run off to?"

"Can't say that I do. I'm pretty happy with where I'm at for the moment. Good whiskey, good company, and no one around. I don't see any reason to go anywhere."

"I'll agree with the good company, but I don't know about the 'good whiskey' part. But that's neither here nor there. So how did you end up back in the FBI? Yes, I did my research, I know a little bit about everything that went down. I have a few friends in the bureau."

"Well, I'd rather not talk about it. As much as I appreciate the drink, I really need to get to reviewing that footage." It came out rougher than expected, but I was fighting myself as I was speaking. Part of me was flirting and wanted to see where this could go; the smart part of me was telling me to get out of there.

"Oh. I understand. Well, if you need anything, I'd be happy to help. I'm just a phone call away."

"Thanks, Angela."

I headed back to my room, and in just short of an hour, one of Angela's team members showed up with the discs I needed. Now I can pore through this new information and allow myself to imagine what it would be like to catch Cappelano and stop this madness. It felt great for a few minutes, but then reality and fear set back in. Distractions aside, I need to get these discs loaded into my laptop to make sure I get all the feeds. Technology is great, but it's not always fast. It will probably take me a couple of hours to load everything into my computer; let's see what's on TV. It looks like I'm going to be able to enjoy this process while watching *Road House*, one of my favorite movies of all time. If you haven't seen it, I suggest that you rent it today. This movie reminds me of the bar fights I used to get involved in when working as a bouncer through college. One of my favorite fights was when I was working at this two-story club called DJ's. That night will always stand out in my mind because I still have the scar to remind me of it.

It was a couple weeks before Christmas, and it was starting to get really busy with the holidays, which means people getting drunk and doing stupid things. On this night, though, it was a guy on a mission to piss someone off. He was fresh out of jail and looking for a fight. He wasn't big by any means; he was quite small, probably five-seven, 160 pounds, with a tattoo across the back of his neck that said "Sinner." He had bad news written all over him, and I just knew there was going to be a problem with him that night. About an hour or two after he came in, he started breaking our pool cues. Normally I could care less because we get them for free, but he wasn't even breaking them in the middle. He was breaking them up at the tip, where it's nice and thin.

I was the head of security at the time, and I remember approaching him calmly, asking him to stop breaking the pool cues. All he did was look at me and ask me why he should stop. I told him that you don't go into someone's place of business and start breaking things and not expect them to get upset about it. Then he got in my face and said, "Make me stop," to which I replied that he needed to leave right now, one way or another. Right at that moment one of my bouncers saw what was going on and stepped between us. About two weeks earlier, I had thrown a guy off the second-story balcony for trying to sell drugs in my club, so my bouncer didn't feel like having another incident on our hands. I went downstairs and let my guy handle the situation any way he wanted, as long as that asshole was thrown out of the club. About twenty minutes went by, and I ended up at the door training one of our new guys on the ability to catch fake IDs. Then our friend with the tattoo came up to the door screaming at me for kicking him out. If that wasn't bad enough, he started pounding on the glass doors, trying to break them, which is when I stepped outside, and the night took a turn for the worse.

After a few minutes of him jawing at me, I looked at his friends and told them to get him out of here before I called the cops. Then he lunged at me, trying to tackle me, and this is where I made my mistake. I put him in a headlock under my left arm, so that his head was right next to my rib cage, under my arm. As I tried to calm him down, he proceeded to turn his head and bite me as hard as he could, breaking through the skin. It took me a moment before I had a grasp of what he was doing. It's not every day that a grown man bites you. His friends looked at me and started yelling at their friend to stop, but he wouldn't, so I did the only thing I could: I reared back and let his jaw up with one punch, breaking and dislocating his jaw in three places. It was one of the nastiest things I've ever seen in my life, just seeing his jaw hanging there from his head. Even though I ended up in the emergency room and had to get a tetanus shot in my ribs, which hurt like hell, I was the lucky one. He ended up having to get his mouth wired shut for almost nine months while it healed, not to mention a couple of metal plates to rebuild his jaw. I felt bad for him at first, but hey, he was biting me.

Seeing as the movie is almost over and my clock is showing

6:47 a.m., I think it's time for me to go to bed. I uploaded six of the ten discs and started the facial recognition program the bureau put on this laptop for me; it should be pretty busy for the next couple of hours. I'll finish uploading everything after a couple of hours of sleep, since I won't be able to sleep in past eleven. I need to get a lot done today. There's a lot of ground to cover and a lot of footage to look through.

22

Agent Dickerson . . . has been in the FBI for almost twenty years, so he knows that a big case like this one takes a lot of patience.

I finally rolled over and pulled myself out of bed, and to my surprise, it looks like the facial recognition program needed more time to load into this laptop. Though convenient, the technology isn't quite there for what we need. It's slow, but then again, justice and the law process are slow, and we wouldn't want it any other way—fast can be inaccurate and sloppy. This process will give me plenty of time to get ready and multitask, such as take a shower and get ready. Hey, at least we're past the days of dial-up when you'd have time to run to the corner store and back before your picture would load.

There really is nothing like a cold shower to wake you up in the morning. However, right now I'm still running hot water to keep me relaxed. Before I get out, I'll turn it to freezing cold water to give me that shot in the arm I need to get going today.

Holy shit, that's cold; even though I know it's coming, I still freak out when that first burst of cold water runs down my back. I guess I should shave, since I'm starting to look pretty bad with this scruff, not to mention I haven't so much as combed my hair since we've arrived in DC. I might even dress up a little bit today. I'll probably just half-ass it and throw my jeans on with a T-shirt, suit jacket, and my dress shoes.

Time to go change out the CDs, so hopefully I can get out of here by noon. I really need to get a jump start on today. I want to go check out blind spots in the surveillance as well as the locations where the cabdriver said he picked Cappelano up. That might help me to centralize a location or at least a comfort zone for Cappelano. Without realizing it, almost everyone has a comfort zone when it comes to public places, as well as recurring habits within those places. With killers, we can use this theory to track down a place of residence or an area where they might look for their next victims. I may not be able to focus on Cappelano's habits. Still, I can focus on Hendrickson's habits, knowing that Cappelano was probably following him for several days. Thanks to credit cards and bank statements, I should be able to piece together the past week or so when Bob was alive. Let's face it, he's probably dead, even though we haven't found a body yet.

In the case of Cappelano, it's a safe bet that he tried to stay within Capitol Hill because he knew Hendrickson would be in the same area. Bob didn't know anyone out here, and he was staying at a hotel only blocks from where he was working. This narrowed Hendrickson's comfort zone dramatically, making it that much easier for Cappelano to keep tabs on him. More than likely, Bob didn't go to a variety of places. In fact, he probably kept a routine schedule to help him get acquainted with the area and build as many relationships outside of work as he could. Most people, when in a new place or location, will keep a very strict routine without even thinking of it. We do this because we like familiarity and we like to be recognized. If we visit the same places over and over, soon people will recognize us and start to remember us, making us feel a little more at home, or at least a little more comfortable. It's this common human trend that made it quite simple for Hendrickson to be a target. The move to DC was probably the worst thing to happen to Bob for many reasons, and a streak of good luck to someone like Cappelano.

Imagine for a moment you were observing the behaviors of an eagle, an animal known for covering a lot of territory. Eagles will become extremely familiar with the territory in which they live so that they can become efficient hunters. If you were to take that very same eagle from its territory and put it in a new one, the eagle would limit itself until it became comfortable with its new surroundings. We as a people are very similar; this phenomenon made Hendrickson a sitting target for Cappelano.

It looks like the discs are all done copying to my hard drive, and now I can start running the facial recognition program to cover all the files. It should be done in a couple of hours; I'll check back around dinnertime. As for now, I'm going to take a ride out to Capitol Hill as well as walk around to all of the local spots Hendrickson frequented, or at least the ones I can tell he frequented from his credit cards. It's amazing that something we look at as an easier way to pay for things actually puts us in danger in ways we weren't before they came out.

Credit cards aren't just bad if you're not financially stable, as the interest can bury you in debt that can take years to escape. They're also bad because almost anyone can hack our identities nowadays, find out our spending patterns, and run up charges in our names. Stealing a person's credit card information is easier than you'd think; a lot of the people who do it are garbage divers. It may sound strange, but our garbage tells our whole story. Think of what you've thrown away this week, from financial statements, bills, receipts—almost anything you can think of is in your trash, and someone can get to it.

It's time to make my way to Capitol Hill to map out Hendrickson's comfort zone. This will give me a better idea of where to canvass for information that might help me track down Cappelano's whereabouts. But first I needed to call the DC bureau office and place an order.

"Hello, is Agent Dickerson there? This is Agent Baggio."

"Yes, one minute. He's been expecting your call."

"Thank you."

"Neil, Agent Dickerson here. Getting another late start

today, I see?"

"Not really, I was up until seven this morning working through surveillance footage. I'll fill you in on it in a couple of hours. Are you going to be at the office around three this afternoon?"

"I can make sure that I am. What do you need?"

"I need to get a blown-up map of the DC area; I'm talking about something extremely large. I guess a computer map will work for now, but it has to have all the local businesses on it."

"No problem. I can get you both, just to be safe. Want to tell me where this is going?"

"I want to build a comfort zone for Bob Hendrickson. Knowing Cappelano's habits as a hunter, I know he would want to be in the same area as Hendrickson at all times. Even when he wasn't tailing him, just to build up appearances around town for when he makes his move."

"Makes sense to me. I'll have one of the agents go through all of Hendrickson's transactions since he's been down here and map everything out for you."

"Thanks. That will be a huge help. I'll see you around three."

"No problem, Baggio. We'll be here; take your time."

Take your time? That's odd. Usually there's more of a sense of urgency in situations like this. Then again, Agent Dickerson—or "Slick," as he's called around the office—has been in the FBI for almost twenty years, so he knows that a big case like this one takes a lot of patience. I have to confess; I didn't think I'd be working with anyone like Slick down here. He's a good guy with a lot of wisdom to share, and I'm glad I've gotten a chance to work with him. He's giving me a little hope in the FBI. Not a lot of hope, but enough to make a difference.

The cab ride up to Capitol Hill was a short one, which was lucky for me since I didn't grab a lot of cash before I left. It was still snowing outside, but at least it's not a blizzard out here, just a light dusting coming down on my head. The streets are plowed, and there's ice melt on the sidewalks. Actually, it's quite beautiful outside, especially with all of the white buildings, definitely a sight to be seen. I think I'm going to take a picture with my camera and send it to Sheila to let her and Carol Lynn know I'm okay, since I haven't talked to them since I got down here. The vibrations in my pocket feel like a phone call. Who could it be?

"Agent Baggio here. Who may I ask is calling?" I said jokingly.

"It's Maria. What's going on, Neil? Mike and I were following up on some leads we got from the cab company yesterday. How's your search going?"

"I just started it. I was up until seven this morning. I'm running a facial recognition program back in my room, trying to find Cappelano on the cameras at the hotel. The head of security was nice enough to give me the surveillance from the days when Hendrickson was staying there."

"That's a lot of video to process. Any luck so far?"

"Nothing that I know of. I spent most of my time just loading the files into my laptop so I could run the program while I was out and about today. Why don't you and Mike meet me back at the bureau office around three this afternoon?"

"We can do that. Do you need us to bring anything?"

"Nope. I'll call you if I can think of anything, though."

I know that Ken and I have trained our crew to be a well-oiled machine, but I can't help but constantly compare them to the way the bureau has taken the initiative out of their people, especially once they get higher up. They've put so much work into getting where they are, they slow down a bit once they're there. That's the nice thing about dealing with my guys at CB, Inc.; all I have to do is tell them what I want, and they'll figure out where to go next. They don't need me to hold their hand along the way.

It seems like Maria is afraid to lose me again like the bureau is afraid to lose me again. They are waiting for me to make every decision, and I can't tell if it's because they trust me, or if they are trying to put it all on my plate if it goes bad. Ever feel like someone is waiting for you to make a move so they can follow suit? That's how I feel. It's like the bureau is waiting for me to make my move on Cappelano, to ensure that all collateral damage is put on my shoulders. I guess it doesn't help that I'm keeping the bureau in the dark with the photos my men pulled in Mexico. Speak of the devil, Ken's calling on my cell.

"Hey Ken, how's everything back in Detroit?"

"Nothing too major here. But down in Mexico, that's a different story."

"Don't toy with me. What did the guys find down there?"

"They found Cappelano's house, Neil. From what the locals are saying, he built the house in 2000 and has lived there ever since. The guys also said that the people down here know Cappelano very well, but they know him as 'Señor Costa'; it's his alias down here. They're going to do some more checking and see when the last time Cappelano was there. I'll get back to you when I have more."

"Thanks, Ken, you and the guys are kicking ass. I'll talk to you later; I have some things to get in order here in DC."

I think it's almost time to make my move. I need to flush Cappelano back into hiding. Normally when you're hunting someone, you try to get them *out of* hiding and into the open. But if you already know where they're hiding, it makes a very big difference in strategy. And I know just the way to send him back to Mexico. Soon, very soon, I'll have to taint his name, ruin his legacy, or at least the legacy he believes he is leaving.

Capitol Hill was beautiful, but I didn't get anything done; the only useful news I received out here was the call from Ken. I should go to the office and continue as if I haven't gotten any new information at all. The FBI would ruin everything by wanting to raid Cappelano's house, and the Mexican government would probably keep us from raiding the place anyway. Time to get creative.

Hopefully, the ride back to the office will give me time to think. I even turned off my phone for a while to keep my head clear of distractions. If only the cabdriver had taken a shower in the past week or so, I might have been able to think a little better, but that stench was just killing me. I doubt it's just bad hygiene, my bet is he's working double if not triple shifts trying to earn money for his family. I guess it's too late to focus on anything since I'm in front of the FBI building now. I tipped the cabbie, got out, and made my way upstairs to the fourth floor, where Dickerson, Maria, and Mike would be waiting for me; at least that was the plan.

"Hey Neil, you're actually early. That's a rarity these days. Did you find what you were looking for at Capitol Hill?"

"Can't say that I did, Slick. How about you guys? Have you narrowed down an area where Hendrickson lived?"

"Yes, and you were pretty close in your assessment. It seems that Bob didn't go outside of a four-block radius unless he had to. He only changed his routine with his walking distance from the hotel when he had to go to work. We have it up on the screen in the other room."

Dickerson and I made our way to the conference room where Maria and Mike were working with a younger man. Let me rephrase that—a kid, probably an intern. The computer screen was projected onto a nice big pulldown screen on a wall, to make it easier for all of us to look at it. From the looks of it, Dickerson wasn't kidding, Hendrickson's brief, tragic stay in the nation's capital was centered on just four city blocks.

"Hey guys, nice work on the map. How much of his credit card activity do you have up there?"

"Actually, all of it," Maria said. "Mike and I are cutting out some of his visits because they were one-offs, or were made for the job, which would force him outside of his comfort zone for work, not because he wanted to. We are getting a little help from this first-year agent." The kid nodded at me with one of those polite half smiles. A real go-getter. When I was his age, I was getting bitten by drunks for a living.

The five of us spent the rest of the day and night going through the map, breaking down every nook and cranny of the area we had mapped out until we had a small enough search area that we could knock out in a day. There were a few hotels and apartment complexes in our target area. Luckily for us, the majority of the buildings were office high-rises and commercial buildings, which made our search even easier.

"All right, Slick, this is how we'll do it tomorrow. You and your guys will hit all of the commercial buildings and apartment complexes, while Maria, Mike, and I will cover all the smaller places where the residents might have noticed more. Since you have the numbers, you can cover more ground. Sound good?"

"Sounds good to me. Tomorrow morning at eight, we'll all meet back here and go over the plan one more time, and I'll have you brief the agents who will be working with us tomorrow."

"Anything to add, guys?" I said, trying to get Mike or Maria to offer any insights of their own.

"No, I think we covered everything we needed to for tonight," Maria said. "How about you, Mike?"

"I can't really think of anything. If I do, I'll make sure and call you, Neil."

"Smart-ass," said Maria, once again jumping in to diffuse the rising tension. "Joking aside, let's get out of here. It's almost midnight, and tomorrow is going to be a big day."

Agent Dickerson went back to his office and got his things ready, while the three of us decided to walk back to the hotel and get some fresh air after being cooped up in those offices for six hours. Tomorrow is a make or break for us. If we come up empty, I might have to push my hand sooner than I wanted to. If this were a game of Texas hold 'em, I would have just seen the flop, and now I'm waiting to see what comes up next. If it's not a card I can use, I might have to bluff and go all in. It might be the only shot I have at catching Cappelano.

I got back to the room to find the laptop had finished searching the discs and came up inconclusive for any facial recognition, but there are hours of surveillance footage that I can still sift through manually. I started to look through everything, but after a few hours I realized it was going to be a bust. Even if Cappelano had gone inside the hotel, he would have concealed himself enough or turned from the cameras. So it's time to get some rest and work on better options. I sent an email with a link to all the footage for the guys back at the Detroit office to continue working on, just in case they find something.

23

It seems as though the first stop of the morning was going to be a view into the rest of our day. It was almost noon, and the three of us had come up empty.

I don't know how, but I actually fell asleep at a decent time last night. It might have been the late-night visit from Maria that wore me out, or it could have been the fact that I'm so mentally drained right now I can barely think. Either way, I couldn't care less. The important thing is that I got a good six hours of sleep last night. Right now I'm sitting in a conference room about to give a briefing to all of the agents helping out on the canvass this morning.

"And now I'll let Agent Neil Baggio fill you in on everything we'll be covering today," Dickerson said to his team. "Neil? Come on up."

"Hello, everyone. I'm sure we all know the seriousness of what we are about to do, and how important it will be to stay focused. We've narrowed the search down to four square blocks, and we've narrowed *that* down to specific areas that might interest Cappelano based on his profile. With the number of agents we have today, we should be able to cover everything. All of you will be handed a packet with the full list of canvassing targets, with individual orders for you and your group to follow, including maps and designated areas. If you have any questions or come upon any information, my cell phone number and those of Maria Garcia and Mike Ponecelli are on the last page of the handout. Good luck everyone, and be careful. We don't know what to expect out there."

That went a little easier than I had expected. Luckily for me, it was a cut-and-dried presentation. I was tempted to hand out the new photo of Cappelano that myself, Maria, and Mike have, but I knew it would end up in the wrong hands and ruin the element of surprise. The renderings are close enough to what Cappelano actually looks like; most people don't remember a complete face.

I don't expect anyone to remember seeing him one time, but if he had frequented a place more than once—as regularly as Hendrickson did—then there's a good chance that someone may have remembered him. But that's also assuming he was interacting with the people in the area where we're searching. If he was just following Hendrickson and keeping to himself, chances are that nobody will remember seeing him. Without a reason to remember seeing Cappelano, virtually no one in the area will recall seeing him, even if they passed him on the street regularly. It's about the emotions of an event that make the memory stand out; basic interactions are hard to remember. If someone almost gets hit by a car or run over by someone on a bike, it's an event that startled you. There's an emotion attached to it, creating a strong memory that you can draw from later. Without that emotion it's hard for the memory to form.

I remember in college watching a video that dealt with eyewitness testimony; I believe it came from one of those nightly national news shows. It featured a professor who was doing research on the topic at one of the Ivy League schools. During one of his lectures, without his students knowing ahead of time, he had a man run in from outside of the class, grab his briefcase, and run back out of the classroom. Just after the man left, the professor asked the class if the man had a goatee or if he was wearing a hat. He didn't tell the students anything, he just asked them if he had those characteristics about him. What he didn't tell them was that the thief didn't have a goatee *or* a hat on.

Shortly after the exercise, the professor brought the students into another room one by one and showed them a photo lineup. Interestingly enough, there was a picture of a student from that class in the array. It was removed from the lineup when that student was in the room to do the ID. There were also photos where a man was wearing a ball cap and had a goatee, as well as just a goatee or just a hat. The disturbing findings were that the majority of the students (more than 80 percent of them, if I remember correctly) picked the wrong guy, and 60 percent of the incorrect identifications were of the guy with a goatee and a hat. Memory is an amazing thing. When you're a witness to something like a robbery, your brain absorbs as much information as possible, but without proper training, it usually will remember useless information, especially if someone asks you leading questions, as the professor had done with his students shortly after the thief ran out.

This brings me to the point that I doubt we'll find anyone who just remembers seeing Cappelano. It will have to be someone who remembers seeing Cappelano because of something that happened. For example, if Cappelano was tailing Hendrickson at a coffeehouse and he spilled his coffee, or he had an extremely odd or detailed order that he got several times, that would help a witness remember seeing him. Otherwise he would be just another face in a crowd.

"Hey Neil, where do you want to start? Any ideas?"

"Let's see how about we start at the farthest point from the agency and work our way back toward it. Sound good? How about you, Mike? You've been quiet since we got to DC. Any ideas?"

"Actually, I was thinking of hitting all the places that close early first, so if we get caught up, we can hit up the others later with no problem."

"Have you already done the research, so we know when all of these places are closing? Judging by your demeanor, I'm guessing you've got a plan all set and ready to go."

"As a matter of fact, I do. I couldn't sleep last night, so I called around and got the operating hours of all the places on our list and then arranged them in the most efficient manner distance-wise."

"Then let's get going. What's first on the list?"

"A place just up the road called Vic's Diner. They're only open until four p.m., and they only serve breakfast and lunch."

"Sounds good. I could use some breakfast to start off the day. You guys game for getting some grub while we're there?"

"No problem with me, I could go for an omelet. How about you, Maria? You game?"

"Food? Count me in."

It seems as though the first stop of the morning was going to be a view into the rest of our day. It was almost noon, and the three of us had come up empty. From the few conversations I've had with Dickerson, nobody on his team had come up with anything either. Mike explained to Maria and me that the next stop was a little coffee shop right up the road. It wasn't too far from the hotel Hendrickson was staying at, and from the looks of his credit receipts, he stopped here almost every morning before work, which means if we are going to find anything, this is going to be a good spot to start. If only we started here and not Vic's Diner, although that breakfast was pretty damn good.

"This looks like the place," Mike said. "Let's get inside. I'm freezing my ass off."

"I second that one," Maria said. "I still don't understand why you wanted to walk everywhere, Neil. We would get more done if we drove."

"Hendrickson walked almost everywhere; that's why it was so easy for Cappelano to follow him. He wasn't driving anywhere unless he had to. So if we are going to get into the mind-set of Hendrickson and Cappelano, we need to be walking, not driving. As for the coffee shop, you two go inside. If they have a white chocolate mocha, I'd like one."

"Where do you think you're going?" Mike said. "You're not coming in with us?"

"Nope. You and Maria can go inside and ask around. I'm going to go across the street to that diner. See if anyone remembers seeing Cappelano in there."

"All right, you're the boss," Maria said. "We'll see you when we see you."

I hope I'm not the only one out of the three of us who noticed that the coffee shop had a big window. With couches and chairs in it that looked directly into the window seats of the diner across the street. It would be a perfect place for Cappelano to wait for Hendrickson every morning; no one would think anything of it. The diner's staff and regulars would just think Cappelano was an early riser who was killing some time before work. As for Hendrickson, he wouldn't even see Cappelano across the street. Let's cross our fingers and hope we find someone who remembers seeing Cappelano.

"How are you doing today, sir?" the hostess greeted me as I walked in. "Will there be just one of you dining with us this morning?"

"Actually, I'm here for a different reason. Is your manager here?"

"Is there anything I can help you with?"

"It's nothing about the restaurant; don't worry. I just need to talk to your manager about something real quick."

"No problem. I'll go get Rick. Give me one second."

Rick? That's an older name. Most people you meet with the name Rick are older. Usually, thirty years old will be the youngest someone will be with the name Rick; it's just not used as much as it used to be when it comes to naming sons. I can see him making his way toward me; he really is a Rick, if that really makes sense. In my mind it does, and that's all that matters right now. He's probably in his early forties, close to 270 pounds, and not very tall, maybe five-nine. Needless to say, he's a very stocky man.

"Hi, I'm Nick, the manager. What can I do for you?"

Oh, she said Nick, not Rick. I don't know if that really matters, but right now I'm overthinking so much that I'm analyzing this man based solely on his name and the first sentence he just sent my way. It's a bad habit I have, psychoanalyzing people the very instant I meet them. I'll even analyze total strangers based on their posture and the way they interact with others. I know I need help, at least a hobby or something.

"Hey, Nick, nice to meet you. My name is Agent Baggio. I'm working a case for the FBI out of Detroit, and it's brought us to DC. Do you mind if I ask you and your employees a few questions?"

"No problem; we're pretty slow right now. As long as you can do it within the hour before we get our lunch rush, I don't see why not."

"Is there anywhere I can talk to everyone in private? Maybe an office or something. I don't want people to think they can't tell me something because you or another employee might hear them. This is very important."

"Yeah, you can use my office in the back. No problem."

"All right. How about I start with you, since we'll be going back there together?"

"Sounds good. What's this about? Can I ask?"

"I'll let you know in your office. I don't want anyone to hear us talking; it could mess up people's memories of what I am going to ask about. I need everyone's mind to be free of suggestions."

"I'll make sure no one talks to each other about their interviews with you, Agent Baggio."

Both Nick and I quickly addressed the employees on what we were going to do with the interviews. I also made sure both of us stressed that no one should talk to each other until this whole thing was over. I needed everyone's memories to be free from suggestion and interference. First up was Nick himself; he turned out to be pretty helpless, but I had guessed that from the start. He didn't seem like a front of the house type of manager, but instead more of the "hang out in his office all day playing computer games" type. I had noticed when we entered his office that he had shortcuts to a couple of different games on his computer. Just before he shut off the screen, probably to keep me from seeing what I had already caught.

Next up was the cook. Not surprisingly, he hadn't seen Cappelano around, since the only time he was out of the kitchen was when he went out the backdoor to have a cigarette, so needless to say, he was a bust. I spent the next ten minutes talking to the busboys and other kitchen help. After that was Florence, a server in her midsixties, and for an old bird, she was still working it. You could tell in her earlier days she was stunning; hell, if I were twenty years older, I might ask her out. Florence noticed Cappelano's photo right away and shouted "Egg whites, dry wheat toast, and a cup of coffee!" as soon as she saw it. She couldn't remember his name, but she did remember he was in there almost every morning, from five until seven or eight. She said he was usually her only customer, and he would generally get up and leave without saying good-bye when he was finished.

I spent a good twenty minutes talking to Florence about Cappelano's habits, from his overall fidgety nature to his incessant note-taking. She brought up a lot of things about him that most people don't notice; I could tell she was a very observant person. Florence also said she learned quickly to leave him alone and not talk to him very much. He always looked busy and rarely liked small talk. She said he always sat in the same seat, ordered the same thing, and usually paid his tab before he even got his food. She thought nothing of it except that he might not like to be bothered. ("Some people prefer their own company," she told me.) I was just happy that I found someone who could place Cappelano in the same vicinity as Hendrickson, even if Maria and Mike have no luck at the coffee shop finding anyone who saw Cappelano. If they can place Hendrickson there at the same time, I can place Cappelano here, and it will help our case a lot.

"Thanks, Florence, you've been a great help. I wish I could tell you more, but he's an old friend, and I've been trying to track him down for some time."

"I know that's not why, but I'll assume there's a reason why you're not telling me the truth." As I said, she was pretty damn observant. "Good luck finding him. Do you happen to have a card, so I can call you in case he comes back?"

"I like the way you think, Florence. Thanks again for everything. If you think of anything else, just call me."

I spent the next twenty minutes finishing up with the rest of the employees who were there, knowing they probably weren't going to help me, at least not like Florence had. But I still needed to follow through just in case someone remembered seeing him in here, even if they didn't wait on him. I wonder how Mike and Maria are doing at the coffee shop. I guess I'll just walk over there and see what's up. Just as I made my way across the street, I saw Mike and Maria heading out and making their way toward me. I waved them to stop and wait, since I was already halfway across the street. I know that technically I am jaywalking, but if any local cop gives me grief about it, I'll just flash my FBI badge; high card wins, as they say.

"Hey guys, how was your luck at the coffee shop? Get anything we can work with?"

"We didn't get anything on Cappelano, no one remembers seeing him there, but pretty much *everyone* remembered Hendrickson," Maria said. "It seems he was very sociable at the coffee shop; almost everyone had a story about him being there."

"I was just as surprised as Maria. From what everyone told me about Hendrickson, he was never the social butterfly that everyone there was describing. I guess he took the move to DC as an opportunity to reinvent himself. How about you? Did you have any luck at the diner?"

"I almost gave up, but there was a sweet lady who remembered Cappelano very well. In fact, she described him to a T. She said he was there almost every morning for the last two weeks from five until seven or eight. She also said he would usually pay his tab before he even had his food, which would make sense if he was tailing Hendrickson. He couldn't waste time waiting to cash out if Bob were making a move."

"Well then, I guess we can move on to our next stop," Mike said. "You'll like it, Neil; it involves food. It's a sandwich shop about a block and a half from here. According to Hendrickson's invoices, he ate there almost every day. The guy seemed to keep a pretty routine schedule."

"You would too if you were in a new area where you didn't know anyone or anything about the town you were in."

"True. Let's get going, I'm hungry."

"Geez, Maria, aren't we the fat cat today? We just had a big breakfast a couple of hours ago."

"Fat cat?! You better be joking. You know better than to tell a girl she's fat, even if she's as skinny as I am."

"You crack me up, Maria. I was just messing with you. Thank you for the reaction I was hoping to get. Mike, I believe you owe me five dollars."

"I can't believe this shit. I'm not paying you, Neil, that shouldn't count. Calling her fat is just cheating."

"What?! You guys made a bet about me? What the hell? Someone better start talking before I start shooting."

"Calm down. I made a bet with Mike this morning that I could get you so bad that your face would get all red. I've been trying all morning, and I had to do it before lunch, so I pulled the emergency switch and called you fat. Hey, I didn't want to lose five dollars."

"All right, you're off the hook. But you're still an ass, Neil. As for you, Mike, pay the man. He won fair and square."

"This is bullshit. I almost made it, and then he had to go and call you fat. You know you're not fat, right? Hell, you need to put a little weight on, if you ask me."

"Enough about my weight, let's just go eat. And don't say it, or I'll knock you both out."

"Calm down, Maria, we're just messing. I'll tell ya what, if it would make you feel better, I'll let you hit Mike right now, a free shot. I won't even block you."

"Hey, wait a minute. What kind of deal is this? I don't like this at all."

"I like it. How about you, Maria?"

"I think I might like punching Mike in the gut, maybe a good kidney shot. But I'll let you go. Don't worry, Mike, I'm not like that."

As we began walking toward the sandwich shop, Maria slowed a bit and slugged Mike right in the back of the kidney, dropping him like a rolled-up rug. I tried so hard not to laugh, but it was just so damn funny. Picture a 110-pound girl dropping a guy walking around at nearly 300 pounds; you'd be laughing your ass off, too.

"Holy shit, girl! You just dropped his ass. Nice job. I didn't think you had it in you."

"That was awesome, it felt so good. I haven't hit someone like that in a long time. Did you see his face as he fell down? I wish I had a camera on me. That was great."

"Shut up you guys, and help me up. Fuck, that hurt. I guess I had that coming, but son of a bitch, for a little shit, you pack one hell of a punch."

"Hey, watch it. Don't make me hit your other kidney. I'm just messing with you. But seriously, I'll do it."

The rest of the walk there, Mike made sure that Maria was in front of him at all times. It was quite funny, if you ask me. At one point he was debating crossing the street to get away from her because she kept faking punches at him. He was as jumpy as a cat on catnip. At least from the outside, the deli looked nicer than our experience at Vic's Diner. As good as my breakfast was, I had a classic case of stomach grumbles that usually come when you get a fast food breakfast, you know, with all that grease. I could go for something a little healthier for lunch. I'll probably settle for something along the lines of tuna salad on whole wheat, something a little lighter than the eggs, sausage, bacon, and hash browns I had this morning. Mike is still limping a little bit; it looks like Maria really laid a shot on him. We're like a bunch of middle school kids waiting in line for lunch, joking around and laughing; you wouldn't think we were in the middle of a serial killer investigation. I guess I should check in with Dickerson and see what's happening on his end of the canvass.

"Hey Neil, how are things going? Any luck?"

"Yeah, we lucked out at a diner across the street from the coffee shop Hendrickson frequented almost every morning. It just proves that Cappelano was following him for almost ten days, something we pretty much already knew. It doesn't bring us any closer to finding him, unfortunately."

"It's a start. We had a few bites but nothing that panned out. A couple of my agents came across a hotel that Cappelano had stayed at. They remembered him because he paid cash up front, and that's not something many people do. But the room had been cleaned several times since he left. He stayed there for only a couple of nights, they said."

"At least we're starting to get a timeline. Just keep pushing; we'll meet back up with you at the office later tonight. Keep me up to date."

"Same here, Neil, I'll talk to you later. And good luck."

Let's hope that we get something soon that we can move on. Right now we're just finding the few things that Cappelano is letting us find. I'm going crazy trying to catch a lead. I think I'm starting to lose my patience. I just pray to God that my guys in Mexico can get a grasp on Cappelano's movements down there. Without them I wouldn't even be as far along as I am; I'd still be playing with my prick. I swear I'm going nuts. Maybe I'm not ready to come back to the FBI. I hate waiting around to do things by the book; it's so much easier to just kick a few doors down without having to worry about the legalities of the evidentiary process.

"So what did Slick say? Did they find anything that could help?"

"Judging by Neil's face, I'd say they didn't find jack shit."

"Shut up, Mike. Don't make me drop you again."

"Would you two stop acting like kids? I swear I'm going to scream. Just get me a tuna on wheat, with nothing on it. I need to step outside and think for a minute."

"Are you all right, Neil?"

"No, I'm not all right. We haven't found shit. We're just reinforcing what we already know. I mean, what the fuck are we doing?"

"Keep your voice down, man, we don't need a scene. Just calm down."

"Don't tell me to calm down, Mike, just back the fuck up. You too, Maria. I don't know why I even came back to the FBI. If it weren't for my guys at my company, we wouldn't even have a photo of Cappelano. Hell, the fucking FBI is still talking to the Mexican government working on diplomatic resolutions to searching for a killer, and that will take months. Give me a break, I can't work at this pace. And yes, I'm making a scene, so leave me the fuck alone. I'm out of here."

"Neil, wait a minute. Where do you think you're going? And please calm down."

"Maria, get out of my face. You guys finish the canvass. I have a copy of the list. I'm going to work it on my own and track down a couple of hunches. Just leave me alone."

As I walked away from them, I put my cell phone in the air and turned it off to make it clear to Mike and Maria that they would not be hearing from me anytime soon. I'm just fed up with the way everything is being handled. I think I'm going to snap— I guess I already did, but you get the point. The stress is killing me. It's not like the movies; it isn't all action, it's a lot more waiting and reacting. It is a true test of the human character being in my shoes, or those of any other agents, for that matter. I need a drink to calm my nerves. Calm down, I'm not going to get drunk, I just need one drink to refocus my mind, slow me down a bit. As you can tell, I can get wound up pretty tight; the problem is I eventually blow up. I guess it comes with the job and being a loner. I don't rely on people for help very much, I just give them jobs I think will keep them busy and out of my way. I like to do things myself; it's easier that way. And one more thing: I miss my girls. They'd know how to calm me down with those puppy dog eyes.

24

*They kept me from catching Cappelano four years ago. I'm
not letting history repeat itself. I've learned my lesson*

After walking around for about an hour, I finally found a place
that looked at my speed. It was an old Irish pub, just a little hole
in the wall, and from the outside it looked like the bar had been
there a while. I've come to find over the years in my extensive
study of different taverns across the country that the smaller
and older the bar, the better the bartender. I think a lot of it
comes from the history and experience one usually comes
across when entering a seasoned establishment. I saw a lot
during the few years I worked in the bar business myself, so I
can only imagine what a bartender who's been doing it for ten
or twenty years has seen. That's why I love talking to them;
they're the perfect shrink for a guy like me.

"How's it going, man? It looks like you could use a drink. Let
me guess: a whiskey man, probably on the rocks?"

"Damn, barkeep! Not half bad. I'll take a Jack on the rocks
with lemon. It's been a rough morning, actually a rough couple

of weeks."

"I'm just guessing, but it seems like you're not from around here. Are you here for work or pleasure?"

"I guess a little bit of both. I work for the FBI, and I'm chasing down a killer whose trail led us here. And honestly, it would be a pleasure to catch this motherfucker."

"That doesn't sound like a good reason to be drinking. But it's not really my place to say. I just fill orders."

"Don't worry, I'm only going to have one, then it's on to coffee. I just need something to slow my brain down enough to help me focus my thoughts. Jack's usually a good friend in helping me do that."

"How long have you been chasing this killer? If you don't mind me asking. Just an interested party, I love watching those crime dramas."

"Don't we all, though? We know they're fake as hell, but we still love to watch them. It actually started back in 1998. I know, almost seven years have gone by, so you can imagine why I'm going nuts. The worst part is I had him in my grasp back in 2001, but I was stopped from getting him because of government policy, and then I was asked to leave the FBI. I guess calling out my employer on national TV wasn't a good career move, but I needed to vent, and there just happened to be a TV crew nearby."

"No wonder you need a drink. Just remember, life could always be worse. You could be stuck on the streets being chased by someone like you."

"That's a good point. I knew I needed to come in here. It's a nice little place you have here."

"Thanks. I'm the owner and operator. I do as much as I can by myself—it makes it easier to get around—and I have a loft upstairs. My wife passed away several years ago, and I needed something to do, so I bought this place from an old friend, and I've been running it ever since. I can't complain. It pays the bills and leaves me with a little something extra. I'm Phil, by the way."

"Good to meet you, Phil. I'm Neil."

I stayed longer than expected and talked with Phil for a couple of hours. We talked about family, friends, children, and life. After a good hour of talking to him, he asked me, "If you could do anything right now, no paperwork, where would you be, what would you do?"

"I'd probably be in Mexico with my team, tracking down Cappelano's base of operations and finding a way to flush him home, so I could catch him." Why the fuck don't I just do that?

"I'm no investigator, but I'd say that's a good idea. What's stopping you?"

"You mean besides a shit ton of legal loopholes, the bureau tracking me, and passport issues? It's not that simple, but it's not impossible either. Thanks, barkeep, I needed this. Sorry about your wife."

It was almost eight at night, and my phone had several

missed calls and messages. I didn't bother checking them, I just let my phone keep vibrating in my coat pocket. I just wasn't in the mood. I gave Phil my card and told him to call if there was anything I could ever do for him, and he wrote his number down for me to call if I ever needed someone to bounce things off of. I might just have to do that. He helped quite a bit.

"Thanks for everything, Phil. I'll be talking to you soon."

"No problem, Neil. Anytime you need an ear, I'm here for you. Remember that. And good luck with the case."

I began to check my messages as I left the bar and noticed that Mike and Maria had found a few things. Turns out, they found a pattern to how Cappelano was tracking Hendrickson. They're hoping that with the right data, they might be able to find where Cappelano's center of operations is. The problem is, it's more than likely past tense. By the time they figure it out and find it, he'll be long gone.

Surprisingly, they did something positive for the case. I don't mean to sound negative, but this case has really been all me, at least it feels that way, and although I'm a loner, everyone needs a little help from time to time. I guess it's time for me to call Ken and see how things are in Mexico City with the guys. I could check the message he left me, but why do that when I can just call him?

"Hey Ken, how are things back in Detroit? Is that smell finally gone from the warehouse?"

"Yeah, the guys put up with the cold for a few days so that

the smell would dissipate. As for the guys in Mexico, I have some good news and bad news."

"Start with the bad."

"Bad news is apparently Cappelano hasn't been at his place for a couple of weeks now, but that's to be expected since he's here killing people again."

"What's the good news?"

"He's planning a return to his house."

"Why do you say that? Is there anyone down there who can corroborate that?"

"The guys have been keeping an eye on his place down in Mexico," Ken said. "They did a little snooping and found out he's bought his way into the government down there. We're talking millions of dollars' worth."

"Which means there's no way we're getting him out of there with the FBI's help if he gets back over that border?" I had a sudden urge to head right back to Phil's bar for another round.

"Pretty much. But at least you know where he's going to end up."

"True, very true. Hey, next time you talk to the guys, have them call me. I need to talk to them. Can you do that for me?"

"No problem. But I thought you didn't want them calling your phone, in case the FBI is monitoring your cell."

"I *know* they're monitoring my cell. I'm going to stop and pick up a prepaid cell on my way to the office today. I'll message you from the phone when I get it. Have them call me on that one."

"You sneaky son of a bitch. It's probably not a good thing that you're hiding all this from the bureau."

"I don't care. They kept me from catching Cappelano four years ago. I'm not letting history repeat itself. I've learned my lesson."

"Glad to hear it, Neil. I've been telling you for years the government has too much policy. It's just as much a good thing as a bad thing these days. And it's only going to get worse."

"Don't get me started on that, not now, Ken. I need to focus. Just wait for my call or message later."

"All right. Until then, Neil. I'll talk to you later."

I hate having to keep the FBI in the dark on everything, but I really don't have much choice. As I told Ken, I'm not going to let history repeat itself. There's only one thing worse than failing at something, and that's failing for the same reason you did the first time. Not me, not ever. I took a cab to a cell store to pick up a burner phone, then took another one back to the bureau's office. It was almost ten by the time I got back to the FBI office, and from the looks of it, the place was empty. That can only mean one thing. Something has probably happened, and it's not good; otherwise there would still be people here working around the clock. I pray to God they haven't found Hendrickson's body, and if they did, then it looks like my decision to go to Mexico will be the right one.

I didn't even get to grab my coffee before I got my ass

chewed out by Slick and Maria.

"What was that shit you pulled earlier, Neil?" Maria said, looking quite pissed. "We need to work as a team on this case; you're not alone in this."

"This is why I didn't want to come back to the bureau; it was this high school shit. I'm focusing on the case, and I'm about to hit my stride, and now I have to deal with this shit? You know what? You guys can kiss my ass. I'm not in the mood."

Slick wasn't having my attitude. "Would you just shut up for one second, Neil? We just got a call about an hour ago. They found Hendrickson's body."

"Where? When? Why didn't you guys call me?"

"We *did*," Maria said. "Check your cell. I called you almost ten times."

"Oh yeah, I just deleted those messages, I figured you guys were just going to be barking at me." I had started to listen to the messages, then deleted them, not realizing it was about this.

"Well, you'll have to get the next flight out to Detroit. Mike and I are heading out in an hour. It's a full flight, but we can try and make a call—"

"Don't worry about it, guys. I need to finish up a few things here before I head back to Detroit. I'll fly out first thing in the morning. I'll just get a ride from my friends at the military base."

"Are you sure, Neil? Mike and I can wait until tomorrow to head back with you."

"Maria's right; I'm sure we can get three tickets for tomorrow."

"Seriously, I'm fine. I'm a big boy. I've just got to get to a few things. I'll be there in the morning. Did they send any photos of what the scene looks like?"

"Yeah, we have everything in the other room. Let's go; we'll fill you in when we get there."

From what I gathered in the photos and files sent up by the agents in Detroit, Hendrickson's body was found stashed in front of the "Spirit of Detroit" statue downtown, with a message spray-painted around his body: *"This was for you!"* Pretty sadistic, if you ask me. Cappelano is starting to turn into a careless killer. Not to mention he would have had to drive the body from DC to Detroit, which means most of the time we were running around DC, he was out of town. The thing about these killers is that the majority of them are cowards, for lack of a better word. They kill for power, the power of taking a life, but none of their victims sees it coming; it's always a surprise attack. If the victim put up any fight, the killer would run, just like when Cappelano ran and disappeared for almost four years after I almost caught him back in Detroit. He will run back to his shelter in Mexico, his safe haven. He's made sure of it by paying off the local government down there.

I still can't believe he went after Hendrickson; that was a brash move. And I can't help but think it's partly my fault. If I hadn't come back to the bureau, they wouldn't have transferred

Bob to DC, and he'd probably still be alive. But I can't keep questioning the past. I know what I have to do, and I only have one shot at it. I need to make sure this is done just right. It needs to be timed perfectly.

It was about three in the morning when I got back to my hotel. I was exhausted, and I needed a good night's rest because tomorrow I'll be heading out to Mexico, not Detroit. I can't do anything here, and the only place I can catch Cappelano off-guard is in Mexico. Everything is coming together; I'm beginning to see what Cappelano was seeing. This is all about me now. He came back to get me to return to the bureau, and now that Hendrickson is gone, the only reason I would leave the bureau would be on my own accord. Cappelano's not going to be around much longer. I need to get him to Mexico; that's where this is going to end. I see it so clearly now. And I know just how to get him there, on my terms.

Judging from the photos that the Detroit field office sent to us, it looks like Cappelano's ego is starting to consume him. This is the time. Very soon I'll flood the media with his picture, and with the bureau all over his ass, he'll have nowhere to go but Mexico. If he's as connected as my guys say he is, then I've got to be extremely careful to make sure no one tips him off on what's going on down there. Wait a minute: what the hell is ringing? Oh shit, that's my prepaid phone. Where the hell did I put it?

"Hello? Is this who I think it is?"

"Yes! It's your guys down here on vacation. We'll keep it brief and vague just in case."

"Thanks, guys. I'll need you to pick me up down there late tomorrow night. I'm coming down. I'll message you tomorrow with the time and information. This is going to end soon. Thanks for everything."

"No problem. The CB teams always got your back."

"I'll talk to you guys tomorrow."

I hate being unclear like that, but I'm still in the hotel that the FBI has me put up in, and there's a good chance that this room is bugged. Especially after the last time I was working for the FBI, I'm sure they're keeping all the tabs they can on me. Son of a bitch, I need to relax, and I'm just too high strung. I want to call Sheila and talk to her, but I don't want to wake her up so late. Screw it. I need to take my mind off everything for a few minutes.

"Hello? Neil, is that you? Why are you calling so late? Is everything okay?"

"Everything's okay, Sheila. I just wanted to call you and talk to you before the next couple of days. Things are going to get really messy and really busy, and I won't be talking to too many people. If you need anything or you're worried, just call Ken. He'll let you know what little he can, but you'll have to drive out to talk to him, he won't be able to talk over the phone."

"I know the drill, Neil, just take care of yourself. You promised me you weren't going to go and get yourself killed, remember?"

"I remember. And don't worry about me, I'll take care of myself. I promised you I'd be there when Carol Lynn graduated from college, and I'm not just talking in spirit, I'll be there. And you know I hate breaking promises."

"I know, babe. I miss you, and I can't wait for you to be back home so I can curl up with you in the middle of the night."

"I can't wait either, babe. Go back to bed. I just wanted to let you know what's up. I'll call you when everything's over. Until then, talk to Ken. 'Night, babe."

"'Night, Neil."

Laying on my bed with my luggage next to me, I started to drift off to sleep. Just talking to Sheila puts me in a good mood. I know the next couple of days are going to go by extremely fast, and I have to get ready for everything. First things first: I have to call in a huge favor in the morning. The bureau is going to kill me if this doesn't work out. If I'm lucky, I'll just be blacklisted from the government and not thrown in jail.

25

Now let's go get us a beer and a gun.

Fuck! Six in the morning comes really early, but then again, I have to get a few things done today before I head out to Mexico late tonight. For starters, I need to call an old friend who's a national newscaster. He was there for me when everything blew up in my face back in 2001 with the bureau and helped me piece my life back together and spin things in a better light. He should be up by now; I hope he hasn't changed his cell phone number.

"Hey, Larry, how's it going? It's Neil. Neil Baggio."

"Holy shit, Neil. What are you doing calling me at six a.m.? I haven't talked to you in months. Last I heard you were back on the Veritas case. How's that going?"

"That's actually why I'm calling. I need you to help me. I can bring you the biggest story in a long time. No bullshit, Larry, this is huge."

"All right, what do you need from me?"

"Meet me with a camera crew in an hour. Can you do that for me? I know you're in DC covering the White House right now. That's why I called you."

"Sure. I'll get a room downtown. Remember the hotel where we were the last time I interviewed you? Meet me there. Same room. I still keep it as a home away from home. I'll have a crew set up with everything within the hour."

"Thanks, Larry. I'll see you in an hour."

I packed everything up and grabbed a cab. I had it drop me off across the street from the hotel and waited for a minute to see if the bureau was tailing me, which they were. It looks like I'll have to get creative. I need to call Larry.

"Larry, it's Neil. I'm across the street, and I've got a tail. Is there any way you can get me a lift around back in five minutes?"

"Done. Look for a white unmarked van."

Larry had one of his crew guys pick me up out back, circle around a couple blocks, then pull up behind the hotel where we had planned to meet. National news crews are used to having to hide interviews and identities. It comes with the territory. Lucky for me, I know Larry has a good crew who won't leak anything to anyone, mainly for their own glory in the end, but it works for me. I finally made it up to the room, and Larry had everything set up so that he could make it look like he was doing a satellite interview. That way no one would know where I'm being interviewed; we could pretend like I was anywhere in the world. I'm telling you; the guy knows what's up.

"Hey Larry, thanks for everything. I see you got the general idea of what we're doing here."

"I had a feeling you wouldn't want people to think this interview was being done today in a hotel room in DC. We'll shoot it now, but I'll play it whenever you want me to."

"Thanks. I want you to interview me as though I'm giving you the photograph of the Veritas killer of what he looks like today. I've had my hands on it for a little while now, but I had to keep it quiet. But I don't want him to see his face all over the news until I can get where I need to be to catch him. Do you get it?"

"I get it. But what do I get for doing this for you?"

"If I catch the bastard, I'll make sure you're the only one to get an interview with the killer."

"And if you don't get him?"

"You'll get the only interview with me. A guy that single-handedly pissed off the entire government and let a killer get away twice. Sound good to you?"

"Sounds good. All I need now is a copy of the photo for my guys to put onscreen."

"I already sent it to your phone this morning. It's there. Just check it."

"Yup, there it is. All right, let's do this."

We spent the next hour shooting an interview that was perfectly timed and presented so that Larry can go on air Sunday night and act like it was an interview shot that day. This way I can make Cappelano think I'm in Detroit when I'm actually in Mexico waiting for him to show up. Thank God for technology, not to mention the media. I never thought I would ever say that, but thank God for the media.

Larry and I wrapped everything up around noon. His crew was kind enough to offer me a ride to the airport, where I'll get on a plane to Detroit, then on a flight to Chicago, then on a flight to Atlanta, then on a flight to Mexico. Needless to say, the rest of my day is going to suck, but I need to put as much space between myself and the bureau as I can. Luckily I packed a couple of backup identities and credit cards that Ken and I set up with the help of some of our investigators who let us use their names and Identities. This way I can't be tracked by my credit cards, passport, or ID. I feel like I'm in a fucking movie, but the sad thing is I'm just risking my career, my life, for a hunch. I guess this is what those action heroes always feel like when they are about to defuse the bomb with a few ticks left on the timer.

Finally, I made my way to the airport and got on my plane to Detroit. The flight attendants were very nice, but that's why I spent the extra money on a first-class flight. This ticket is on the bureau's dollar; I want them to think I'm going to Detroit. Technically I will be, at least for a little while until my next flight leaves for Chicago. Then the fun begins—changing names as many times as I change planes. The pilot got on the PA system and informed us that we will be landing soon at Detroit Metro Airport and that we should put our trays in their upright position and buckle up.

Once off the plane, I made my way to the next plane. I'm not worried about my bag. I grabbed all the important things I needed and put them in a backpack that I'll be lugging around with me for the next couple of days. One of Ken's guys works security at the Detroit airport, and he's going to grab the bag. I checked and drop it off to Ken in a couple of days to make sure the bureau doesn't see a bag with my name traveling to Mexico. As I said, I'm good at being sneaky. It might be because I've watched too many movies, but who cares? It works, and that's what matters. It's time to make a phone call to Maria. I've got ten minutes before they start boarding my next flight, so I need to make this quick.

"FBI field office Detroit, this is Jen. How may I direct your call?"

"Hey Jen, it's Neil. Is Maria around?"

"Yeah, no problem. Just give me a second to find her."

I know Maria is in her office right now, and that I'll be on hold for exactly one minute and thirty seconds so they can set up the tap to record the call and track where it's coming from. Sometimes these guys can be so predictable. She'll be picking up the phone in four . . . three . . . two . . ."

"Hey, Neil, it's Maria. What's up? Are you in Detroit?

"Yeah. I'm at the airport. I just got in. But I need to get going in a minute. I have a lead to run down. Can you do me a favor?"

"Yeah, anything, Neil. Do you want me to meet you somewhere?"

"No, don't worry about that. I need you and Mike to track down a guy named Brian Dilger. He was the boyfriend of Anna Walton, the girl who survived Cappelano's attack, at least for a couple of days. I'm almost positive that he will be Cappelano's next victim. He's finishing off old business."

"We'll get on it right away. You aren't pulling my leg, are you, Neil?"

"There's no time to play around; just do it. I've got to see an old friend in Ann Arbor, Cappelano's sister-in-law. I'll be there for a couple of days. I'll talk to you later."

"All right, Neil. Mike and I will get going on this ASAP. Good luck."

"You too, Maria, and get on this fast; his life is in danger."

I guess I should feel bad for sending Maria and the FBI on a wild goose chase after Brian, and then again after me in Ann Arbor, but it's the only way I can keep them off of my trail. As I said, I like to work outside the lines and as independently as possible. It's not my fault I can't trust them; they're the ones who keep fucking everything up, not me. Let's just hope everything falls into place. For now I need to start on my tour across the United States a few times to make sure that no one knows where I'm headed.

The rest of the night was a combination of airport bars and sleeping on the flight. That way I wouldn't slip up and say something stupid to a flight attendant about who I really was. I can't help but laugh, because right now one of my guys from CB, Inc., is in Ann Arbor using my credit card and ID to buy gas, a few meals, and a hotel room, to throw off the bureau completely. I'm so fucking good at this job, it's scary. I hate to say it, but I've definitely picked up a few things from Cappelano over the years.

It's almost 1:00 a.m. local time here in Mexico City, and customs are taking forever. I hope they still take bribes, because I don't want anyone to know I'm here. From the looks of things, I should be all right. Hell, I'm sliding a thousand dollars in hundred-dollar bills to this guy. But will he take the bait? Yes, he did. Score! As I made my way outside, I saw Carl and Tony—or Carlos and Antonio, now that we're in Mexico—waiting for me. Finally the case brings me somewhere warm. Things are starting to feel good, that confidence is coming back. I'm sure being with my team has something to do with it.

"Hey Neil, good to see you," Carl said. "All you have is a backpack, huh? Are we going to need to make a stop?"

"We can pick up everything I'll need tomorrow. I hope you guys have found a good place to get a gun around here. A beer wouldn't hurt, either."

"I know a place where we could get both for you right now if you want," Tony said. "You got to love Mexico; mixing beer and guns, what a great country."

"Nice to see you guys are in good spirits. Thanks for doing

a great job down here, by the way. How much money have you had to spend so far to get the info?"

"Including our own expenses, close to a hundred grand. I know it's a lot, but information costs a lot down here."

"Don't worry, guys. If we catch him, it will be worth every penny. Now let's go get us a beer and a gun."

The guys have done a good job blending in with the locals, seeing as people knew their faces and weren't surprised to see me. Thank God I can still speak enough Spanish to get by. I may have let Maria think I couldn't speak Spanish, partly because I liked it when she spoke for me; also I like to keep some things close to the vest. Most people won't think I'm a government agent right off the bat. But for now, I'm just glad I got a Glock 24 at the tequila-and-pistols joint that Tony recommended. Just like the one I have at home, except this one is threaded for the silencer I picked up there as well. It has a laser sight built into the barrel. They do good work down here.

With my gun in my backpack and enough ammo to take down a small cartel, I was ready to get some sleep. The guys took me to the house they'd been staying at since they got down here. Not bad for ten grand. It's still a shit hole on the outside. There's nothing in the way of creature comforts. No air conditioning, not even a TV. They do have all of their weapons, as well as surveillance equipment in a hidden closet. Along with three beds, so I couldn't be happier. It didn't feel like this back in 2001. It just feels right this time.

26

I feel this rage inside of me building every day. It's getting harder and harder to stay focused and not do something rash.

It's almost noon, and Tony wakes me up with a cup of coffee, which smells fresher than anything I've ever smelled in my life. I'm all sweaty from sleeping in a hot room with no air conditioning, but I really can't complain. This is better than I expected to stay in when I got here.

"Hey Tony, where's Carl? Or Carlos? Whatever we're calling him down here."

"He's keeping an eye on Cappelano's house to make sure that nothing has changed. He's been there almost all night. We've been rotating twelve-hour shifts watching it."

"Nice work. You're not too close to the place, are you?"

"Not at all. There's a set of buildings about half a mile away that are on a higher elevation than Cappelano's house, and we've got a top-floor office space rented out in one of them. They think we're working on some city planning things. That's why everyone is so nice to us down here."

"Not bad, guys. I like the way you've set up."

"With the equipment we have, it's pretty easy to keep an eye on the house. And every couple of hours, we do a drive-by through the neighborhood. We usually do it at night, so no one notices us."

The shower wasn't the prettiest thing I've ever been in, but I've been in worse on stakeouts. I'm missing my house back in Detroit an awful lot right now, but I can't waste any time thinking about being home; I need to focus on the case at hand. It's the fourth quarter with only a minute left in the game. I've got the ball in my hands, and it's up to me to make the other team bite on the play fake so I can get the pass off. I know sports clichés are what they are—clichés—but that's the best way I can describe things.

Sadly enough, the shower reminded me of the high school showers I had in the dormitory. Nothing special, just really old, and lacking enough hot water, but you learn to get by. I'm already on my second cup of coffee, and I've barely made it out of the shower, but this coffee is just so fresh. It doesn't taste anything like the crap I've been drinking all these years back home. Hell, I don't even need to throw creamer and sugar in my coffee, it tastes that good. I can only imagine how good it tastes in Colombia, freshly ground. Just before I started making love to my coffee mug, Tony started yelling from the kitchen.

"How do you like your eggs, Neil?!"

"I'll take them over easy with toast if you have it."

"Coming right up. Get dressed; we need to get going in a bit. I'm due to give Carlos his break. I figured I'd have you come with me so I can fill you in on everything with all of our tech at the office."

"All right. I'll be there in a minute; it's not like I have too many clothes to choose from."

I reached into my bag, grabbed some underwear, and got dressed. I didn't pack any clothes other than a couple of different shirts and some underwear. I didn't even pack socks; I'm just barefooting it in my running shoes. I think I'll fit in just fine down here. By now my dirty blond hair is pretty shaggy, down to my ears, and I haven't had a decent shave in a couple of days, so I have a good five o'clock going on. Mix that with my worn in and torn jeans, wrinkled shirts, and beat-up running shoes, and you'd think I've lived here for years, except for the fact that my tan is starting to fade pretty quickly after all that cold DC weather. I know it's bad for you, but I still love to tan once or twice a week; it's very relaxing. There I am staring at myself in the mirror, with enough stubble to look like a high school freshman trying to grow a beard. My steel blue eyes just kept staring back at me, reminding me of all those who have died because I couldn't catch Cappelano back in 2001. I feel this rage inside of me building every day. It's getting harder and harder to stay focused and not do something rash to ruin everything I've put into this case.

"Eggs are done. Get your ass in here, Neil."

"All right . . . all right, I'm here, don't get your panties in a twist. Thanks for the grub. I need something in the old stomach after last night."

"No problem, boss man. I'll get the car ready. Hurry up and eat. There's one more cup of coffee left in the pot, knock yourself out. You've got five minutes."

"Look at you, bossing your boss around. Feels good, doesn't it?"

"A little bit. Let's get going, though. We've got to get there before Carlos starts to fall asleep."

"I'll meet you at the car in two minutes. Just let me hoof this food down."

"Clock's ticking."

I'm so proud of the guys right now, they're doing an awesome job down here. If it weren't for them, I wouldn't be in the position I'm in to take down Cappelano. It's a Saturday afternoon, and by this time tomorrow, Cappelano's face is going to be plastered all over the national media, forcing his hand. If I know him, and I do, he'll run and hide like the bitch he is. Before I headed out to the car I ran into my room, pulled my underwear and clothes out of my backpack, then threw in the gun I grabbed last night along with some extra clips and a couple of boxes of hollow-tipped rounds, and an extra shirt just in case. It will help keep the gun and clips from bouncing around and rubbing all over each other.

"Nice bag, Neil. How long you had that thing? It looks worn as hell."

"That's because it is. It's a leather backpack I've had since college. I've had it repaired countless times, but I love it. It's perfectly worn down, nice and soft. Let's get going."

"Boss man is back to bossing. We just have one stop to make on the way."

We made our way toward the high-rise where the stakeout was being held. The stop wasn't anything important, just a payoff to one of the local authorities to make sure nobody bothered us—nobody with a badge, at least. The building was being remodeled, which helped with the cover because cars were going in and out of there all day. No one would think twice about Tony and Carlos staking out Cappelano's place.

"We're here. Can you grab those blueprints in that box back there and follow me?"

"Blueprints. What the hell are these for? Are these of Cappelano's place?"

"That's what that stop was for. It was a hush bribe to make sure he didn't spill the beans that he gave me the blueprints. The beauty of this place is that green speaks louder than bullets. If you have the dough, you can get anything you want."

"That's probably how Cappelano's been able to hide and move in and out without anyone saying a word."

"That, and he helped the local officials assassinate a couple of rebel leaders. He did it as a favor to them, for protection, and in return they won't touch him with a ten-foot pole."

In the beginning I thought Cappelano was down here killing for fun. Now I'm starting to think he was doing it as a means to an end. It was a way for him to keep doing his research, as he likes to call it. Working for the cartels and the government buys him credit, cash, protection, and the anonymity he needs to operate.

"No one ever said Cappelano was an idiot," I said.

"That's for certain, but what he didn't count on was us finding his hideout in Mexico."

"Don't be so certain of that. Never assume anything with Cappelano."

We made our way to the top floor and into our office. As soon as you walk in, there's a small lobby similar to a doctor's office, probably to keep up appearances. But once you go through the doorway it's a whole new world; it's nothing but equipment, computers, and scopes. They even have a high-powered telescope hooked up to a computer recording the house 24/7, just in case they miss something or fall asleep. Not a bad setup. Too bad this is going to cost me a lot of money, but I would have to say it's worth it. Maybe I can do a media tour or write a book when this is all done just to help cover the costs.

"Nice pad, guys. How much did this set me back?"

"Neil, you're always worried about money," Carl said. After a twelve-hour shift, he was looking even more ragged than I was, but the excitement of our little adventure was keeping him afloat. "Don't worry. We did a couple of side jobs down here to raise a little dough so we could pay for our new toys. Didn't

Tony fill you in?"

"No, I didn't. I was waiting until we got here to talk to him about it."

"What are you guys talking about? You ex-military boys are always looking to kill something, aren't you?"

"Only if it will make us some money," Tony said. "We helped out the local officers by taking out a small rebel group. It was thirteen men, but they didn't see it coming, so it was a pretty easy hit."

"Neil, it may not look like it, but it's a constant war zone down here," Carl added. "They just know how to hide it really well."

"Don't tell me anything else; I don't want to know. I'm just glad we're getting shit done, that's what's important. Now fill me in on everything, even the things you don't think are important."

The rest of the day was spent going over blueprints of Cappelano's house as well as the guys getting me up to date on what they'd been doing since they arrived in Mexico. It turns out they've been pretty busy, getting involved in rebel battles, military coups—it sounded like they were competing with Cappelano for business down here. They were even saving the newspaper clippings dealing with the events they were involved in for mementos of their trip down to Mexico City. They described it as a gun head's dream vacation and thanked me for having Ken send them down here.

"You guys are freaking nuts. I'm just glad you're on my side and not Cappelano's. Have you gotten into the house at all yet?"

"Nope, we just got the blueprints yesterday," Tony said. "It looks like he's got a pretty high-tech security system. Luckily for us, the power goes out all the time in this area, and this building is a short distance from the main circuit."

"But doesn't Cappelano have a backup system?"

"Yes and no. He has an emergency generator, but it's only good for thirty minutes. It's just a backup in case the power flickers on and off."

"So what's your plan?"

The guys informed me that they were going to knock the power out by setting off a small electrical disturbance at the main circuit. They said they've already timed it, and it takes the local utility company forty-seven minutes to get power back up. This leaves us a seventeen-minute window to get me into his place and set up shop before his security system kicks back on. This is going to have to be timed just right so that I'm not stuck sitting in his house too long. Anything longer than a day and I'll go nuts.

"Well, I guess we need to go run a couple of errands tomorrow. I need a few things to help me with the waiting I'm going to have to endure inside his house."

"We have a bunch of meal replacement bars that you can take along with some water," Carl said. "They taste like crap, but they'll keep your strength up. Not to mention they're small, so you'll be able to pack a couple of days' worth in your pockets alone."

"All right, and we'll also need to have a small communication device. In case of an emergency, you guys will be able to earn that bonus money," I said with a grin.

"Already got it. We got our hands on the same communicators that we used in the Army Rangers. That way you can whisper to us to help keep your presence unknown, and we'll hear you loud and clear."

"Looks like you have all the bases covered. Where's the best place for me to stay once I'm inside the house?"

"You'll have pretty free rein once you're inside, but you'll have to stay either upstairs or downstairs the whole time. The alarm is set to go off if anyone uses the stairway without disarming the security system first. And of course, you won't be able to get out of the house without tripping the alarm."

"So I need to decide if I want to wait for him upstairs or downstairs? Survey says . . . downstairs."

Around seven or eight at night, Carlos finally headed out to get some sleep back at our place, leaving myself and Tony to keep an eye on the house. From the outside, Cappelano's house looked immaculate. If he built something like that in a big city in the States, we're probably talking a couple of million dollars. There really isn't any landscaping; it's more of a fortress. If you were to make your way up the long driveway, you would first be stopped by a gated entrance with cameras and pin codes. Then you'd have to cover about fifty yards from the entrance to the front door.

The house has tall columns reaching from the ground to the roof, giving you a feeling of money and power. At first you don't notice it, but the windows are bulletproof glass reinforced with steel bars on the inside. It looks like Cappelano has built his own personal prison, keeping himself in just as much as keeping his enemies out.

It was around 3:00 a.m. when I finally dozed off to sleep—as I said, I suck at stakeouts—while Tony stayed awake and kept an eye on the house. Don't get me wrong, he wasn't just sitting there staring into a screen. He had monitors set up, along with a satellite so they can watch American TV, and a few video games to keep himself and Carlos busy during the long shifts. As for me, I just gave in and curled up on the couch, knowing I needed my rest for the next couple of days ahead.

The whole night I kept having a recurring nightmare of Cappelano walking in on me and laughing while I was in his house, knowing I was already there. Every time I would wake up just as he was pointing a gun at me. I know it's my subconscious bringing my worst fears to the front of my mind; scary as it might be, it's not a bad thing because it will help me to be extra careful. As long as I have Tony and Carl watching my back, I'll be just fine. At least that's what I keep telling myself.

27

With each passing ring, I could feel my breath get a little bit weaker, a little bit heavier, and I knew this was the easiest the next twenty-four hours were going to be.

It was almost noon when I was abruptly awakened by Tony and Carl laughing their asses off. It looks like Larry kept his end of the deal and put our interview on the news, as I knew he would; he's always been one of the few media personnel I could always trust and count on. As for the two-gun twins, they were hitting each other and laughing at me on the TV like a couple of idiots.

"Holy shit, Neil, you are not photogenic at all. Didn't they have a makeup artist there to help you out?" Carl was giving me some well-deserved shit.

"No, I filmed that just before I headed out to see you guys at like six in the morning. I was a little tired. How does it look?"

"You wouldn't know that you're here right now, that's for sure. It was a nice touch leaking the photo of Cappelano during an interview. Is this why you're the boss, because of ideas like this one?" Tony was trying to play it straight while fighting back laughs in his voice.

"Shut up, guys, and get me my coffee; I'm dying over here. I need some caffeine to get me going."

"Get up off your bum and get it yourself. There's a fresh pot in the other room."

"Are you guys tapped into the local airports? I need to know all the flights coming into Mexico City from Canada."

"Canada? Why there? I thought he'd be flying out from Detroit."

"No. He wouldn't risk it. He's probably grabbed a fake passport, just like I did, driven over the border, and made his way to the Toronto airport. Find out all the flights coming in from Toronto with at least two stops."

"Wouldn't it be less hassle if he took a direct flight?"

"Just the opposite. He's going to throw on a disguise, probably something latex but simple like a nose; he was always good at that stuff when he was with the bureau. We're not talking complete masks, just simple changes sush as a wig, maybe a mole or two, and a different nose. You'd be surprised how little it takes to change your appearance."

"All right, we'll get on it right now. As for you, get ready. We're getting you into his place tonight at midnight, so whatever you need to take care of, do it now, because who knows how long you'll be stuck in there."

"Understood. I'm going to need one of you guys out at the airport as a spotter looking for Cappelano. You don't need to follow him back to his house, just let us know when he lands."

"Can do, boss. By the way, I took the liberty of grabbing your cell back at the house, and you have a bunch of missed calls. You might want to check them."

"I already know who it's going to be: Maria and Mike from the bureau bitching me out about keeping them in the dark about what's going on. All right, give me my phone; I need to make a call. Can we scramble the signal so that I can talk to them and keep them from tracing the signal?"

"No problem. Just give me a minute to set everything up. Go clean up in the bathroom. I'll have it ready for you when you get out."

My heart rate keeps increasing with every passing minute, knowing that this is going to end here one way or another. I have to prepare myself for this moment. I need to sit down and meditate. But first I need to call Maria and make sure they don't mess this up.

"Hey boss man, it's all set. You ready to do this? You'll have four minutes to talk to her and then you'll have to get off, to keep them from tracing the call."

I sat down next to Tony at the computer, grabbed my cell, and started to dial Maria's cell phone number. With each passing ring, I could feel my breath get a little bit weaker, a little bit heavier, and I knew this was the easiest the next twenty-four hours were going to be.

"Hello? This is Maria Garcia speaking. Who may I ask is this?"

"It's Neil. Before you say anything, just listen—"

"Neil, where the hell are you? The bureau is going nuts trying to figure out what this news stunt is all about."

"Shut up or I'm hanging up this phone. Don't worry, I have everything under control I just need forty-eight more hours and I'll have this whole thing wrapped up. I can't tell you where I'm at because I don't trust you guys, not after last time. If he gets away, this is all on me, so I'm not taking any chances of the bureau fucking everything up again. You'll either hear from one of my associates or me when everything is completed. As for now, I need to get going. 'Bye, Maria."

"But Neil, wait—"

CLICK

I hated ending the conversation that way, but I had no choice. I can't waste any more time. If I'm going to make it through the next twenty-four hours, I'm going to need to prepare my mind, body, and soul. I know it sounds corny, but I need to meditate for a while and refocus my mind.

"Nice job, Neil, quick and to the point. Just so you know, the clock is ticking. You've got ten hours left before this goes down, so do what you need to, but be ready by eleven p.m. 'cause we need to get everything ready by midnight."

"No problem, guys. I'll make a list of things I'm going to need for my stay at Château Cappelano tonight."

"Just give it to Carl, and he'll make sure that everything gets taken care of. As for me, I have a lot of work to get done for tonight."

I took a few minutes and wrote out a list of things I would need to get me through the night at Cappelano's residence. It was a shor tlist consisting of my gun, cleaned and oiled; three clips of backup ammo; the communication device; and some of those meal replacement bars. I'll just get water from Cappelano's place and take my chances with Montezuma's revenge. If they say I'll have free rein downstairs, I'm not too worried, and if not, it's probably for the best. I don't want to have to piss right before he shows up.

I made my way down the hall of our house and found an empty room. I closed the shade, turned off the lights, and sat in the middle of the room, eyes closed, breathing slowly and deeply, focusing on the task at hand. With every breath I took, I focused deeper and deeper until I put myself into a state of focused sleep. Although my body was resting, my mind was very much awake and going through every scenario that could play out when Cappelano shows up. I guess I might be too confident about him showing up, but I've known him for so long, I know this is his only move. He'll probably call my cell phone, but I'll keep it off to upset him even more. This will put his sole focus on getting to Mexico so he can rethink and reassess everything. My mind wandered off into every possibility I could think of. I played through scenarios involving a shoot-out between myself and Cappelano, or the possibility that he knows I'll be there, and he brings backup. I even played through a scenario where Tony and Carl get picked up by Cappelano's guys before they have a chance to tell me he's coming. I thought of everything I could.

"Hey Neil, it's time. It's eleven fifteen p.m., we need to get everything going. Tony is already at the main power grid for the area. We've got an hour to get you within striking distance of his house. Are you ready?"

"I'm ready, Carl. As ready as I'll ever be. Let's get going."

Carl opened the door and threw in a change of clothes for me. It was a dark urban camouflage that would help me stay undetected while approaching the house as well as once I'm inside. It had pockets for all of my needs. Carl had packed everything for me and made sure that my gun was good to go. He said he cleaned it and took it out practice shooting to ensure it wouldn't jam, and he guaranteed me it was in pristine shape for the night ahead.

"All right, Neil, this is it. Do you have everything?"

"Cell phone. Communicator. Meal replacement bars. Glock with a laser sight. Extra clips of ammo. I think that's everything."

"This is a one-time shot we have here. I'll help you get over the wall with a grapple and rope when we get there, but once you're over the wall, it's all you. I've got to get out of there and clean up everything so Cappelano doesn't suspect anyone has entered. And try not to leave any footprints in the grass or pathways."

"I got it. Let's get moving."

Carl and I made our way downstairs to the car, then drove to Cappelano's house and waited for Tony to trip the power. He was right on time: it was eleven forty-five, and all the power in the area shut off at once. Then, right on cue, the porch lights and a couple of interior lights at Cappelano's house flickered back on as the backup generator took over. Now we just have to wait thirty minutes for the generator to turn off, and then it's showtime. Then it's up to me.

"You ready, Neil? We have three minutes left. Just keep an eye on those lights. Once they shut off, you'll have seventeen minutes."

"I know, I know. Let's get to the wall and get the grapple ready."

"There go the lights. Let's go."

Carl made his way to the wall, tossed the grapple over the top, pulled it tight, and I took off as fast as I could up the wall. When I got to the top, I tossed the grapple back to him and dropped down. That's when we went silent, except for the communicators. They were high-tech, all right. All you had to do was press the communicator to your voice box and whisper, and the other people could hear you clear as day.

"Good luck, Neil. We've got your back."

"Carl, get your ass out to the airport and scout for me, and

Tony, get your ass back to the office and keep an eye on me. I'll contact you when I get in and situated."

Without power, it was pretty easy to get in through the window. The guys had shown me a couple of years earlier how to pick a lock without scratching the handle, so Cappelano won't notice that someone broke in. With the lock picked, I said a little prayer and opened the door. Luckily nothing went off; let's hope there isn't a silent alarm. I'll know very shortly if the Mexican military shows up at Cappelano's door and starts to hunt me down.

"You've got eleven minutes left before the power kicks back on, Neil. Now's your chance to check anything upstairs before you're stuck downstairs for the night."

"All right, let me know when I have four minutes left so I have enough time to get downstairs."

I made my way up the stairs and down the hallway. The house was surprisingly well kept, though I guess that's not *too* surprising. Cappelano is pretty anal; everything has its place for him. I want to look for his files or mementos of all his killings, but I'll have time for that later. Once I end this once and for all, I can take my time. I took a brief tour of the upstairs before Carl warned me that I had only four minutes left. Ever so carefully, I made my way back downstairs to check the main room and kitchen. It looked like Cappelano bought this house from someone else. He doesn't have this good taste. To him, things must be practical. If Cappelano designed this house, the decor would be in stainless steel from top to bottom. I noticed very quickly that there wasn't a basement, not even a small crawl space.

"Hey Tony, do you see a basement on those blueprints?"

"No. Out here, the ground is too close to sea level to dig a basement, plus I don't think Cappelano wanted there to be any other way for someone to get into his place."

"A lot of good that did him, seeing as I'm making my way around his house. Oh, fuck, Tony. This isn't good."

"Neil, you've only got two minutes before the power kicks on. What's up?"

"There are cameras all over his house, on the inside. Of course, Cappelano would put cameras all over his house! Fuck! Fuck! Fuck! I'm in the kitchen right now. Look, is there a closet anywhere, a big one, maybe a front hall closet? Check the blueprints quickly, Tony!"

"Neil, head back toward the front door; there's a walk-in closet right by the front door, according to the plans. Hurry, you've only got forty-five seconds and counting."

"I see it."

"Thirty seconds . . . twenty seconds . . . ten seconds—"

"I'm in, I'm in."

"Four . . . three . . . two . . . one." Nice job, Neil. You might as well get comfortable; you're going to be there a while."

"Thanks, guys. At least I have enough room in here to spread out. Carl, when's the next flight coming in that

Cappelano might be on?"

"The first one is at nine thirty a.m. local time and then eleven thirty p.m. If he's not on either of those, then we're screwed, because it will be three days before the next flight comes in, at least from our guess."

"Just keep me posted."

"Get some rest, Neil. We'll wake you if anything comes up."

"Sounds good. Thank you."

I spent the next several hours in and out of sleep, thinking of Sheila, Carol Lynn, Maria, and almost everyone else in my life. I kept having flashbacks to the day I lost Cappelano, over and over again. Being in his house just gave me the coldest feeling; you could feel the deaths in the air. I couldn't help but remember my years at Orchard Lake St. Mary's Prep. During my one semester in the dorms, I roomed with a Korean exchange student named Jae Sub Pahk, who taught me so much about his culture and so much about myself. That's where I learned how to meditate on a deep level. It is an amazing tool to learn.

I saw my life slowly flash before my eyes, from my courtship of Sheila to the birth of my daughter. The emotion within me kept building, more and more, until I started to get a restless heart. The more I thought of my family, the more I kept thinking of all the families Cappelano had ruined over the years. All of the deaths, all the pain and loss. All for his own righteousness, his belief that he was helping humanity by learning the mind of a killer. All he'd done is turn into a self-glorifying monster. The anger, the rage kept building inside me. I don't know if I'll be able to control myself when I see him. If I kill him, I'll be no better than he is, just a waste of a human being, nothing but a killer. A void of feeling.

"Neil, wake up. It's Carl. The first plane just landed, and there was no sign of Cappelano among the passengers. If he's in disguise, though, Tony will get an ID on him as he pulls up, so be alert. It's just a fifteen-minute drive from the airport to your location."

"Thanks, guys, I'm up. Just keep me informed. I'm going to prep myself."

The next fifteen minutes felt like an eternity. Was he going to be here, or was I going to have to spend the rest of the day in this closet? This compiled with all the scenarios that could happen. How smug was he going to be? Was he going to be calm and collected? Would he act like he knew everything the whole time or be surprised? I couldn't stop my brain from racing all over the place, trying to work through all the scenarios my imagination and my Cappelano Rolodex could come up with.

If he did get off in disguise, how do I know he's going to come straight home? Maybe he'll make a stop or two first. Only time will tell, but I can't stop my mind from racing. It keeps trying to catch up to my heartbeat.

"Neil, it doesn't look like he got off on this flight. If he did, he's not coming directly home, he might be making stops. I'll keep a close eye on the house until the next flight lands."

"Thanks, guys. I'm not going anywhere."

With my gun in hand, I started picturing my girls at home laying in front of the fire while I sat in my chair listening to Frank Sinatra, sipping on a Jack and just letting go. Once this is over, I am definitely going on a vacation, a long vacation, and not to Mexico. Maybe somewhere in Europe. I'd love to go to Italy and see where my family's ancestors come from. I'd love to be anywhere right now but here in Cappelano's coat closet, waiting for him to show up if he even shows up at all.

As the morning turned to day and the day to night, I started to question my thought process. Maybe he isn't coming back to Mexico at all. Maybe he's going somewhere else to start over. Maybe he was just setting me up to be here. It wouldn't be the first time I got played by him. But this just feels so right; I can't help but feel that this is where he'll be. I looked down at my watch, and it was almost 8:00 p.m. The next flight isn't due in until 11:30 p.m., so I might as well catch some sleep.

"Hey guys, I'm going to catch an hour or two of sleep before the next flight lands; wake me up if something changes."

"You got it, boss. How you holding up in there?"

"I can only imagine how it must have felt to be in a tiger cage during the Vietnam War. Those guys are amazing to have survived that. But for now I'm going to try and sleep."

I started to doze into and out of sleep when Carl woke me up, babbling about something, but I couldn't hear him because

I was barely awake. It sounded like he was saying that Cappelano's not on this flight either, it looks like we struck out, so I rolled over and closed my eyes again.

"Neil, wake the FUCK UP! He's pulling into the driveway. He's pulling up the driveway, I've got a visual. It's him. Get your ass up! He's already out of the car."

"What?!"

I pulled myself together as quickly as possible, checked my gun, and made sure I had the chamber loaded. I fastened on the silencer barrel and stood up in the closet. This is it. This is the final moment, everything I've been waiting for. If it goes wrong, this is all on me. Cappelano and I have done this dance many times. The thought of ending it once and for all in a country I can sneak out of in the night is very tempting.

"Neil, he's at the door. The door is open, he's making his way in. It looks like he's disarming the alarm. Now he's walking into the house. Now's your chance. He's got his back to you."

I pulled in a few more deep breaths, in and out, in and out, focusing. This is it, there is no more time, no more waiting. Now is the moment of truth. As I started to slowly open the closet door, I could hear Tony telling me that Cappelano still hasn't turned around and that it looked as though he didn't hear me yet.

"Hello, Franklin. Long time no see."

"Neil. What a charming surprise," Cappelano said sarcastically.

"Put your hands up right now and slowly turn around."

"You know you can't arrest me in Mexico. What do you plan to do? Kill me?"

Just as he turned around and I saw his cold, dark eyes, the faces of all his victims flashed before me, filling me with rage, unlike any other. I was furious. I wanted him dead. This was it; this was the moment. No one would know. I could shoot him and end this all right now.

"Neil, this is Tony. I can see you. Don't do it, man. Don't kill him. He's not worth it. If you kill him, you'll give him what he wants."

"Tony, what's going on?" Carl said. "Is Neil all right?"

"I think he's going to kill Cappelano. Call Agent Garcia right now."

As Cappelano looked at me, he just laughed and gave me that crazy-as-fuck smirk he's acquired over the years. I just stared back at him in silence, with my laser sight pointed between his eyes.

"Why don't you just shoot me, Neil? Get this over with. You know you want to."

"Just shut up. Shut up!"

"I'm so proud of you, my student. You have done your teacher proud. The news interview was a nice touch. I really didn't think you had it in you to do that."

"Why'd you come back? You had to know I'd be here."

"Yes, I knew. That's why I made you wait in the closet for so long. I arrived last night, but I thought I'd make you sweat a little bit."

What the fuck? Are you kidding me? That's it. I'm tired of his sick and twisted games. No more, it's over. I pulled my communicator off and threw it down, then walked up to Cappelano, pointed the barrel at his head, placed my finger on the trigger, and started to pull back.

"Hello . . . this is Agent Garcia. Who is this?"

"This is Carl, one of Neil's guys."

"The ones who found the photo of Cappelano in Mexico? That's where you are, isn't it?"

"It's over, Agent Garcia. It's over."

"What's over?"

CLICK